## BADLANDS BRIDE

"Wood crafts a fine read. Strong characters set against a unique backdrop add depth to a[n] . . . enjoyable plot."

—*RT Book Reviews*

"A sensual, emotionally satisfying romance, smooth writing and dialogue, and a plot sophisticated enough to keep readers engaged and invested. A hint of intrigue adds tension, and a few unexpected twists deepen the complexity and texture of the plot. A quick, enjoyable romance."

—*Kirkus Reviews*

"Wood takes readers off the beaten path and on an entertaining romantic adventure. . . . The out-of-the-ordinary setting adds an extra dimension. . . . Although the lovers' initial meeting is explosively snarky, Wood builds their relationship in a wholly believable fashion, and her decision to pair Lily with the penniless but gallant journalist . . . is endearing. Western romance fans should give this change of pace a try."

—*Shelf Awareness*

"An enjoyable Americana romance starring two seemingly opposites falling in love in a fabulous locale. . . . Fast-paced . . . engaging."

—*Genre Go Round Reviews*

"Captivating and kept me turning the pages until the end . . . [with] several surprises that caught me off guard."

—*Ramblings from a Chaotic Mind*

Also by Adrianne Wood

*Badlands Bride*

Available from Pocket Books

# Adrianne Wood

# STOWAWAY BRIDE

POCKET BOOKS

New York   London   Toronto   Sydney   New Delhi

Pocket Books
A Division of Simon & Schuster, Inc.
1230 Avenue of the Americas
New York, NY 10020

This book is a work of fiction. Any references to historical events, real people, or real places are used fictitiously. Other names, characters, places, and events are products of the author's imagination, and any resemblance to actual events or places or persons, living or dead, is entirely coincidental.

Copyright © 2013 by Adrian Wood Liang

All rights reserved, including the right to reproduce this book or portions thereof in any form whatsoever. For information, address Pocket Books Subsidiary Rights Department, 1230 Avenue of the Americas, New York, NY 10020.

First Pocket Books paperback edition December 2013

POCKET and colophon are registered trademarks of Simon & Schuster, Inc.

For information about special discounts for bulk purchases, please contact Simon & Schuster Special Sales at 1-866-506-1949 or business@simonandschuster.com.

The Simon & Schuster Speakers Bureau can bring authors to your live event. For more information or to book an event, contact the Simon & Schuster Speakers Bureau at 1-866-248-3049 or visit our website at www.simonspeakers.com.

Designed by Lewelin Polanco
Cover illustration by Craig White

Manufactured in the United States of America

10  9  8  7  6  5  4  3  2  1

ISBN 978-1-4516-9825-1
ISBN 978-1-4516-9827-5 (ebook)

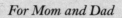

*For Mom and Dad*

**1**

R EALLY, IT WAS ALMOST too easy.

Skirt weighed down by the gold coins she'd sewn into the hem of her dress the night before, Emily Highfill Grant managed to dodge the porters on the train platform and haul herself up into her grandfather's Pullman Palace car without being seen—or at least stopped. She eased the door shut behind her with a puff of exertion and relief and then looked around.

Inside the car, one kerosene lamp was lit, allowing her to see enough to avoid bumping into the gilt-edged chairs and table. Not much had changed since she, her sister, her mother, and four servants had traveled down to New York from Boston last week in the private railcar. The interior looked neater now than when they'd stepped down onto the platform and into the hustle and noise of New York—somehow her sister Annabelle had managed to impose chaos in the single-day trip from metropolis to metropolis. But someone had tidied up, readying the car for her mother's cross-country trip to San Francisco.

It was a trip her mother had intended to take alone (well, alone with two servants), and Annabelle and Emily were supposed to travel back to Boston by themselves (with the other two servants).

But Emily had no intention of missing this opportunity to go west and see the rest of the country. After all, her older sister, Lily, had traveled to Denver when she was only twelve. Emily was twenty and had never gotten farther west than New York.

Tonight, that would change.

Good—they hadn't removed the tablecloth from the card table. Although cards wasn't considered proper recreation for young ladies, Lily had taught Annabelle and Emily games such as euchre and pitch last winter, and they had played for several hours on the ride to New York.

Emily smiled. The long tablecloth would hide her admirably.

A whistle outside blew a long blast, making Emily's heart jump, and the noise level on the platform ticked up. The train was at least two hours away from departure, but not everyone trusted the timetables to be correct, and passengers began to put themselves and their belongings on the train.

Her mother could arrive at any moment.

Peeling her jacket off first, Emily crawled under the card table. Ugh. Grit clung to her palms, and dust crept up her nostrils. Well, it would only be for a few hours. Once they were well under way and she revealed herself to her mother, Emily could go back to sitting in an armchair instead of hiding like a sneak thief.

Emily tucked her jacket behind her and leaned back against the wall. If it weren't dirty, and dark, and cramped, and a bit too warm, this nook would be a nice place to spend some time alone, thinking her own thoughts. . . .

Emily sat up straight, knocking her head on the tabletop. Blinking didn't help her see more—it was black as midnight under the table. The cloth, like everything of her grandfather's, was top-notch quality and woven tight.

Beneath her bottom, the train shuddered like a hypothermia victim. They were moving, and at a fast clip, too. How long had she been asleep?

Outside the tablecloth, the car was silent.

Emily leaned forward, grimaced against the pins and needles that bit her stiffened limbs, pressed her cheek against the gritty carpet, and lifted the edge of the tablecloth.

The windows were black, and the lamps had been turned down so low that shadows curled up in the corners of the car. She must've been dead asleep for hours. Perhaps everyone had already gone to bed in the small bedchambers off the salon.

Waking her mother from a sound sleep was not how she'd imagined revealing herself, but she couldn't wait until morning.

Emily's stomach rumbled. There was another good reason to announce her presence. She'd napped through at least two meals.

Flipping up the tablecloth, she scooted out into the open and took a deep breath of non-dusty air.

A pair of bare feet thumped down inches from her left hand. Emily shrieked. She whipped her head around so fast that her vision blurred, but she instantly knew she was staring up into a face she didn't recognize. She promptly upgraded her shriek into a full-blown scream.

Another scream—not her own but familiar nonetheless—tried to rupture her right eardrum.

Emily whipped her head around again, almost smashing her nose against her younger sister Annabelle's face. Where had Annabelle come from? Well, it didn't matter—not when they were under siege from some . . . some . . . *stranger*. Emily reached behind her, grabbed Annabelle's hand, and dragged the two of them across the length of the car, where she pulled her sister behind her and twisted to stare at the man. A man who should not be there.

"Who are you?" Emily demanded. "You are in the wrong car, sir."

He looked more like a ruffian than a gentleman, with his bare feet and his shirt unbuttoned and showing more male chest than she'd ever seen in her life, but her mother would be deeply disappointed if Emily couldn't retain her good manners even in a crisis.

A tiny part of her—the part of her that wasn't gibbering with a mixture of indignation and terror—

pointed out that she had smuggled herself on the train to gain more adventure in her life, and she was already achieving that goal quite effectively.

Too effectively.

The dark-haired man stood, and he was taller than she'd expected him to be. Emily tried to back up one more step but succeeded only in treading on Annabelle's feet.

"Who are *you*?" he countered. "And I must disagree— I am very much in the right car. I hired it only thirty minutes before the train departed the station. *You* are in the wrong car, lady."

Somehow *lady* coming out of his mouth didn't sound nearly as respectful as *sir* had coming from hers.

"Did you think to steal a free ride in an empty car?" he asked.

Emily shook her head, more to unscramble the muddle in her head than to reply to his question. She looked around frantically. Yes, this was the right Pullman car. Beneath Emily's feet was an autumn-hued rug her grandfather had ordered specially only last summer, and over the desk in the far corner hung an oil painting of her, her two sisters, and her parents that had been commissioned seventeen years ago, when Emily had been two and Annabelle only a newborn.

More confident, she said, "Sir, I am afraid you are mistaken—"

"The lady who was going to take this car changed her mind at the last minute," he interrupted—and rather rudely. "There was not enough time to decouple the car before the train was scheduled to depart, so it was rented to me."

"Oh," she said weakly. It made hideous sense. Her mother hated train travel with a passion. She'd been pale throughout the daylong trip from Boston to New York, and she'd spent most of the past week lying on her bed in the hotel, a cool cloth pressed to her eyes. Emily simply hadn't considered that her mother would refuse to continue her trip. Emily's sister Lily was expecting a baby in a few months, and their mother had been adamant that she would travel to San Francisco to be there at the birth. Apparently that adamantiousness—was that a word?—had evaporated after a single day of train travel.

"Oh," Emily said again. And then she didn't know what else to say, so she looked at the stranger more closely.

The low lamplight concealed most details—for instance, she found it difficult to judge his age precisely—but the way he stood with his hands propped on his hips, uncaring that his shirt was open, and the impatient manner in which his dark eyes drilled into her spoke volumes about his personality. If the meek were to inherit the earth, he'd be lucky to get a measly half acre in the deal.

"Emily," Annabelle said breathily from behind her, "introduce us, please."

She'd completely forgotten about Annabelle. It was an unusual thing to do—Annabelle loved being the center of attention and took pains to stake a claim on that spot—but apparently Annabelle had correctly deduced that being quiet for a change was the smart thing to do. At least until now.

Emily flicked a glance over her shoulder. Annabelle was looking at the inconvenient stranger like he was a French dessert.

When Emily turned back, the stranger was, finally, buttoning up his shirt.

Somehow that gesture, that minor attempt at decency in an awkward and bizarre situation, gave her the courage to say what she did next. "We are two young ladies escaping to a new destiny, and we throw ourselves on your mercy, sir."

At least *she* was escaping to a new destiny. Why Annabelle was there, she had no idea. Annabelle's destiny was to be the Belle of Boston, and while Emily didn't envy her that role, it had never seemed much of a hardship.

Being "the nice sister of the Belle of Boston" . . . well, that was absolutely not a role to be envied. An easy role? Oh, yes. Interesting? No.

He didn't look impressed by her speech. "Names?" he said, and buttoned the final top button of his shirt. Emily got the impression from his brief grimace that he rarely used that button, but she would have concealed as much skin as possible if Annabelle were ogling her so voraciously, too.

"Emily." She pointed at herself. She couldn't use a fake name, as Annabelle had already called her Emily. "And my sister . . . Anna." Better not to use Annabelle's real name, in case it helped the man identify them.

Annabelle, bless her heart, didn't blink at having to relinquish the part of her name that meant "beautiful," though it must have been a blow to her dignity.

The stranger waited, clearly expecting Emily to supply her surname.

"And you are . . . ?" she asked quickly.

"Lucien." And he raised his eyebrows a fraction, daring her.

She took a step forward, closer to him. From the way his eyebrows popped up all the way, she knew she'd surprised him. "Mr. Lucien, we are in the unfortunate position of needing to entrust our good reputations to a man we do not know. We must know more of you than your first name." She paused. "And at the same time, we must not tell you more than we already have."

For as soon as he knew their identities, he would put them off at the first train stop, send a telegram to their grandfather or their stepfather, and leave them there to be picked up and hauled back home like misplaced baggage.

She had gotten on this train. And she was going to stay on it until she reached San Francisco.

"Are you always so dramatic?" Lucien asked dryly. "Or is this a special performance just for me?"

Emily smiled at him. No one had ever accused her of being dramatic before. "Just you," she assured him.

He stared at her, and then the corner of his mouth quirked up. "All right. Have it your way, Miss Emily the Mysterious. I am Lucien Delatour."

The name was familiar, but Emily couldn't pinpoint why. "Are you a businessman?" Her stepfather and grandfather were well-known among the most successful industrialists in the entire country. It would be quite unfortunate if Lucien Delatour traveled in the same circles as they did.

"Isn't everyone?"

"I'm not," Annabelle said coyly.

"Indeed," Lucien replied with a little bow.

Emily was going to press him for more details but her stomach growled at that moment in an embarrassingly noisy fashion. Well, in for a penny . . . "Would you happen to have any food?" she asked.

"Your wish is my command." There was an edge to his voice that hinted he was being more sarcastic than courteous, but Lucien padded out of the salon on his bare feet and disappeared into the small hallway that held the pantry. Hopefully a well-stocked pantry that included many of her mother's favorite foods, such as biscuits and lemon curd. The thin door snicked shut behind him.

Emily rounded on Annabelle. "What are you doing here?" she hissed.

"I saw you sneak out of the hotel, and so I followed. I thought you might be meeting a man." Annabelle sniffed, and her lovely brunette curls bounced around her equally lovely face. It was a face that artists in the public parks chased after, begging Annabelle to sit for them. "I might have known better. And then once you do find yourself practically alone with a handsome man, you ask him for *food*?"

Emily put her hand on her stomach. "I was hungry!"

"This is why you've remained unmarried, Emily."

Because she ate when she needed to? Surely a good husband would want an intelligent wife, not one who forgot to eat and fainted on a regular basis.

Annabelle settled into one of the plush seats. "Where are we going?" she asked, sounding completely unconcerned.

"*I* am going to San Francisco to visit Lily and help her with her new baby. Where are you going?"

"With you, I expect. We should not tell Mr. Delatour who we are, though. He'll send for Mother or Grandfather to come get us."

"Precisely!" Emily heaved a sigh of relief and suffered another furious stomach growl.

The door to the salon swung open, and Lucien appeared balancing a tray practically overflowing with bread, butter, and cheese.

"Let me handle him," Annabelle whispered, and then flowed gracefully to her feet. "My, what a feast!" she gushed. "You did a wonderful job choosing the food."

Emily was fairly sure she managed not to obviously roll her eyes. Well, if Annabelle could wrap Lucien Delatour around her little finger, it would make the whole journey much easier, she supposed.

Lucien stepped all the way into the room and placed the tray on the card table. "I'm sorry, Miss Anna. This is for your emaciated sister. Did you want some victuals as well?"

The food he'd brought in could have fed four people. Had her stomach truly growled that loudly?

"Thank you," Emily said, and took a slice of bread and cheese. Then she proceeded to eat as much as she could while her sister babbled away and Lucien watched both of them with an expression on his face that she couldn't quite identify but thought might be amusement from the way his eyes occasionally crinkled in the corners.

Lucien Delatour. A French name, of course, which loosely translated to Light of the Tower. He was not light in any way, with walnut brown hair trimmed fashionably short, dark eyes and brows that she thought could be mightily intimidating, and skin that had spent a fair amount of time in the summer sun. Only his feet, still bare and bright against the dark-hued carpet, were light in any way. Presumably he didn't frolic with his boots off very often.

The "tower" part of his name suited him. While he was not alarmingly tall, he held himself in a way that added several imaginary inches to his height. A most effective tool to convey superiority, or at the very least confidence.

Her grandfather Charles Bertrand Highfill held himself the exact same way.

Emily swallowed the last bit of bread she could fit inside her happily full stomach, waited for Annabelle to finish her monologue on how tedious she found all the horse manure on the New York streets to be, and asked, "Are you a self-made man, Mr. Delatour?"

He nodded, then drawled, "My mother and father had an early hand in the process as well, I understand."

Humph. He was either making fun of her or trying to

embarrass her. Well, Highfills were made of sterner stuff than that. She blinked at him innocently. "Oh, no, Mr. Delatour; you must have been misinformed. *I* understand that hands are rarely essential to that process."

Again his eyes crinkled. "Not essential, no—but certainly helpful."

Annabelle was staring at Emily like she'd decided to douse her head with kerosene and light her hair on fire. *What?* Emily mouthed at her when Lucien turned away to snag a piece of cheese for himself, but Annabelle shook her head.

As Lucien reached out one of his tanned hands for a second piece of cheese, Emily noticed a map was on the table. She leaned forward to get a better look. It was not a map she'd seen before, so it must be Lucien's.

"What is this?" she asked, touching one finger to the paper. The plate covered the heading of the map, but she could see dark, straight lines crisscrossing its width. Lines she recognized from other maps. "A railroad chart? But of what area of the country?" She bent closer to read some of the town names. "Oh! This is Iowa, of course."

"You are well educated in your geography," Lucien said.

"I love maps." She traced the path of the Illinois Central Railroad. In her position at the Boston Immigrant Aid Society, she'd recommended that route to many headed for the Dakotas. Would they be following that line themselves? Her decision to join her mother on her cross-country trip had been made only two hours before she'd sneaked out of the hotel and onto the train. She hadn't had time to examine the train's route in detail.

"Bedtime, I think," Lucien said. "You ladies look worn-out."

A gentleman never commented when a lady appeared less than perfect, but perhaps Mr. Delatour hadn't ever learned that. Or perhaps he didn't care.

Then Emily seized on the most important piece. "You are allowing us to stay?"

"For now." He looked both of them up and down, and Emily was suddenly aware of how wrinkled she must be after napping for hours under the card table. She glanced down and self-consciously brushed a few dozen bread crumbs off her chest. Given how she looked and acted, it was the height of hypocrisy to be mentally criticizing Mr. Delatour's manners. "I can't in good conscience throw you out the window," he continued.

He could always make them find seats in the passenger section of the train, but Emily wasn't going to tell him that. She'd already slept upright this evening and didn't care to repeat the experience when a flat bed was offered.

She supposed she should be more worried and less relieved that a strange man was giving her and her sister a place to sleep in a secluded private railcar, but, surrounded by the knickknacks of her family and satiated by food, she couldn't stir up the emotion. Besides, he was still in his bare feet. What kind of man would molest ladies without wearing boots?

"Thank you. That is very generous of you," she said.

Annabelle gushed more words of gratitude and admiration at Lucien while Emily fished her jacket out from under the card table. Then she silently followed Lucien to the skinny passageway that led to the tiny private bedrooms for which the Pullman cars were so famous. Lucien pointed Annabelle into one and Emily into another. Another bedroom door was half-open at the end of the passageway, and Emily knew that was the largest room in the car—though calling it large in any way was rich hyperbole. Presumably Mr. Delatour was sleeping there.

Emily stepped inside her room and tossed her jacket on one of the pair of seats facing each other next to the night-black window. Then she propped her hands on her hips and stared at the angled panel attached to the ceiling above the seats. Theoretically, that panel should unfold down between the two chairs to create a flat bed. She'd never seen it operated, though.

"Allow me," Lucien said, reaching past Emily to flick open a latch on the left that she hadn't noticed. He then had to lean to her right to open another latch. This near to him, she could see a glimmer of beard stubble on his chin.

She tucked her arms around herself. She'd been close to men before, of course, during parties, picnics, and dances, and the like. Never with a man with naked feet, though. In a bedroom.

"Can you show your sister how to open the bunk?" Lucien asked. As he stepped back, he touched the top button on his shirt as if to verify that it was still fastened.

Emily squelched a smile. A man with a healthy sense of self-preservation around her sister was almost as rare as one who didn't wear his boots around ladies. "Yes, I can. And thank you again."

"Good night, and see you in the morning." He stepped backward into the passageway. Before he disappeared toward his own room, he added, "If you get hungry again, feel free to plunder the pantry. It's quite well stocked."

With her mother's food. "I will indeed," she assured him. "Good night."

Emily listened carefully until she heard his door click shut, then hustled across the passageway to Annabelle's tiny room. Annabelle was struggling with the bunk the same as Emily had, and Emily released it for her. Annabelle flopped down full-length on the mattress with a sigh, and Emily perched next to her hip. While she would have dearly loved to lie down and be rocked to sleep by the motion of the train, they had Things to Discuss.

Emily spoke in a low voice, even though the sound of wheels on the tracks would certainly obscure their words enough that Lucien wouldn't be able to pick them out through the thin walls. "We didn't conclude our conversation. Why do you want to go with me to San Francisco instead of back home to Boston? The trip will be long, the city is not very sophisticated, and unless I'm mistaken, you have no deep love for babies."

Annabelle seemed to be trying to avoid her eyes, but the room was too small for such a maneuver, so she went on the attack. "I can't believe you were flirting with

Mr. Delatour," she said accusingly. "We hardly know the gentleman—if he is indeed a gentleman at all. Really, Emily."

Flirting? She wasn't—Emily pulled her thoughts back on track. "Annabelle, you're avoiding my question."

"Fine. Did you know that Mother and Mr. Grant want me to marry Judson Bacon?"

Emily tried to recall who he was. "Short, with blond hair and a ridiculous beard?" They had fallen into conversation once in the park about farming in the Dakotas. At least he seemed to have a brain in his head; her sister could do worse.

"No, that's his older brother. Judson is the good-looking one." When Emily shook her head, Annabelle said, "Well, he's completely in love with me, and he doesn't take no for an answer. Someone saw him kissing me, and Mr. Grant is going to marry me off to him. To a nobody!"

Their stepfather's reaction sounded extreme. Annabelle was caught kissing someone, oh, every few months, and Emily was certain that Annabelle kissed gentlemen far more often than she was caught. Emily had once overheard a young man tell his visiting friend that he wouldn't truly sample Boston's delights until he'd sampled one of Annabelle's kisses. "Judson forced you to kiss him?"

"He didn't ask my permission."

Emily had been Annabelle's big sister for a long time; she knew a dodge when she heard it. She waited.

"Oh, all right! I didn't mind it that much, and it wasn't

the first time." She huffed a few times before adding belligerently, "A few of my buttons were undone as well."

"Ah." Perhaps the engagement was Mother and Mr. Grant's not-so-subtle way of reining Annabelle in. "Well, the engagement can be broken later without too much talk," Emily said. "If you truly don't wish to marry Judson Bacon, Mother and Mr. Grant won't make you."

Annabelle didn't seem reassured.

Uh-oh. "Were, um, more than a few buttons undone when you were caught?"

Annabelle covered her face with her hands, confirming Emily's suspicions. "Oh, Emily, it was so embarrassing. And the worst part is, I think Judson *meant* for us to be caught! He had a self-satisfied smirk on his face even while he was helping me get my dress back on."

Emily winced at the words *get my dress back on*. No, Mother and Mr. Grant would not allow Annabelle to wriggle out of the engagement even if Annabelle managed to convince them that Judson had arranged it. Unless:

"Did he force you, Annabelle?"

"Um, not precisely. I didn't expect we'd be caught, though! And for Judson to arrange for us to get caught is the height of villainy."

Annabelle usually tried to deflect blame from herself when she got in trouble, and Emily normally would have disregarded her excuses, but there was something in her sister's lovely eyes that Emily had never seen before.

Fear.

"You see now why I have to come with you," Annabelle said. "I must escape Judson. If he arranged for us to get caught, what kind of husband do you think he'll make?"

"A selfish one." Which would be the absolute worst kind of husband for Annabelle.

Annabelle nodded vigorously. "Yes, exactly. Oh, it's just so unfair."

"Indeed." For everyone. Emily loved her sister, but babysitting her during a transcontinental trip was not how she'd envisioned the next few weeks.

In addition, if Annabelle weren't with her, Emily suspected Mother and Mr. Grant would probably not chase after her. They'd often remarked how blessed Emily was with common sense, and due to her years of work with the Boston Immigrant Aid Society, she had friends in every major town across the country. A telegram at the next station would settle their minds, and Mother might even be pleased that someone from the Highfill family would be with Lily at the birth of her first child.

Unfortunately, Annabelle was both engaged and lacking a modicum of common sense. Mother and Mr. Grant were probably frantic. If a hue and cry was raised to find both girls—as it would be—Emily would have to be clever to stay ahead of the hunting dogs.

She reached out and took Annabelle's hand. "Don't worry. We'll both get to San Francisco. Once we're there, and you're away from Judson Bacon for a while, maybe Mother and Mr. Grant will reconsider your engagement."

Maybe.

"Mother and Mr. Grant are going to be worried about us," Annabelle said.

Emily nodded, trying to conceal a tiny surge of annoyance. She could not allow their parents to think that they were in any sort of danger. A telegram must be sent at the next station to save them from unneeded anguish. After that, they would need to dodge pursuers sent by their parents.

"Why are *you* traveling to San Francisco, Emily? You, too, have no love for long trips, unsophisticated cities, or babies."

"I like babies," Emily said, surprised at Annabelle's certainty. "Not as well as I like children, but babies become children soon enough. And I have never been to an unsophisticated city, or been on a long trip." She leaned forward and touched Annabelle's hand. "I've helped hundreds, maybe thousands of immigrants reach their new homes out in Nebraska, Kansas, and Nevada through the aid society. I research train routes for them, give them timetables, help them learn what supplies they'll need. But I've never been west myself, and Mother has refused to let me go. This trip is my opportunity to see what's happening in other parts of the country. To see how people other than the famous Boston Highfills and their friends live."

Annabelle looked so perplexed by this desire that Emily added in a burst of from-the-heart honesty, "I was living in a cage, Annabelle. And I needed to get out."

"A cage, Emily? Mr. Delatour is right—you have become quite dramatic."

Lucien shut the door to the bedroom and, for good measure, locked it. It was a strange world when a man had to be more in fear of losing his virtue than his life, but that gal, Anna, had the hungriest eyes he'd seen on a young lady. And he wasn't in the mood to be supper.

Unbuttoning his shirt, he threw himself down on the bed. It bounced, but not too much, and he sighed with pleasure. Getting this private car at the last minute had been a mind-boggling stroke of luck. Lucien had been lucky often in his life, and he'd recognized and welcomed the tingle that swept like sunshine over his skin when Lady Luck had graced him again. But perhaps the Lady had been laughing at him behind her hand, for she'd deposited two pieces of unwanted baggage in the Pullman Palace car with him as well.

Lucien slid open the window over his bed, and the gentle thundering of the train's steel wheels echoed into the small bedroom. Some men complained that they could not sleep on a train, but the sound reminded him of why he was on this train in the first place: the Great Mountain Railroad line that he and his partner, Chuck, were building in the wilds of Wyoming Territory.

After the line was built, and passengers and freight were paying to use it, Lucien would be able to afford his own private car like this one.

He probably wouldn't, though. He didn't want anyone at all thinking that he was trying to ape that bastard

Charles Bertrand Highfill, who everyone knew owned a Pullman Palace railcar of his own.

Lucien shook that thought away. He needed to look forward, not backward. And, barring any more construction accidents on the Great Mountain, success was only a half year away. Dreams should come easily tonight.

Except now, even after three nonstop weeks of rushing around Washington, D.C., and Manhattan to gather more financial and political support for his and Chuck's railroad project, his eyes refused to close, and he was thinking about his distracting stowaways.

*We are two young ladies escaping to a new destiny, and we throw ourselves on your mercy, sir.*

A strange contrast, those two girls. Both were lying through their teeth, of course, but there was enough family resemblance that their claims to be sisters were credible enough. Aside from that, though, they couldn't be more different. He'd do well to steer clear of Anna; she looked as dangerous as a mountain lion. But there was something about the Emily girl that reminded him of Chuck's wife, Jacqueline Winthrop, especially when Chuck had first brought her out west from her home in Washington, D.C.

Lucien had visited the nation's capital first in this most recent "money-grubbing dog-and-pony show," as he and Chuck called them. Good thing he had: With Lucien's reputation for building profitable enterprises, and his and Chuck's substantial seed money as proof that they could build a much-needed rail line, the politicians had thrown their support—as well as some under-the-table investments—behind Lucien. The one holdout had been Senator Hutchins from New York.

His daughter had been an enthusiastic supporter, though.

Lucien realized that, even lying down, his shoulders were trying to hunch up to his ears, and he forced himself to relax. Susan Hutchins was a lovely girl, and he was lucky to have met her and, apparently, won her regard.

Well, all right, he hadn't been lucky. Luck had nothing to do with it. Jacqueline had arranged the introduction, and Lucien had been well aware of Jacqueline's not-so-secret intentions that Susan and Lucien make a match of it. From a purely practical point of view, having a senator's daughter in the family would open doors to investors Lucien and Chuck had been turned down by before. People like John D. Rockefeller, James J. Hill, and Andrew Carnegie. Equally important—at least to Lucien, who had a major stake in the whole marriage idea—Jacqueline knew Susan and believed she and Lucien would be "comfortably compatible."

Gossip of an impending engagement had spread ahead of him like a wildfire fed by hurricane winds, and when he traveled to New York for the final week of his trip, his welcome there had been doubly warm because of it.

Damn it, he'd left his writing case in the salon. He'd planned to pen at least ten letters tonight to the top investors who'd bought shares or pledged support and mail them off when they hit the town of Marion, where the train would next stop. But the two girls without last names had distracted him. Well, he'd just have to write the letters tomorrow morning, as well as ten more letters to the second-tier investors. In all, Lucien had gained about twenty investors during his New York and D.C. trips, including several key politicians. Keeping all of them apprised of the railroad's progress would suck additional hours out of his day. And as the cofounder, president of the board, and lead engineer of the Great Mountain Railroad, he already didn't have enough hours.

One investor he had not called on was Charles High-fill. A few of the other investors had asked if Highfill or his son-in-law William Silas Grant was involved, and upon Lucien's abrupt no, their expressions had flickered toward . . . well, he wasn't sure what. On some faces he thought he'd read satisfaction. On others, concern. But none of those people had declined to join the Great Mountain, and no one had suggested outright that he approach Highfill, so perhaps he'd been imagining things. Good thing Highfill's participation had not been a requirement, because Lucien wouldn't ask Highfill for money even if Lucien had less than two pennies in his pocket.

He'd done it once and ended up as close to ruined as a man could be. Jacqueline had even lost her brother because of that decision.

Never again would he put his fate in the hands of a Highfill. Never again.

Annoyed, Lucien punched his pillow and rolled over. He usually managed to avoid thinking of Highfill—so why was the man haunting his thoughts tonight?

He would think of Susan instead. Tomorrow he should write Susan as well and tell her he was safely away from New York. She'd laughingly told him to be on guard against New York's marriage-minded society maidens. Or maybe she hadn't been joking—Lucien often found it hard to tell. Either way, he owed her a letter, too.

Hmm, he probably shouldn't mention his stowaways to her. If she was worried about New York maidens ensnaring him, the news that he had two of them cozily ensconced in his private Pullman car would not be well received.

Before he dropped off to sleep, Lucien made another resolution. He had to get rid of the mystery sisters. While their cross-country flight was intriguing, and that Emily girl had a sense of humor that made him smile almost against his will, he had too much to do and too much at stake with Susan.

Tomorrow, they had to go.

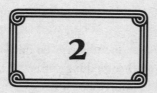

**2**

WHEN HE ENTERED THE salon the next morning, Lucien was somehow unsurprised to find Emily awake and eating breakfast. A lot of breakfast. She was quite trim in form and precise in mannerisms, yet managed to consume food at the same rate as a stray mongrel. If she weren't clearly a lady, he'd imagine she'd been deprived of regular meals while a child. Much as he had.

She blinked a few times when she saw him. Either she had forgotten that he, not she, was the one leasing the railcar, or she was surprised by his change out of his black woolen city suit and back into his everyday clothes: leather vest, white shirt, and buff-colored canvas trousers. His guns and gun belt he'd left back in his room, assuming—perhaps incorrectly—that these young ladies wouldn't be a threat.

"Good morning," she said after swallowing. She gestured to the table. "I prepared coffee. Would you like some?"

Just as he expected—she had completely made herself at home.

"Thank you." He poured himself a cup and took the seat next to her.

One sip and his mouth screwed up. This was coffee? Or had she scraped something rotten off the bottom of a metal bucket and poured hot water over it?

"This is the first time I've ever made coffee," Emily said gaily. "It didn't turn out nearly as terrible as I expected it would."

He cleared his throat and tried to couch his next words politely. "The next large town is Marion. Trains running east stop there frequently."

"Yes, I know of it." Emily took another bite of a sugary bun.

Apparently he would have to be blunt. Just as well—it was his preferred mode of communication. "If you neglected to bring money with you, I'd be happy to pay for your and your sister's train tickets back to New York City. From Marion. Because you should get off the train there and go home."

Emily slowly blinked velvety brown eyes at him. Although she was the less beautiful of the two sisters, she was good-looking enough to be momentarily distracting. And he didn't know why, but somehow her wrinkled fancy dress made her even more appealing. To keep his mind on track, Lucien focused on her hands, which were twisting her napkin in her lap. Good. A show of nerves.

"Mr. Delatour, we are not going to New York City. We are going west."

"Not with me, you aren't." Hmm, that might have been *too* blunt. Lucien took a swallow of coffee to conceal his frown and then immediately regretted it. God, this was the worst coffee he'd ever tasted, and he'd tasted a lot of hair-curlingly awful coffee in his time.

His statement was true, though. He had too much to do without also worrying about the well-being of the two sisters. Or even just spending time talking to one of them. He had letters to write—lots of them.

But Miss Emily appeared unfazed by his gruffness. "I admit that it is an awkward situation. Had I realized that this car had been rented, I would not, ah, have come aboard as I did. But we seem to scrape along with each other tolerably well, don't you think?"

"I'm a bachelor and not prepared to house two nice young ladies."

"Do not worry yourself. I've found the pantry to be quite well stocked."

Lucien ground his teeth before realizing that Emily's brown eyes were a bit too wide and innocent. She was deliberately misunderstanding him. "Your and your sister's reputations are nothing to make light of," he growled. "And, more important, I'm a busy man and find the whole situation to be damned inconvenient."

She flinched at his swearing. "I beg your pardon!"

He leaned closer. "We. Do. Not. Suit."

"We're not seeking marriage to each other, Mr. Delatour. You have a very large and mostly empty private car, and my sister and I would like decently comfortable accommodations on our trip west. It seems like a reasonable partnership."

Lucien settled back in his chair and reached for his coffee before thinking twice and setting the cup down again. So they were negotiating now. He was extremely good at negotiating. "In good partnerships, each party gains. What do I get out of it?"

She looked around the main salon, obviously seeking inspiration. "We, ah, can help relieve your boredom. Train travel can be tedious, can't it?"

"I do not find it tedious. In any fashion."

She sighed. "Neither do I. It's quite lovely, in fact. Did you know that when train travel first began, some doctors feared that people would go insane from the speed at which the land was rushing past their windows? They worried that people would suddenly feel untethered from the earth and panic. I don't feel that way at all. It feels like flying to me."

"Have you stood between the cars yet?"

"No. Is it wonderful?"

"It will be wonderful for a green rider like yourself."

Eyes shining, she said, "Can we do it now?"

How had he become so easily distracted? "No." He seized one of the rolls and the excuse it offered. "I haven't eaten yet. And we haven't finished our conversation. What are you offering in this partnership?"

"Stimulating conversation?"

He snorted. "I do not mean to cause offense, but

young ladies of good social standing rarely provide *any* stimulating conversation."

Her eyes narrowed. "How many young ladies of good social standing have you spoken with, Mr. Delatour? From your rough mode of conversation, I would venture to say less than a handful. Or, if more than that, those ladies surely fled your company quite quickly."

He grinned at her, enjoying her annoyance. "Perhaps you're right. So, to spare your tender feelings, I suggest you and your pretty sister disembark at Marion."

Emily plucked a pear from the platter of food. "Luckily for me, my feelings are not so tender."

"Are you sure you are a young lady of good social standing, then?" He was either being very rude—or flirting. At the moment, he wasn't sure which.

She looked at him through long, dark lashes. A smile played peekaboo in her eyes, and his pulse staggered like a drunkard. "And are you sure you do not find my conversation stimulating?"

Gulping the last of his coffee and regretting it immediately, he pushed away from the table and stood. "I'll show you how to stand between the cars." A head-clearing burst of fresh air was essential. Right now.

"Wonderful!"

The small passageway that led past the bedrooms and to the front end of the car seemed even cozier than before. Lucien could hear Emily's skirts swishing gently against her legs even over the racket of the train's wheels.

Anna popped her door open as they went past. "Where are you going?" she asked past a yawn. Even with her ebony hair mussed and her eyes sleepy, she was absurdly beautiful. Too bad there wasn't much brain matter residing under the hair.

"We're riding between the cars!" Emily sang.

"Oh." And Anna shut the door, leaving them alone again in the passageway. The cozy passageway.

"Fresh air, only ten steps away," Lucien told Emily grimly, and forged on. Her silk skirt *swish-swish*ed behind him as she followed on his heels.

Lucien twisted the handle on the door to the outside platform and shoved it open—a little too quickly. He stumbled on the sill and pitched forward. Behind him Emily shrieked, and he felt hands scrabbling at his back as she tried to catch hold of him.

Too surprised to swear, he reached out to grab the rail one was supposed to grab when one was enough of an idiot to practically jump out the safety of the car and into the precarious open area where a single bad decision could tumble you under the train's merciless wheels. But the handrail wasn't there, and Lucien catapulted forward into inexplicable darkness.

When he hit the ground, he did swear . . . and then swore once again when Emily landed full-length on top of him, driving his chin into what felt like a gritty metal floor. It was not a gravel rail bed. Somehow, they were alive.

Emily swatted him on the shoulder as she climbed back to her feet. "Really, Mr. Delatour. Your language!"

"I was praising our Maker because we're both still alive. Ow." Lucien rolled onto his hands and knees—both now bruised—and stared around them. His eyes soon adapted to the lack of light. "Aha. Now I understand." They were in an enclosed passageway that was designed to keep the wind off passengers as they moved from one car to the next. He'd seen them on other trains but never experienced one himself, and it hadn't occurred to him that this Pullman Palace car would be equipped with one. But of course it was. It also had a wider traversing platform than he was used to, most likely so that ladies could walk back and forth without worrying that their broad skirts would conceal a dangerous misstep.

He stood and took a closer look at how the telescoping passageway was attached to the neighboring car. Ingenious, really.

Behind him, Emily said, "That was exciting, but aren't we supposed to be able to see outside?"

"I wasn't expecting this to be here," he said as he turned to face her. She was quite close. This dim corridor between the cars was even snugger than the passageway past the bedrooms, and there seemed to be a strange lack of air in here. When he took a deep breath, a flyaway strand of her golden hair tickled his nose and clung there.

"Other end," he said abruptly, and barreled past her and into the safety of the Pullman car. Weaving past the bedrooms, through the main salon and then back to the lavatory area and the pantry, he reached the tail end of the car and flung open the sliding door. This time he had sense enough to poke his head outside instead of charging into the unknown.

Ah.

Perhaps luck was smiling on him again, for they were at the very end of the train. Not even a conductor's caboose obscured the view of the land unrolling behind them like a runaway bolt of green and brown velvet.

A small platform with handsome polished brass handrails formed a kind of balcony off the back of the car. Somehow Lucien knew that if there had been room to fit a chair, the owner of the car would have placed one here. Lucien would have, anyway.

He squeezed himself to the side and waved Emily forward. "Is this more to your liking?"

Emily had to turn sideways to get by him, and her body whispered against his as she sidled past. "Pardon," she murmured.

The insane part of his brain that apparently had a weakness for blond, adventure-minded young ladies took over his body. He reached out a hand and stopped her as she was halfway past. If either of them moved even a quarter inch forward, they would be plastered against each other like new paint on a canvas.

Then the insane part of him relinquished control, and he scrambled for a reason why he was practically pinning her against the side of the train.

"Thank you for trying to stop me from falling. Back there. At the other end of the car." He didn't especially like reminding her of his earlier idiocy, but it was the first thing that popped into his mind. Plus, he did owe her his thanks.

She looked up. Lucien stared back. His body felt tense, as if he were waiting for something.

What was he doing? He practically had a fiancée back in Washington, D.C.

"Um, what?" Emily said after a long moment. Rather than sounding demanding, she sounded dazed.

"Thank you," he said again, and then reluctantly dropped his hand to allow her to move all the way past him.

Maybe train travel had given her a touch of motion sickness. Emily was having trouble finding another explanation for why her arms and legs felt strangely disconnected from her body and her thoughts were moving like molasses.

Or maybe she had fallen between the cars harder than she thought she had. Lucien had broken her fall quite capably with his entire body, and at the time she'd felt more shocked by hearing him swear—twice!—than she'd been shaken by her fall. Yet, perhaps she was having a delayed reaction. It wasn't every day that she fell on top of a handsome man.

Nor was it every day that she simply stood so close to a handsome man, frozen like an ice sculpture. There was enough room for her to move past Lucien, but she was stuck, like her shoes had been nailed to the floor.

"Simply beautiful," Lucien whispered, and her whole body began to prickle. The prickling sensation wasn't awful, like the time when she'd acquired poison ivy at age twelve, but more like feeling a cool breath of air on her skin after getting out of a lukewarm bath.

She stared at him. Tiny lines around his eyes crinkled as he gently took her chin in his hand and turned her face . . . a quarter turn to the right. "Look," he said, a smile warm in his voice.

She looked. "Oh, goodness," she managed to say even though the breath had been snatched out of her lungs.

They were hanging off the back end of the train on the tiniest platform Emily had ever seen, much less stood on. Surrounding them was emerald green grassland broken here and there by gingery brown bushes. Everything flew out behind them at an incredible speed. It was like walking the plank of a pirate ship while it was under full sail—and feeling an odd compulsion to throw yourself off into the sheer beauty that surrounded you.

The train gave a small hopping lurch, and Emily grabbed the handrails at her side. All right—so she didn't *really* want to throw herself off.

"What do you think?" Lucien said in her ear. Out of the corner of her eye, she saw his hands settle on the rails a few inches behind hers.

"I can't tell if I'm scared to death or awestruck or both," she said honestly. "I might have a little motion sickness, too."

"You have motion sickness? Surely not. Your appetite has not suffered at all, and that's always a first sign."

"You're laughing at me," Emily grumbled, but she didn't dare remove her hands from the rail and turn around to frown at him. She was still about seventy percent terrified and thirty percent awestruck.

A white house a quarter mile off the track swung past her eyes. Then more and more houses began to appear, and before she knew it a whole herd of cows, standing much closer to the rails than she ever would have expected, whipped past. They didn't even raise their heads from their grazing. Those cows were more used to trains than she was.

Something about the way that Lucien effortlessly stayed balanced made Emily think that he, too, was far more used to trains than she was. Of course, as this was only her second trip in her entire life, she supposed most people she knew would have more experience with train travel than she.

However, she believed that she had now traveled farther west than most of her female friends or their mothers. In fact—

"Where are we?" she asked. She half twisted, keeping her grip tight on the handrail, and looked back at Lucien.

"Pennsylvania or perhaps even Ohio."

Emily smiled. "Excellent."

"Indeed? And why? Are you a criminal fleeing justice? Is that the true reason why you won't reveal your name?"

"I've simply never been so far west."

"Really? Most New Yorkers I know have ventured at least this far."

She almost told him that she was from Boston, not New York, before remembering that she was still incog-

nito. Emily wrinkled her nose at him. "New Yorkers who
are men or women?"

"Men. As you suggested before, my acquaintance
with women is slight."

He was teasing her again. She gave him a mock glare
and changed the subject. Carefully lifting one hand from
the brass rail, she gestured to the landscape flashing
past. "How long can we stay out here?"

"You can stay out here as long as you like. I need to
work."

"And what is your work?"

"Today, writing."

"You are a . . . novelist?" Emily said, unable to contain
a doubtful note from creeping into her words. Lucien
Delatour looked like a cowboy, not a writer. He seemed
so very physical that she couldn't imagine him sitting at
a desk all day, pen in hand. On the other hand, her sister Lily's husband was a journalist, and as Lily was expecting a baby in a few months, Mason must be physical
enough for certain activities. Emily had caught a glimpse
of Mason only once, a moment before Emily had shoved
him off her family home's front steps and into a Boston
blizzard, and he hadn't struck her as scrawny.

That encounter hadn't been one of her finer moments. As she was planning on climbing Mason and
Lily's front steps in only a week, Emily hoped he'd forgiven her.

Slowly, still keeping one hand tight on the railing,
she turned in a half circle so that she was facing Lucien
fully. Sliding one foot back and then the other, she felt

the rearmost guardrail knock against her waist, and she settled against it. The wind pressed against her eyelids and cheeks and pushed her hair away from her face, and she felt quite daring, lounging at the very end of this speeding train.

Lucien said, "No, I'm not a novelist. I'm writing letters today. Twenty of them. Or more, if I can fit them in."

He looked so morose that she almost laughed. But a better reaction struck her. "I could help you," she offered. "Unless they are personal letters, of course." But who would write twenty personal letters a day?

"How is your penmanship?"

*Barely legible.* She said firmly, "Marvelous."

"All right. We'll give it a try." He stepped backward and began to disappear into the depths of the Pullman car. "I'll get a few letters started, and then when you're ready to come in, you can copy them and put others' names at the top."

Standing at the back of the train was exhilarating in a way she'd never experienced before, but it might quickly become terrifying again if she stayed out here alone. Perhaps tomorrow she'd venture out onto the platform alone. That is, if she could convince Lucien Delatour to allow them to stay.

"I'll come in now and see to those letters," Emily said. "And perhaps have a snack. I'm feeling a bit hungry again."

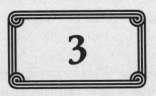

**3**

THEY WERE ONLY A few hours outside of Marion, and still Lucien would not relent in his plan to put them off the train.

Emily was getting desperate.

They had passed a fairly pleasant day writing letters, although Lucien commented more than once that he'd expected her penmanship to be better. Emily ignored it; his mood lightened bit by bit with every letter she finished, and she decided her lack of lovely handwriting was not as sore a subject as he was pretending. He was even humming to himself while she finished up the last three letters, and he spent his newly free time poring over a map that appeared to be of a portion of Wyoming Territory.

Now, though, as she was sitting at the desk with nothing to do except worry about how to convince him that she and Annabelle should stay on his train, Lucien put aside the map, took up a pen, and grimaced furiously at a blank piece of stationery. He was not in the sort of mood she wanted him to be in while they debated—again!—his decision to toss them off the train at the next station.

Why was she even fighting him about it, though? She and Annabelle could always catch the next train heading west or even find seats on this train in another car. While they almost certainly wouldn't be in a private car, they could hire a sleeper berth and ride somewhat comfortably to San Francisco. The immigrants whom she helped always traveled west in public cars. She should experience what they experienced.

But . . . those other trains didn't have Lucien on them.

Her eyes swung back to him, as they always seemed to do.

Staring morosely at the unpenned letter on the card table, he was slouched in her grandfather's favorite chair with his sleeves rolled up and his top shirt button unbuttoned. Unlike his bare feet, his arms and throat were the same tanned color as his face. This amount of casualness in his attire was, apparently, quite usual.

If she was going to be honest with herself—and she did try to be at all times—Lucien was fascinating. He didn't mince words, he sometimes swore in her presence, and even when he was sitting still, she could practically sense the energy vibrating through him. He was a person who liked to get things done.

Still, it was the age of the pioneer industrialist, and plenty of men projected an attitude of being ready to leap onto the next horse or steamer to tackle a new challenge.

So why did she find herself staring at him when she had nothing else to do? And why was she still trying to convince him to let them stay?

Lucien sat up again and picked up the pen. Then he didn't do anything more for a full minute.

"I can write that for you," Emily offered. "I'm all done here."

"No, no. I have to do this one myself."

"Is it another investor letter?"

Although he dressed like a cowboy, she had divined from his correspondence that he was building a railroad and seeking subscribers to a stock offering that would fund the construction. If the people he was writing to were the same people he'd been visiting in New York City and Washington, D.C., she'd have to stop mocking him for his lack of social entrée. He'd met many powerful men.

Lucien shrugged, not really answering her question.

Annabelle had a reputation within the family for being stubborn. Emily had a reputation for being persistent.

"A personal letter, then?" she said with an encouraging note in her voice.

There was no other way to describe it: Lucien squirmed.

That was odd. And just as oddly, Emily suddenly had no desire to continue to pursue that line of questioning.

"I can start now on the letters you wanted to write tomorrow," Emily suggested. "You *do* have more letters to write, don't you?" She had seen a list, and they certainly hadn't gotten through all of them.

"You're just looking for a reason why I should keep you here," Lucien said, not looking up from the blank letter. "But I'm not going to, for several reasons. Yes, I admit you've been very helpful, but I don't need a full-time secretary. One who eats enough for two secretaries, by the way," he added.

Emily, who had just started sliding a half-eaten plate of lemon cake toward herself, quickly put her hands in her lap. "But imagine how much more you would do if you had a full-time secretary. I can write two dozen letters a day for you. Or more! Surely you want as many people to become part of your company as possible."

"Usually it's easier to manage a few people's expectations than it is to manage dozens upon dozens."

"You already are planning to manage dozens."

He shrugged. "I can do it. I've done it before."

"But did you *like* it?"

"Not especially, but that's not the point. Getting you and your sister back to the bosom of your frantic family is the point."

Annabelle sauntered into the salon at that moment. She'd stayed in her room most of the day, reading a novel. "Perhaps our family isn't as frantic as you think, Mr. Delatour. Perhaps we're leaving to make their lives better."

Lucien got to his feet, snapped his cuffs shut, and closed his shirt all the way. "Miss Anna. Nice of you to join our discussion. Your suggestion is one that had not occurred to me, I admit. How would your departure make your family's lives better?"

Emily stared at him. Why was Lucien suddenly being so proper and . . . and couth?

Annabelle's beauty was like a tornado: It threw people into chaos, and it couldn't be stopped or turned aside. Even wearing the same dress she had on yesterday and with her hair pulled back into a simple bun, Annabelle sucked all attention to her.

Normally Emily was grateful for Annabelle's appearance. As the "nice" sister, Emily was often given the dubious pleasure of speaking to newcomers to the Boston social scene, whether they were guests of residents or young pups new to the social whirl. Hostesses around the city knew that Emily could be counted on to be pleasant and set people at ease.

Often newcomers were interesting, and Emily didn't mind being their first introduction to Boston; but just as often Emily got stuck in tedious conversation. Sometimes, she suspected, a hostess would send her most socially inept guest her way just to keep him or her away from the others. But upon the arrival of Annabelle and her perfect face, Emily usually managed to mutter her excuses and slip away while a gentleman was picking his jaw up off the floor. Having a beautiful sister did come in handy.

For the first time in her life, as she watched Lucien run his fingers through his dark hair to tame it down, Emily wished that Annabelle's beauty was just a bit less showy.

"How would our departure help our family?" Annabelle repeated. "Our father is extremely old-fashioned and refuses to let our youngest sister marry until we are married before her. It's like we are living in the Middle Ages. First Emily, as she is the eldest, must get married, and then myself, and then finally our youngest sister."

A complete fabrication, though an interesting one. Which novel had Annabelle been reading today?

Lucien waited until Annabelle had gracefully sunk into a chair before seating himself again. Emily scowled. This afternoon Lucien had hardly moved a muscle as Emily popped up and down out of her chair.

Lucien turned his dark eyes on Emily, and her stupid heart gave a twist. "Of the two of you, I thought you were the younger sister," he said.

"Why?" she asked baldly.

He tapped his finger to his chin and continued to regard her. "I don't know. Your enthusiasm, perhaps. I'll have to think on it."

Her enthusiasm? Perhaps he thought of her enthusiasm in the same light as Emily regarded that of the young gentlemen in their first social seasons: with amused tolerance and a dollop of pity.

Emily felt her back stiffen. "If you would enlighten me when you solve that question, I would appreciate it."

Lucien tilted his head as if he were perplexed by her icy tone. Men: completely unobservant. "All right," he said agreeably.

Annabelle cleared her throat.

"Hmm?" Lucien said, still not taking his eyes off

Emily. Perhaps he was looking for additional signs of her enthusiasm. It was all she could do not to stick her tongue out at her, but that would only make her seem younger than he already believed her to be.

"As I was saying, our youngest sister has found the love of her life, and only if Emily and I remove ourselves from our family will she have a chance at true happiness." Annabelle heaved a sigh. "She's a bit cross-eyed, so it might be her one chance for a love match."

Lucien burst out laughing. "What a load of horse— uh, poop."

"Mr. Delatour!" Annabelle gasped, and covered her ears.

Emily snorted. They were lucky he hadn't used the word he'd originally had on the tip of his tongue. If they did manage to stay in this Pullman car with Lucien, their vocabularies would be broadened before their trip was over.

"She's both cross-eyed and star-crossed?" Lucien said, still chortling. "Miss Anna, please stop treating me like an idiot. Let's try this again: Why would your family want you to leave?"

"They don't," Emily interjected, throwing Annabelle a let-me-do-the-talking glare. "To be very honest with you—"

"A nice change."

"—my mother had originally planned on taking this car on her trip west. And she didn't want me to come with her, but I had to. I wanted to see the West. I've heard so many stories . . ." Emily bobbed to her feet and began to pace along her grandfather's lush carpet. "So many stories of adventure and hardship and success, and I needed to see it myself. So I snuck aboard, expecting to surprise my mother after we left New York. But instead I surprised you."

Lucien's expression was unreadable. "What about her?" he asked, cocking his thumb in Annabelle's direction.

"She followed me and snuck aboard as well. Please, Lucien. Let us stay."

Annabelle squinted at her, and Emily realized that she'd called Lucien by his first name. It wasn't the only time she'd done it today—she'd hollered his first name when she thought he was diving headfirst between the train cars. And she'd probably used his name a half dozen times since then while writing his letters. Odd that she hadn't noticed until now that she was addressing him as casually as she did longtime family friends.

Maybe this was what going west did to people. It stripped away the veneer of fancy eastern manners, revealing . . . what?

Lucien broke into her thoughts. "And where do you intend for your adventure to end? I'm not a sentimental fellow, but even I cannot leave you two on a train platform at the other side of the country and simply wave good-bye and good luck."

"We have a sister who has a house in San Francisco, and she will take us in at the end of this trip."

"And," Annabelle added, unable to stay quiet, "our parents are trying to make me marry someone I don't wish to marry. You must help me escape that fate."

Lucien looked like he was going to laugh again, so Emily said quickly, "That's actually true."

He shook his head, and Emily's stomach dropped. He was going to say no. Again.

He started, "I admire your adventurous spirits but—"

"We'll rent our bedrooms from you for the duration of the trip," Emily interrupted. "What would it cost?" Before entering the salon that morning, she had picked open her skirt hem and retrieved the three dozen gold double eagle coins she had secreted there.

Lucien gave her a basilisk stare that she suspected he'd perfected over years of hard negotiation. "Two hundred and fifty dollars. Each."

Emily sat back down in her chair and tried not to obviously sigh in relief. That would leave them with a bit more than two hundred dollars in their pocket, and she was sure they could easily survive on that—at least until they reached San Francisco. "Done."

He gawked at her, and Emily belatedly realized that the price he had asked was an exorbitant sum. Oh, she should have known better. She had helped many immigrants purchase train tickets to new homesteads out west.

Rising to his feet, Lucien sauntered over to where Emily was sitting. He braced one hand on the desk and loomed over her and her plate of cake. "Who *are* you?"

Emily blinked innocently at him and said in a reasonable tone, "I am a young lady of good social standing who wishes to travel west. In comfort. And, if possible, escorted by a clearly competent gentleman such as yourself."

"Competent?"

"I should have said *exemplary*. And keenly knowledgeable." Was she laying it on a bit thick?

Lucien rolled his eyes. All right, yes, she had gone over the top.

"And handsome, too," Annabelle cooed.

This time Emily was the one who rolled her eyes. She caught Lucien frowning at her, and realized he might be insulted by her reaction. "And handsome, too," she added. She almost added specifics like *With your dark eyes* and *With your strong arms* but caught herself. When he was standing so close, he muddled her thinking.

She poked a finger into his chest. Clearly surprised, he backed off, allowing her brain to work again. "So," she said, determined to get everyone back to the primary question, "do we have a deal?"

"No."

Annabelle evidently decided that Emily needed help. She threw herself on her knees in front of Lucien, clasped her hands to her heaving bosom, and gave him a soulful look. Lucien's eyebrows jumped up so far, they almost flew off his head.

"Oh, Mr. Delatour, please reconsider. We will not be a bother or get in your way. We'll buy our own food, prepare meals for you—"

That should be interesting. Neither one of them had

ever prepared a meal beyond making sandwiches at picnics on Boston Common.

"Do my laundry?" Lucien suggested.

Annabelle didn't flinch. "Yes, that, too."

Poor Lucien. If he wanted his clothes to be clean, she and Annabelle would need to find a porter or other railway attendant to subcontract the washing to.

Lucien reached out, took Annabelle's hands, and raised her to her feet. "Ladies, I appreciate your perseverance, but the answer is still no. I'm putting you on the platform at Marion, buying you tickets back to New York, and saying good-bye. It's been . . . interesting meeting you."

"Likewise," Emily murmured. Why was Lucien still holding Annabelle's hands?

He lifted one of Annabelle's hands to his lips. "I wish you a pleasant return trip." Releasing his hold on Annabelle, he turned his dark eyes on Emily. "And I hope that if we meet again in New York, you will wish to continue our acquaintance."

Despite his fine words, he made no move to kiss *her* hand. Older, enthusiastic sisters must not be as appealing to him.

Emily inclined her head, trying to look regal instead of aggravated.

Without another word, he turned and left the salon.

Emily sniffed and flapped a hand after him. "There is a good example of a strategic retreat. Also known as running away."

"He's the victor, though. We're headed back to New York."

Emily smiled and speared another piece of cake with her silver fork. "Indeed? What makes you think that?"

Marion was grimier than Lucien remembered it—or perhaps he was just more aware of the run-down station house, the loud shouts of the salesmen touting their wares to train passengers, and the oily smell from the food carts lined up just off the platform as Emily and Anna daintily walked beside him to the ticket counter at the end of the platform. Not that the girls were shiny pennies—both of them wore the same wrinkled dresses they'd had on yesterday. For stowaways, they were remarkably unprepared . . . aside from the large amount of cash that Emily was apparently hauling around with her. He'd strapped on his gun belt before leaving the car just in case someone in Marion realized that Emily was a walking bank vault and decided to rob her.

Lucien shook his head. The sooner these two were off his hands, the better. Now that their departure from his company was only a few minutes away, he didn't mind admitting to himself that Emily was far too distracting. And attractive.

He'd been a breath away from kissing her on the platform on the back of the Pullman car. Only the thought of Susan had stopped him: Susan, who considered them well on their way to an engagement. And who could blame her? He'd certainly left Washington, D.C., with that expectation as well.

Lucien caught himself staring at Emily again and yanked his gaze away. He'd spent most of the day watching her while she wasn't looking. As she wrote his letters, she would nibble on a thumbnail, or a lock of hair, or the end of the pen. In fact, she was constantly putting things in her mouth. His pantry was probably bare by now.

Well, these mystery girls weren't his problem anymore. At least, they wouldn't be his problem as soon as he put two tickets to New York in their hands.

"When's the next train to New York?" he asked at the ticket counter.

"Tomorrow, seven a.m.," the ticket seller replied. He scratched his graying head. "Didn't you folks just get off the train that came from New York?"

The girls would have to stay here overnight, then. The cost of returning them to their family in good health was rising. "Is there a good, clean hotel nearby?"

The ticket agent looked affronted. "This isn't the backside of beyond, you know. Several fine hotels are only a two-minute walk away."

Lucien turned to the girls. Emily had her hands folded primly at her waist and had her attention on him. Anna was, naturally, ogling a young porter who was unloading baggage from the train and displaying impressive arm muscles as he did so.

"You'll have to stay here overnight," Lucien said to Emily. "I'm sorry."

She shook her head. "No need to be sorry. We shall

be just fine. Good-bye, Mr. Delatour." She stuck out her hand to shake his.

"I'm buying your tickets," he reminded her.

"No, we would rather not be indebted to you."

This was the woman who had just devoured most of his foodstuffs without a qualm. A wave of suspicion prickled over his skin.

He turned back to the ticket seller. "Two first-class tickets to New York on the next available train, please."

Emily squeezed herself next to him, edging him away from the ticket window and close to the edge of the platform. She smiled at the ticket agent. "Please ignore him. We would like two first-class tickets to San Francisco, please."

"This is the window for gentlemen to purchase tickets," the ticket agent said disapprovingly. "Ladies use the window to the right."

Emily plunked four gold double eagles down in front of the agent and smiled at him again. "We would like tickets on this train, if possible."

"Yes, ma'am!"

Lucien bumped his hip into Emily's, scooting her sideways and away from the window. He swiped up the coins and forced them into her hand. "Two tickets to New York," he growled at the ticket seller. "*Now*."

Emily said loudly, "Mr. Delatour, you are not our father, our guardian, or our husband. You—"

"I could be husband to only one of you, not both," he pointed out.

"—have no say over our travel plans. You may purchase tickets for us and you may even escort us to the local hotel of your choice if you truly wish to, but we will be taking the next train to San Francisco as soon as you are out of our way." Emily lifted her chin.

Lucien had engaged in enough negotiations to recognize steely resolve when he saw it gleaming in his opponent's eyes. And he had no leverage here at all, damn it.

"Do you want me to alert some of the porters, ma'am?" the ticket seller asked Emily. "They'll make this fellow stop bothering you."

"No." Emily paused and skewered Lucien with a warning look. "Not at the moment, that is. Thank you for your concern, sir."

"Fine. Get your own tickets," Lucien snapped. Damn stubborn girl. "If you have a hankering for cake, you know where to find me."

He stepped back and away and, for the second time that day, plunged into empty space. This time off the edge of the train platform.

"Lucien!" Emily shrieked. She made a grab for him and missed.

Lucien landed on his feet this time—like a cat, he thought proudly—and then one ankle crumpled beneath him. He staggered and grabbed the wooden platform edge. "I'm all right," he told Emily.

He tried taking a big step up onto the platform, but his stupid right ankle refused to hold his weight. Feeling like a fool, he propped his rear end on the platform and then swung both legs up. Grabbing the edge of the ticket booth for support, he managed to haul himself upright. His ankle felt like it had been wrapped in barbed wire that had been heated in a campfire and then spit on by a rattlesnake. Not good.

Without asking permission, Emily ducked under his right arm and draped it over her shoulders, making herself his living crutch. "Lean on me. We'll get you back to the car."

Carefully, Lucien allowed Emily to take some of his weight.

"I'm not going to break," she said chidingly.

Lucien leaned more heavily on her, and both Emily and his ankle seemed much happier with the situation. Like this, he could probably get back to the Pullman car. What he'd do once he was inside, he couldn't imagine. He'd essentially be an invalid, trapped on the settee in the salon or in his bedroom.

"I can take his other side," Anna offered, stepping forward.

"No!" Emily and Lucien said at the same time.

"Then what can I do to help? Buy our tickets?" Anna said.

"We'll do it after we get Lucien back to the car," Emily said as she nudged Lucien forward. "This is more important. Anna, can you just walk on his other side to make sure he doesn't fall?"

"I won't fall," Lucien ground out. God, this was embarrassing.

Emily quirked a smile up at him. "Good. I'm not sure that Anna could catch you anyway."

The ticket seller was shaking his head as they hobbled away. "We'll be back," Anna called to him over her shoulder.

Lucien didn't hear exactly what he muttered in return, but it sounded suspiciously like "I doubt it."

It took a good ten minutes for them to make it back to the Pullman car. A porter jumped forward and helped Emily haul Lucien up the stairs to the car like an overlarge piece of baggage. It was not, Lucien thought, one of his finer moments, and he was annoyed to the core of his bones that this was likely to be Emily's final memory of him once they parted ways.

The only bright spot was having Emily snugged up close, pressed to his side from hip to shoulder for the entire trek.

Emily, breathing heavily, maneuvered him onto the salon's love seat before detaching herself. She pushed a chair into place before him and then gently raised his damaged foot onto the chair. "There," she said with satisfaction.

The train whistle blew, signaling the train's departure in ten minutes, and the satisfaction wicked out of her expression. "Oh, no. We still have to buy tickets and send a telegram to Mother so she doesn't become alarmed." Dark eyes wide with worry, she said to Lucien, "Will you be all right if we leave you?"

Some kind of wild madness overtook him. Perhaps it had been brought on by the pain of his twisted ankle or his overall concern about the two sisters traveling across the country on their own. Or perhaps it was the effect of spending the past ten minutes pressed as close to Emily as a lover would be. In any case, madness swamped his normal good sense, and Lucien heard himself say, "No."

Emily halted halfway to the entrance to the car and spun to face him. "No?"

"No. I don't think I will be all right. If your offer is still open, I would like you two to stay." He gestured at his ankle. "I'll need your help getting around."

Emily slowly walked back toward him. Her hips swayed and her skirts swished. Lucien's mouth went dry.

"All right," she said. "But we'll pay you only fifty dollars each. Since we'll be helping you so much."

His brain started working again. "You eat a lot. I'd be beggared at fifty. One hundred each."

"Seventy-five."

"Add in three hours of letter writing a day, and we have a deal at seventy-five each."

Emily nodded. "Deal." She held out her hand to shake.

The same madness that had hit him earlier came back for an encore performance. He took her hand and brought it to his mouth. "You're an angel of mercy."

Emily started to look concerned. "Lucien, we'll stay, but I still need to telegraph my mother. I'll come back in five minutes." Before she departed, she said to her sister in a whisper that Lucien was probably not supposed to hear, "I think he may be getting feverish. Make sure he drinks some water." Then she descended to the platform and disappeared into the crowd of scurrying passengers, porters, and hawkers of wares.

Lucien frowned. Maybe he *was* getting feverish. With Emily out of his presence and cool, lucid thought rushing in like a snowmelt flood, he was having second thoughts.

Well, what was done was done. If his ankle improved rapidly, they could always revisit their deal and he could refund to Emily part of their fee. But if his ankle was broken, having an on-site assistant pay *him* for the chance to help him hobble around, to feed him, and to write his letters would end up being the best bargain of his life.

Emily made a mad beeline toward the telegraph station through the rapidly dispersing crowd on the platform. She'd spent the last hour mentally searching for just the right words that would reassure her mother and Mr. Grant and keep them from pursuing her and Annabelle. Whether it would work . . . well, they would find out soon enough.

There was no line at the window when she arrived, and Emily said bluntly to the young man inside the little room, "How do I send a telegram?"

"You tell me who to send it to, then you tell me what to put in it, and then you pay me for each word," the young man said promptly. "Easy as pie." He scanned her, and Emily wondered what he thought of her fine dress, which was wrinkled as an old apple. "How much money do you have?"

"Enough for a lot of words." Emily put a double eagle in front of him, and he nodded quickly.

"Indeed. All right: Who and where?"

"Mrs. Mary Grant, Imperial Hotel, New York City." Odds were that her mother was still there. Her daughters had been missing for almost a full day, and she was likely combing the streets of the city.

Emily's stomach shriveled. Mother must be frantic with worry. No telegram she wrote would be able to take back the last twenty-four hours of panic her mother must have experienced. While her mother was imagining all kinds of disasters or crimes that must have befallen them, Annabelle had been reading novels, and Emily had been eating lemon cake and writing letters.

"And what do you want to say?" the telegraph operator prompted her.

Emily took a deep breath. "Please write, 'Dear Mother, we both are in good health and happiness and are on our way to San Francisco. Do not worry. We will write again when we arrive. Very sorry for making you worry.'"

He read it back to her and then said, "If I were you, I'd make it shorter, like, 'Mother, we are fine. Going to SF. Will write on arrival. Don't worry.' It's more than half as short, which means it's half as expensive."

"Can I afford the note I wrote?" Emily asked, and nodded at the double eagle.

"Oh, absolutely."

"Then please send mine."

"You said *worry* twice," the telegraph operator said, apparently unwilling to let such extravagance go.

"I said it twice, but she must be twenty times as worried as that," Emily told him. "Please send what I wrote."

With one eye on the train, she shifted from foot to foot as he counted off her change and then began tapping in her telegram.

"Will the receiver of the telegram know where it came from?" Emily asked as she scooped the coins into her purse.

"Oh, yes."

She'd thought so but hadn't known for sure. Well, it would take her mother and Mr. Grant a very short while to realize she and Annabelle were on a train. And if they wanted to find them and bring them home, all they would have to do was telegraph ahead to the next major station, alert the stationmaster to their suspected presence on the train, and ask him to remove them.

She and Annabelle would have to be very, very careful.

Emily hurried back to the train.

Anna sauntered across the length of the salon and put her hand against Lucien's forehead, apparently checking for fever, although he'd never heard of a man getting a fever from an injured ankle. "Poor Mr. Delatour," she cooed.

Lucien gently but firmly removed Anna's hand. "Miss Anna, I appreciate your, ah, concern, but I'm feeling quite in good health, thank you. Aside from my twisted ankle." He paused. How to say this without being overly offensive? "Miss Anna, we will likely be spending a great deal of time with each other in the upcoming days, so I'd appreciate it if you would treat me as an old family friend." *An old, ugly, poor, and uninteresting family friend.* "Maybe a friend of, say, your father's. Or grandfather's."

"My father's dead," Anna said absently. She wrinkled her nose at him in a way that reminded him of Emily. "I wouldn't be surprised if you were a friend of my grandfather's, in fact."

"Yes? What's his name?"

She laughed. "I'm not that easy to trick."

Shrugging, he said, "I had to try." But if Emily and Anna were from the social circles he thought they were, it was possible that he knew their grandfather. He'd spoken to a lot of men with a lot of money in the past few weeks.

She tapped a finger against her cheek and regarded him thoughtfully. "Mr. Delatour, just now, were you trying to politely ask me to not flirt with you?"

Such bluntness could only be matched with bluntness. "Yes."

"Well, I'll consider it. As you say, it's a long trip, and we will be with each other quite often . . . and I flirt much better than I write letters. But it's not as much fun when the gentleman doesn't know how to flirt back."

"I know how to flirt," Lucien defended himself.

"I don't believe you do. A man has to have a little romance, a little fun, in his soul to flirt. You, sir, are the smoldering type."

Emily climbed up the stairway. "I'm back," she said breathlessly.

"Oh, good," Anna said. "Emily, I was just telling Mr. Delatour that he doesn't flirt, he smolders. What do you think?"

"I think it sounds like you've been having an interesting conversation," Emily said slowly as she closed the door.

"No, no—what do you think about him smoldering?"

"Well . . ." Emily said, looking at him.

For fun—because he did have fun in his soul, damn it—Lucien tried out a smoldering look on Emily.

"Oh," she said in a tiny voice. She looked, he thought smugly, like an ox that had been hit in the skull with a tree stump.

Anna clapped her hands in delight. "Marvelous! I knew it."

Emily shook herself. "Yes, um, quite impressive, Mr. Delatour."

Uh-oh. When Emily called him "Mr. Delatour," something was wrong.

The train whistle gave two long blasts. With a jerk, the car lurched forward. The station slowly slid past the window, and then a row of two-story hotels. One of those hotels would have hosted the sisters tonight if Emily hadn't been so stubborn about sticking to her plan to go west. And if her stubbornness hadn't gotten him so riled up, he'd have two working ankles now instead of just one.

As he watched Emily settle into the chair she favored, he realized he wasn't as annoyed as he'd normally be when he lost a battle of wills. He'd underestimated her, and she'd used that to her advantage, surprising him at the last moment with her plans to continue west with or without him. It was admirable, really. And he wouldn't underestimate her again.

"What did your telegram say?" Anna asked Emily.

"I wrote Mother that we were on our way to San Francisco and that she shouldn't worry. I promised to telegraph her again when we arrived there."

"How did you know where to send it?" Anna asked Emily. "Mother might not be—" Then she shut up.

Lucien's antennae quivered. Emily sending a telegram to their mother instead of their father supported Anna's statement that their father was dead, but why wouldn't they know where their mother would be? Now that he would be traveling with the sisters longer than he'd expected, these questions had grown more important.

Just who was he sharing his Pullman car with?

He leaned forward to question Emily. The move jostled his raised leg, sending a firecracker explosion off in his right ankle. "I think I need a drink," he told Emily through clenched teeth. "I hope the owner of this car isn't part of the Temperance Union. . . ."

Emily stood and moved close to him. So close that her skirts brushed against his healthy leg and a lemony scent—probably from the cake—whispered in his nostrils. She leaned in. Lucien focused on her lips, which were now only six inches away. Beautiful lips, plump and quick to smile. Delicious lips, he was sure. All she had to do was bend down . . .

She rose up on her tiptoes, pressed on the carved wooden panel above his head and to his left, and revealed a small cabinet containing several bottles of spirits and some glasses. She seized a bottle and plunked it on the table next to him.

"How the hell did you find that?" Lucien demanded.

Pink dotted her cheeks. If he hadn't been so close, he might have missed the panicked widening of her eyes. Either she was feeling guilty about something, or his rough language had startled her again.

Not meeting his gaze, Emily brought down a glass and placed it next to the bottle. "My mother had been told about it by the person who was letting her use the car, and she mentioned it to us."

Lucien had a hard time imagining a high-society mother telling her unwed daughter where the spirits were secreted in a Pullman car, but suddenly he was tired of being suspicious. His ankle ached like a bastard and Emily had found alcohol to help dull the pain. That was all he needed to know now. If she wanted to keep her secrets, she could. It was no matter to him.

At least until tomorrow.

4

THEY STOPPED AT THE next station shortly before
dawn. Emily hopped off the train and went in
search of a cane, a doctor . . . and a disguise.

The cane was Lucien's idea, and a good one. The
doctor was her idea, and it was a good idea as well, she
thought, even if Lucien wasn't convinced. "I'll be fine in
a few days," he'd insisted as she'd helped him from his
bedroom to the salon, his arm slung over her shoulder.
"And you have no idea of the level of quackery that some
doctors descend to out here." But he'd had creases of pain
around his eyes, and Emily had resolved to ignore his in-
sistence on having no doctor, just as she'd been ignoring
his unsubtle forays into discovering who her family was.

Emily scowled. Assuming that her mother had received the telegram, her family had almost certainly figured out by now that she and Annabelle were on this
train. Hence the need for disguises.

*Exciting* was beginning to feel like an understated way of describing their travels across the country.

Forgotten fliers and discarded railroad tickets fluttered in the morning breeze along the nearly deserted train platform, some catching in cracks in the boards and others darting away across the tracks to freedom. Emily lifted her face to the predawn sky and sucked in a deep breath. Dozens of scents danced through her senses—the dust of the town's roads, manure from the livery stable she could see beyond the station, a hint of upcoming rain—but the one that overrode them all was the smell of living plants. Trees, bushes, long grasses: all exuded an invigorating smell that made Emily breathe in even more deeply and put a bounce in her step.

Boston had its famed gardens, including the Public Garden, but never had the scents of living plants wrapped around her and seeped into every pore like they did now.

If this was what a town on a busy rail line smelled like, what would she experience once they moved deeper west and farther from civilization?

Sucking in another deep lungful of the predawn air, Emily reached the end of the platform, descended a few steps onto the boardwalk that ran past the shops that fanned out from the station, and headed for the general mercantile that stood three stories tall and loomed above every other storefront on the street. Already several horses and wagons were tied up to the hitching post in front of the mercantile, and Emily could see lights on inside and bodies moving around behind the glass-paned windows. One fat drop of rain plunked against her shoulder and then another on her cheek in the moment before she slipped inside the store, the bell chiming softly as she shut the door behind her.

Emily gaped.

She'd been shopping before, of course. She'd been fitted for countless gowns; she'd helped her mother choose new Tabriz Persian carpets for the downstairs parlor; she'd even watched her stepfather, Mr. Grant, purchase a pair of matched ponies for their best carriage. But this . . . this was amazing.

Great big barrels marked "Salt," "Sugar," "Kerosene," and "Nails" stretched along one wall like fat soldiers arrayed for battle. Boots, hats, ready-made clothing, and bolts upon bolts of material squared off against the barrels on the opposite wall, and between them was a mishmash of gloriously interesting items: barbed wire, axes, glass lamps, chairs, playing cards, an oil painting of a female dancer—most certainly not a ballerina—rifles, and a stuffed buffalo head.

She would never be able to find a cane in this gorgeous circus of a store.

She searched for help. At the back of the store, a handful of men lounged around the big brass cash register. Most wore hats and jackets, like they'd come in off the street, but the shortest one wore shirtsleeves and a vest, and a watch chain stretched across his thin chest. The shopkeeper, she guessed.

For the first time since she'd sneaked into her grandfather's private car instead of plunging forward into the unknown, Emily hesitated.

She'd never actually gone shopping by herself before. Either an older servant or her mother had accompanied her. Their experience and ease must have given her false confidence. Now, in a shop she'd never visited and facing a handful of men she'd never seen before, she felt as skittish as a mouse who sensed a cat was lurking in the room.

It didn't help that the men looked quite fearsome. One had a scar across his face that had deadened an eye. Another had hair so long, he looked like an Indian. In fact, she realized as she looked closer, he was an Indian in white man's clothing. A third man looked fairly ordinary, but his eyes wouldn't settle on anything and his hands twitched constantly.

Just another part of the adventure. She could do this.

Emily swallowed and then fastened on her best smile as she strode forward. "Gentlemen, would you help me? I'm purchasing a cane for my, uh, employer, and I'm unsure where the canes are located."

"Right this way, miss," the shopkeeper said, edging past the small pack of men. He led her to a pile of merchandise next to the boots and began rooting around. "What size do you need?"

She didn't know canes came in sizes. "It's for a tall man—"

"Aha!" The shopkeeper pulled out a black wooden cane. "This might do."

Emily tried it herself. It seemed short even for her. She shook her head and handed it back.

Out came another cane. "This one, then."

It seemed better, but without Lucien here with her, it was hard to tell if it would be right.

Her eyes fell again on the men at the back of the store, still chatting away. Taking a deep breath, she approached them again.

Emily offered the cane to the Indian. "You, sir, seem closest in size to my employer. Would you mind trying this cane for me and telling me whether you think it would suit?"

Eyes fastened on her like horseshoe nails, the Indian took the cane, tested his weight on it, thumped it a few times on the wide wooden floorboards, nodded, and handed it back to Emily. All without speaking a word.

Emily offered him another smile. "Thank you." Her legs wobbling only a tiny bit, she returned to the shopkeeper. "This one will do."

"Do you need anything else?"

"A doctor. Do you know one?"

Emily paid for the cane with a few coins that Lucien had given her. Feeling four—no, three and a half—pairs of eyes on her back as she walked away, Emily heaved a sigh of relief as the door shut behind her.

Some parts of this adventure were more nerve-racking than others.

She decided to forgo another nerve-racking encounter—this time with Lucien, who would be annoyed that she had pursued a doctor on his behalf—and shamelessly instructed the doctor she had located to knock on the Pullman car door, introduce himself to Lucien, and inspect his foot. With twenty minutes left before the train's departure and a gold coin burning a hole in her pocket, she had some real shopping to do. And it wasn't going to be at the general mercantile.

She spent five of her precious twenty minutes finding an open store, another five looking at and selecting merchandise, and then another five looking at even more merchandise because the storekeeper did not have enough cash money to give Emily the correct change for her twenty-dollar coin, leaving Emily with the choice of buying more than they needed or leaving money on the table. And as her grandfather had told her over and over again, Highfills never left money on the table.

The train's warning whistle blew as she exited the shop. Her early-morning shadow stretched in front of her as she raced back to the Pullman car, her arms loaded with brown-paper-wrapped packages.

"You went shopping," two voices said at once as she stumbled into the Pullman car. One voice was delighted—Annabelle jumped up to take some of the packages from her. The other was disgusted. Lucien had his foot wrapped in bulky white bandages, and the pain lines around his eyes were back.

Emily took a few steps toward him to check his foot before realizing that she still held most of the packages. The man had an unfortunate effect on her mental faculties.

"Indeed. Some necessities." Emily stacked the rest of the packages onto a chair, and the brown paper made a satisfying crinkling noise. "What did the doctor say about your foot?"

"I told you, I didn't need a doctor," Lucien grumbled.

"I forgot," Emily said, not even bothering to lie well.

He muttered something under his breath that Emily was glad she didn't hear. Her vocabulary of curse words had expanded enough recently, thank you very much.

"The doctor said that he should stay off it as much as possible and keep it wrapped strongly but not tightly," Annabelle said after it became clear that Lucien wasn't going to reply. "It should be much better in a week or two."

"Good."

"That's what I said, too," Lucien reminded Emily.

Really, he was acting like a baby. Emily tried on her mother's favorite disapproving expression. It felt strange on her face, but she said anyway, "Mr. Delatour, gentlemen do not tell ladies 'I told you so.'"

Lucien scowled. "One: I never claimed to be a gentleman."

True enough. Was that the reason why she found him so fascinating? Even when he was grumbling at her, she couldn't take her eyes off him.

She pulled her gaze away, and it settled on a tray of steaming sausages and warm bread slices. Where had those come from, and how had she not noticed them until now?

"Two: Ladies take deep pleasure in telling gentlemen 'I told you so,' and what's good for the goose is good for the gander. Three: Had I known that you had planned to ignore my wishes as you did, I wouldn't have ordered this from one of the station vendors." He gestured at the tray.

"You might not be a gentleman, but I think you are a saint," Emily said, smiling at him.

He didn't smile back. "Hardly."

Why was he acting so grim? Was he truly that upset about the doctor? "Are you an angel, then?"

"No."

"A philanthropist?"

"No."

"A mongoose?"

He blinked. "A mongoose?"

"Yes, I've been reading about them. Indians in India keep them to eat snakes, so they don't have to worry about snakes biting them in their own houses."

He blinked again. "What does that have to do with breakfast?"

Nothing, but at least he'd lost that forbidding expression on his face. "Well, mongooses are helpful. And speaking of being helpful, what do you need me to do for you today?"

"Improve your atrocious handwriting," he replied, but his eyes crinkled at her, this time not with pain, and Emily grinned back, inwardly whispering a sigh of relief.

She got three plates from the pantry and served sausages and bread to Lucien and Annabelle before loading her own plate with breakfast. "I've had a busy morning," she defended herself when Lucien raised his eyebrows in exaggerated surprise at her haul. "The general store was unlike anything I'd ever seen before. I could have spent hours in there, looking into each bin and opening every box. Anna, the next time the train stops, I'm going to take you to one of those stores. You'll love it."

"You don't have anything like that in your neighborhood?" Lucien asked casually.

Ah, he had resumed the probing questions. "Not that I'm aware of. And you? Tell me about where you live." She'd turned the discussion back on him quite deftly, she decided.

From the quirk of his mouth, she knew that he'd recognized her tactic. But he answered readily between bites of food. "I live on a ranch about five miles outside of a small town in Wyoming Territory. It's a bit isolated, but the ranch is beautiful."

Emily was putting the pieces together, and it didn't make a picture she was familiar with. "You're a rancher? Building a railroad?" Nor did it suit him: Something about him screamed city boy. Perhaps his clothes, which, though simple, had a flair that was missing from those she'd seen on the men at the train stations they'd passed through. Lucien's manners, though, were sometimes little better than those of an uncouth ranch hand who preferred to spend more time with cattle than people. He was a puzzle indeed.

"I'm a businessman who owns a ranch and half of a railroad," he corrected. "I'm owner or part owner of several steamboats on the Mississippi as well."

"You are rich, then." Annabelle stated it rather than

asked it. "Yet I've not heard your name before within our social circles. Why not?"

"Anna," Emily said in a warning tone. If she were Lucien, she would take offense at the possible insinuation that, despite his wealth, he was and would always be an outsider and unworthy of mingling with them.

"Very strange," he agreed. "Who is among your social circle? Perhaps we have friends in common that we are unaware of."

Annabelle opened her mouth, but Emily said quickly, "Nice try."

Shaking his head, Lucien replied with good humor, "I have to keep trying."

"Why?" Emily said. "What does it matter? If you knew our names, would you back out of our agreement?"

"Careful," he said.

She paused and then mentally shrugged. Why start being careful around him now? "We don't know you very well, just as you don't know us very well."

Even as the words left her mouth, they sounded wrong to her ears and, if she was going to be sentimental, to her heart. Half the time she could predict how he would react, whether it was with a scowl or an eye roll or a laugh, as if they had known each other for years. The other half of the time she couldn't predict anything about him, but she waited almost breathlessly to see what he would do.

She gave herself a shake and continued: "Are you the type of businessman whose name is his word, or the type who insists on a written contract to enforce agreements, or the type who thinks a contract isn't worth a hill of beans?"

Lucien was sitting very still, his mouth a flat line. "It's been a very long time since someone doubted a promise I've made," he said finally.

All right. Clearly this was one of those times when his reaction was not as she'd expected it would be. Perhaps it *was* time to be careful. "I'm not doubting your promise. I'm wondering whether you consider our agreement to be a promise."

He exhaled. "Fair enough. As you say, we don't know each other very well." He tapped his fingers on the table for a few moments as he thought. "And I do not consider our agreement to be a promise binding on both parties. You could change your minds at the next stop, hop off the train, and catch the next train back to New York. I could learn something so terrible about you two that I turn you over to the sheriff at the next station. But right now I intend to keep my end of the bargain and take you to San Francisco, where I have business with other potential investors and where I'll place you into the safe hands of your sister."

"What if we're wealthy?" Annabelle asked.

Lucien gave her the smile one would give a silly child. "Your sister promised me five hundred dollars to take you to San Francisco. I know you're wealthy."

"Or was," Emily muttered. She was still annoyed at herself for agreeing to his offer immediately. It was one reason why she'd negotiated their fare harder the second time.

"Think of it as an investment in future adventures. Well-cushioned future adventures."

Emily cocked her head. Where was he going with this?

"Let me guess: Your life back home consisted of afternoon tea with silly ladies, weekend parties with brainless gentlemen, and a shopping trip every day."

Emily's curiosity turned into downright irritation. "I never claimed to have a difficult life, Mr. Delatour, nor a life that I wanted to be less cushioned. I simply had a life I wanted to change."

"Besides," Annabelle cut in, "the brainless gentlemen never talked to Emily—she was always too busy conversing with the smart ones."

An exaggeration but a flattering one, and Lucien's sudden sharp frown was an additional flattery. "Indeed, some gentlemen were quite interesting." Emily gestured carelessly at the list of investors Lucien was corresponding with. "Many of the people you wish to enlist in your railroad are not unfamiliar to me."

Lucien's eyes narrowed. "Then let us put your expertise to work, Miss Emily. As soon as you finish breakfast, we can continue the letter writing."

"I'd like to change my dress first."

He nodded grandly. "You may."

She stood and strode to his side, where she could stare down at him in her most intimidating fashion. "I wasn't asking permission."

He was trying not to smile and failing. "I know."

Honestly, he was infuriating.

The way that lock of hair was falling over one of his eyes was infuriating, too. Emily reached out and flicked it back where it belonged.

Lucien went still.

Quickly Emily pressed her palm against his forehead, as if that had been her intention all along. "You don't seem feverish," she pronounced, and removed her hand. "The doctor I found must have done a good job."

Lucien caught her hand in his and slowly, so slowly, brought it toward his lips.

Emily's chest felt tight, and she couldn't pull in a normal breath.

She'd had her hand kissed uncountable times, and almost every occasion was completely unmemorable. But now, even before Lucien's mouth touched her skin, she knew that this kiss wasn't going to escape her memory so easily.

His lips grazed the back of her hand. Something in her heart spun free, like a dandelion seed soaring in a breeze.

Annabelle cleared her throat, and Emily retrieved her hand. Unsure of what she would see on Lucien's face—a dazed expression like her own, complete obliviousness, or worse, smugness—she kept her face averted as she picked up the brown-paper-wrapped packages and led Annabelle to her room.

Then she shut the door behind them and displayed her new purchases.

Annabelle was not impressed. She held a dress up to herself, wrinkled her nose, and said, "Ready to wear? It doesn't even have a bustle."

"Do you think I should have bought yards of fabric, thread, and needles instead? Annabelle, unless you have a secret life I am unaware of, neither one of us knows the first thing about how to sew our own clothes."

Annabelle shrugged, putting down the first dress and picking up a second. "These will not be as flattering to our figures—I can see that right away."

"That's the point, really. These are our disguises."

Annabelle stopped examining the dresses and stared at Emily. "Disguises? Whatever for?"

"Mother and Mr. Grant are now very likely aware we are on this train. If they want us to return, all they needed to do was leave a telegram for the conductor at the last stop, asking him to search for us."

Annabelle didn't look convinced. "How will ugly clothes help?"

"Our fine clothes will make the conductor take a second look at us. And fine clothes that are wrinkled and worn, as ours are, will be the proof that we are the girls he is looking for."

"What if we simply ask Lucien to tell the conductor that we are his sisters?"

Emily didn't want to admit that she hadn't thought of that, but Annabelle must have read something in her expression. "Honestly, Emily, sometimes you do act like the younger sister. Did you go to all this trouble to find new clothes just because you wanted to put on a disguise?"

"That's not the whole reason. With fresh dresses, we will smell better." This morning, when she'd helped Lucien walk to the salon, Emily swore he'd sniffed her once or twice during that short journey. At one point, his nose had been practically pressed up into her hair. She would have enjoyed it far more if she hadn't been worried about how she smelled after wearing the same clothing for two days straight.

She tugged the dress out of Annabelle's hands. "If you do not want any of these, I will take them all."

Annabelle's eyes lit up. "May I then have the dress you are wearing now?"

"No!" For Annabelle was right: The dresses they had on their backs were flattering, as they were in fashionable colors and styles and of course custom fitted to their figures. While Emily generally didn't consider herself vain and had joked more than once that, when standing next to Annabelle, she might as well wear sackcloth and ashes . . . well, now she didn't want to really prove the theory while wearing provincial-looking ready-made dresses.

Annabelle, as was her style, got straight to the point. "Lucien will stare at you the whole time no matter what you have on, Emily."

"I'm not . . . He's not . . . I mean, I don't think he—"

"He's mad for you. When you were off this morning, he didn't say more than a half dozen words to me."

A lovely warm glow sparked inside Emily's chest. She thought he was interested, but to have Annabelle confirm it—

"And believe me," Annabelle continued, "I tried to engage him in conversation."

The glow went from lovely and warm to sharp and hot in a second. "Why?" Emily demanded.

"Oh, the challenge, I suppose."

Emily searched for a handhold on her anger so that she could stuff it away. It didn't quite work. "Did it ever occur to you that perhaps this one—one!—time that a gentleman might be interested in me, it would be sisterly of you to not try to entice him?"

Annabelle tossed her head. "I wasn't trying to entice him. And many other gentlemen have been interested in you, Emily. You simply were not interested in them. It's been quite fun to watch you and Mr. Delatour flirting."

Flirting? Half the time it felt more like arguing.

"I believe he's quite immune to me," Annabelle said. "It's been lovely. So relaxing. Your idea of stealing onto this train was a good one, Emily."

"No man is immune to you."

"He is. Here, I'll prove it." And with that, she strolled out of the bedroom.

Prove it? What did that mean?

Oh, no.

Emily dropped the dress on her bed and raced to the salon. What if Annabelle was trying to entice him right now?

Lucien glanced up from the newspaper as she whipped around the corner and stumbled to a halt. Annabelle wasn't in the salon.

He smiled, and Emily grabbed the back of a chair for support. Really, it was unfair that he was so handsome that he could turn her knees to mush. She was just lucky he wasn't trying to smolder at her again.

"Where's the fire?" he asked.

In her chest. Racing to her fingertips, which she wanted to trace along his cheekbones and throat.

Emily tried to pull some shreds of sanity together. "I was about to change my dress but thought I'd forgotten something out here." She made a big show of looking around. "Apparently not."

He waggled his fingers at her. "Just let me know if you need any help with the buttons."

She felt her cheeks flame. "Um, no, thank you." She didn't need to look down to know that all her buttons were in the front. And so were the buttons on her new dresses.

Unfortunately.

Not daring to say another word, Emily backed out of the salon and then ran to her bedroom, sliding the door shut behind her. As she undid the final button on her well-used dress, she heard Annabelle's footsteps out in the corridor and then her voice, too low to understand, from the salon. Darn it—Annabelle had slipped past her.

Starting to perspire—which defied her whole plan of wearing clean clothing and smelling fresher—Emily grabbed the nearest dress off the bed and started buttoning it up the front as fast as she could. Some of the new buttonholes were a hair too tight, and Emily felt a big drop of sweat roll down the back of her neck as she jammed the buttons through.

There! She slammed the door open and darted back

to the salon. She had been gone only two minutes, maybe three. Surely Annabelle couldn't have—

Emily's feet practically dug furrows in the carpet as she slid to a dead stop. Annabelle smiled sweetly up at her from where she was cuddled next to Lucien on the padded couch like a kitten next to a tiger. She placed a small hand on Lucien's forearm. "Mr. Delatour, tell me more about your railroad plans. It's just so *fascinating.*"

Emily narrowed her eyes at Annabelle. If anything, it was Annabelle's newfound interest in railroads that was truly *fascinating.*

Lucien stretched out his arm, displacing Annabelle's hand in the process, and beckoned Emily to come forward. "Apparently you did need my help," he said. Without asking permission, he slipped open the top button of her dress.

What—? Oh: She'd misbuttoned her top two buttons in her rush to get dressed.

Emily stared down at the top of his dark head as his fingers tugged at the fabric and buttons, his knuckles grazing the bare skin at the base of her throat and igniting a shiver down her spine.

She felt herself sway and rested one hand on his shoulder for support. The muscles under her palm moved and flexed as he slid home the final top button that she had missed completely.

For a long second they both didn't move, and then he leaned back against the couch, breaking the contact, and looked up at her with an expression she couldn't read. "All fixed now," he said.

"Thank you," she said. Or, really, squeaked.

"Any time," he replied gravely, and then dropped her a wink before shaking open his paper and returning to reading it, placing a shield between himself and the girls.

Emily took a deep breath, touched the top button at her throat, and started to turn away. As she did so, Annabelle's satisfied expression caught her attention.

Annabelle, being Annabelle, couldn't simply be happy with her victory. She replaced her hand on Lucien's forearm and simpered at him. "I'm going to put on a new dress as well. I'll call if I need help with *my* buttons." Then she stood up and sauntered out of the salon.

Lucien immediately lowered his paper. "Is she always so . . . intense?"

Emily wasn't sure her voice was working normally yet, so she just nodded.

"It must be exhausting. I was exhausted after sixty seconds."

A wise woman would let the conversation end there, but Emily had become more daring and, possibly, less wise since she'd hidden herself under the card table two days ago. "Most people find her invigorating."

Lucien opened his mouth and then shut it. After a moment he said, "I'm afraid I don't know her well enough to comment."

"And apparently she's a good kisser." Hmm, she'd perhaps just transitioned from daring into reckless.

"I wouldn't be surprised. I get the impression that she's had a lot of practice," Lucien replied dryly.

Should she offhandedly comment that she herself had not had a lot of practice and would like some? With Lucien, specifically?

"What about you?" he asked, his voice huskier than it had been a moment before.

The perfect opening . . .

Emily inhaled. Her lips parted—

A loud banging from the front of the car made Emily whip her head around.

"Ahoy there!" a male voice shouted over the sudden sound of steel wheels on tracks. The door to the next compartment must have been opened. "Coming through."

The conductor! Emily went up on tiptoe next to Lucien and hissed in his ear, "I'm your sister!"

Then she rushed over to the desk and sat down, busying herself with arranging the fountain pens and stationery there.

She prayed Annabelle would stay in her room. If she appeared in a vastly more stylish gown than the dress Emily now wore, that would give everything away.

The conductor walked into the salon and surveyed Lucien and Emily. He was a thin man with a mustache that reminded Emily of a garden rake, and if Emily hadn't been watching him so closely, she might not have seen his shoulders slump. He was sighing.

"Sir, I apologize for intruding. You will find it hard to believe, but I'm searching for two girls who have run away."

He barely even glanced at Emily, though she was

clearly a girl. If the stakes weren't so high, she would have been annoyed.

Lucien shook his head. "Not a problem at all. I take it you haven't found them—otherwise you wouldn't be here, in the last car on the train."

"Haven't found them, haven't seen them, and no one else has seen them, neither. I considered skipping this car entirely, but I had to be diligent. Not ashamed to admit I'm glad they aren't on this train. Last thing I want to do is manhandle a couple of highfalutin debutantes."

Ah! So the conductor had been sighing with relief, not in despair. Emily's own shoulders loosened a trifle, but she wouldn't relax entirely until the conductor left the car.

"No, they generally don't take to manhandling very well," Lucien said dryly.

Unfortunately, now that he'd dispatched his duties, the conductor seemed to be in a mood to chat. "Bet you know the proper way to handle 'em, eh?" And he winked.

Emily frowned.

Lucien said, sounding genuinely surprised, "No, not particularly." Then he glanced at Emily for a reason she couldn't fathom. Did he want confirmation? If so, and if she weren't in fear of being hauled off the train, she would have quickly nodded her agreement. His manners often left much to be desired.

The conductor followed his look. "Beg your pardon, miss. Didn't mean to offend." Then he turned away, dismissing her from his attention.

"As that 'miss' is my wife," Lucien said, "I assure you she's probably far more amused than offended."

His *wife*? Didn't he recall that she was supposed to be his sister? But Lucien wasn't watching her; he was staring at the conductor with an annoyed expression on his face. He was doing a fine job of acting like a man who thought his wife had been slighted.

The conductor bobbed his head nervously and started to back out of the salon. "Right. Ah, thanks for your time and—"

Annabelle squeezed past the conductor and into the room, breathing "Pardon me" in a fashion that made the conductor's head whip around so fast, Emily thought his mustache might fly off.

Annabelle, bless her heart, was wearing one of the new but ugly dresses. But the conductor didn't seem to be looking at Annabelle's clothes at all. He was staring at her like he'd been whacked on the head with a mallet. Emily prayed his thunderstruck expression was due to Annabelle's usual affect on men—not the realization that he'd found his two lost "highfalutin debutantes" after all.

"My wife's sister," Lucien said. Every syllable vibrating with lack of welcome, Lucien added, "Good day, sir."

"Wait!" the conductor said, and strode deeper into the room. He reached into his jacket, and Emily froze. Was he going to pull a gun and force her and Annabelle to go with them?

Lucien tensed and, broken ankle or not, looked ready to leap off the couch and onto the conductor.

"You are Mr. Delatour, are you not? I have a telegram for you. It was waiting for you at the last stop, and with all the excitement about the missing girls I forgot to get it to you right away." The conductor slipped a piece of paper out of his jacket and handed it to Lucien. "My apologies."

Nodding to all three of them, the conductor backed out of the salon. A moment later Emily heard the outer door open, the sound of wheels on rails, and then the door shutting again. The conductor was gone.

She slumped in the desk chair, relief turning her bones to putty. They were safe. For now.

She straightened up again as a thought struck her. "My disguises worked," she crowed.

"That man was an idiot," Lucien said tersely, and unfolded the sheet of paper. Then his face whitened.

Emily jumped to her feet and hurried to the settee. "Bad news?"

"Yes." He took a deep breath. "There's been another accident on the railroad. Two men died."

"This railroad?" Annabelle asked.

"No, *my* railroad."

"Do accidents happen often?" Emily asked. He had said *another accident*. Clearly there had been more than one.

"Yes," Lucien answered, but he sounded distracted.

Emily waited, and he eventually looked up. "I need to get back to my railroad as quickly as possible, which means I'll switch trains farther east than San Francisco—probably in Cheyenne. I won't be able to personally deliver you to your sister's doorstep. You can stay in this car all the way to San Francisco even though I won't be here, of course—"

"Don't worry about us," Emily said quickly. "We'll manage." She tried to sound as confident as she would be if this were her sixth transcontinental trip instead of her first. "But what about you and your ankle?"

"I'll manage," he said, repeating her words back to her but sounding vastly more grim.

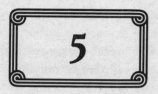

# 5

WHILE EMILY WAS RELATING to her sister Anna the details of the conductor's visit, Lucien unfolded the telegram again. It held only five words:

2 DEAD. SABOTAGE. HIGHFILL. —CHUCK

Sabotage. Before he had left to go east, Lucien and Chuck had discussed that a few recent accidents on the rail line weren't accidents after all—but quickly dismissed it. Clearly Chuck had changed his mind, and he wouldn't have bothered to try to track down Lucien if he wasn't sure.

That Chuck had gone to such trouble to send him a telegram while Lucien was on his way back signaled that Chuck, normally impervious to panic, was deeply worried.

*Two men dead.*

Lucien could feel Emily still staring at him, and he

knew without looking that she was chewing her lip, as she always did when she was thinking about something.

"Is there anything I can do?" she asked.

"No, nothing."

Her face fell. It wasn't a large gesture, like a childish pout or a heaving sigh, but he could tell she was disappointed. Emily was a natural-born helper.

"Well, there's one thing," he said, and she perked up again. "I'll need to send a telegram back to my business partner at the next stop to let him know I got his message and I'm returning with speed."

Emily nodded. "What should it say exactly?"

"'On my way.'"

She blinked. "That's it?"

"That's all that's needed. He'll know what it means."

"Well, that shouldn't be too hard to remember," she said dryly. "When is the next stop?"

"Two, three hours."

Anna, apparently deciding that nothing exciting was going on, chose another novel from the salon's well-stocked shelves and disappeared in the direction of her compartment. Lucien rearranged his ankle on the chair and stared out the window at the green and brown countryside slinging past the train.

Sabotage. Two men dead. And he was stuck at least four days away—probably more like five—with nothing to do but think.

While he and Chuck had considered the possibility of sabotage at the time of the second "accident," it was a moment of black humor instead of true speculation.

Two ropes had snapped on one of the cars that was hauling rails up the mountain, sending thousands of pounds of heavy equipment into a deep ravine. An outfit with deeper pockets might've been able to leave the rails there and simply order replacements, but Lucien and Chuck's pockets weren't that deep. They were forced to take dozens of men and mules off track-laying duties in order to drag the rails up out of the ravine, setting them back ten days in an already tight schedule. They had miles of tracks to lay and were aiming to breach Dead Horse Pass well before winter set in.

A week before the ropes snapped, a rock slide had buried the rails only a quarter mile behind the track-laying crew, stopping the delivery of both railroad and food supplies until the track was cleared.

Accidents happened all the time on every railroad. Chuck had lost two fingers only a few months ago, when a pry bar had slipped and sent a heavy tie down on his hand. But two major accidents so close together?

"Either we're cursed, we're incompetent, or it's sabotage," Chuck said morosely.

Lucien privately thought that the breaking ropes was incompetence—someone hadn't noticed the ropes were rotten or had loaded the cars so that there was too much pressure on them—but Chuck looked so defeated that Lucien said confidently, "Oh, it's sabotage. I'd bet my best pair of boots."

Chuck looked up, startled. "What?"

"Yep. Someone's afraid of us."

Chuck looked even more thunderstruck, and then a

grin twitched his lips as he got the joke. "Afraid of us. Of course. And I know just who it is. James J. Hill!!"

Both men laughed.

Then Chuck glanced around and leaned close to Lucien. "If this was sabotage, I know who would really be behind it. Charles Bertrand Highfill."

Lucien understood why Chuck was practically whispering. His wife, Jacqueline, didn't allow Highfill's name to be mentioned around her. She still blamed him for her brother's death.

"He's back east," Lucien said. Not disagreeing, though. If there was one person who would be happy to see him and Chuck fall into a black hole of bankruptcy and shame, it was Charles Highfill. Jacqueline wasn't the only one who held a grudge after the project with Highfill had ended in failure and death. Lucien had a half dozen letters from Highfill that had cursed him up to the skies and down to hell.

Chuck shrugged. "Then I guess incompetence is the culprit."

"I'll have a talk with Hendrick," Lucien said, standing. "He's the foreman and supposed to be on top of these things. And if he's not going to do it, I will." It wasn't an empty threat. Ten years earlier, Lucien had spent a miserable winter laying track across the Sierra Nevada, and when the foreman had quit, Lucien had taken over. He'd worked his way up the ranks, made several well-considered and lucrative investments, and broken away from the railroad by the time he was twenty-six. Now he was back in the thick of it.

"You're going to Washington next week," Chuck said. "I'll find another foreman if we need to." Chuck then paused. "Stay out of Highfill's way."

"He should stay out of mine," Lucien replied.

"Yes, but with the recent accidents here . . . well, don't go looking for trouble."

If anyone personified *trouble*, it was Charles Highfill. Five years earlier, Highfill, Chuck, Chuck's young brother-in-law, and Lucien had formed a partnership centered on buying up land just outside a booming town alongside the Union Pacific and then building on it or selling it later at a profit. Six months in—and about four months too late—Chuck and Lucien learned Highfill had partnered with others as well, sometimes selling land to Chuck and Lucien and sometimes buying from them. It wasn't illegal, but it was pretty clear that Highfill would screw over one set of partners to get more money through another set of partners. Jacqueline's brother ran into some of Highfill's other partners in a saloon while drunk, started a fight, and ended up with a splinter from a broken chair wedged in his thigh. He died of blood poisoning two weeks later.

Stupid way for a kid to go.

Immediately after that, Chuck and Lucien cut Highfill out of the partnership.

Highfill, realizing that he couldn't play his various partners against each other any longer, vowed revenge. Lucien and Chuck had steered clear of him ever since.

Lucien scrubbed his hand over his face and realized he had turned away from the window and was looking at

Emily. *Again.* Even when he wasn't thinking about her—which wasn't all that often—he turned toward her like she was a lodestone.

Lucien had managed to avoid Highfill while he was back east. He hadn't dodged a pretty girl on the run quite so nimbly.

While Lucien had been thrashing around in his thoughts, Emily was writing more letters. As he watched, Emily whipped a letter to the side and started on a new one. At this rate he could write to every wealthy investor in New York, Baltimore, Boston, and Washington, D.C., before their train trip ended. The investors might not be able to read every word, but they would have a letter from him.

"This list has grown since yesterday," Emily said, pointing to a sheet of paper with the names of people Lucien wished to contact. "Did you add to it?"

"Yes, this morning while you were out."

"As I said earlier, I've met some of these men. I could add some personal touches to their letters if you like."

She could add some personal touches to *him* and he wouldn't object. She could skim her fingers over his skin, murmur his name in his ear, and seal her mouth to his. He'd like those personal touches.

Lucien blew out an irritated breath. *Focus.* He and Chuck had spent years in their pursuit of building a rail line. He had a lot at stake—and it far outbalanced the deliciousness of a few stolen kisses.

Lucien looked up at Emily—again!—and realized she was looking at him expectantly. "What?" he said.

"I could add some personal touches," she repeated. "Mention their other businesses, or their wives, sons, daughters . . . Well, maybe not their daughters. That might sound like you're fishing for more than an investment."

He tried not to squirm. He still needed to write to Susan, damn it. "Better not," he said. "I can't recall who mentioned what about their family. I wasn't really paying attention to those bits."

"My grandfather always says those are the bits you really need to pay attention to, because everyone is pleasantly surprised when you remember, and then they remember you as well."

"He's probably right, but it's a bit late now."

She nodded and bent back to the letter writing.

Lucien watched how her hand moved swiftly—too swiftly for good handwriting, of course—through a bar of sunlight cast across the desk surface, and then lifted his eyes to see a stray beam glimmer on her blond hair for just a moment before a curve in the train's track caused the sun to move away.

Hell's bells, he was doing it again. Watching her instead of doing everything else that he should be doing. Not that there was much he could do, stuck here in a train that wouldn't go faster no matter how much he urged it to.

Emily whipped another finished letter to the side and bent over the list of investor names. With a slight frown, she looked up. "You don't have Charles Bertrand Highfill on this list. Shall I add him?"

"Hell, no! I would throw all my steel rails and locomotives into the darkest ravine before asking that whoreson for help."

Eyes as wide as the moon, Emily stared at him for a few seconds before dropping her gaze to the desk. Without a word, she took a fresh sheet of paper from the stack and began scratching out a new letter, although at a less furious clip than before.

Damn it, he was always forgetting to watch his language around her. But if there was one thing that could strip away the veneer of good manners and social polish that he had spent years building up, it was the mention of Charles Bertram Highfill.

"Have I showed you my railroad?" he asked Emily abruptly.

She gave him a sideways look. "Is this your way of apologizing to me?"

She must be referring to his language. "Yes. Sorry."

Emily left her desk chair and moved to his side. Even those new ugly dresses made a delicate swishing sound that caused the muscles in his stomach to tighten. "Do you have photographs of your railroad?"

"Not photographs, but I can show it to you on a map."

"Oh, good. I love maps," Emily said.

He'd remembered her saying that before. Which was why he was slowly unrolling the map of the Great Mountain and its planned route as if it were filled with precious gems instead of black-inked squiggles. He swore Emily was bouncing in her excitement.

She'd asked yesterday why he'd thought her the

younger sister, and he replied that it was her enthusiasm. That only captured part of her charm, though. She seemed to see only the best in people. She didn't hold grudges, and she forgave quickly. And she had a quick intelligence that wanted to be challenged. He imagined that she opened her eyes every morning thinking, *Hooray, I'm awake! What new experiences will I live and what new things will I learn today?*

"Is that your railroad?" Emily asked, leaning forward and tracing a heavy black line on the map with her fingertip.

Lucien patted the couch next to him. "Sit down."

"Please," she said, not looking at him.

"Please," he repeated with a sigh, and she whisked a smile at him before sliding into a spot on the couch far enough away that they weren't touching but close enough that his pulse kicked into a higher gear.

"Here's the piece that we've already built," Lucien said, tapping his finger on the heavily inked line. "It runs from Desarto City up to Bramble Creek. The plan is that we'll push over the mountains through Dead Horse Pass and then drop down to this valley. There are a few farmers in that valley now, but once we open up the land with the railroad, lots more will come. And timber companies will come, too. By using the Great Mountain instead of taking the longer way around the mountains, people can move their freight to their destinations faster and cheaper."

"The dashed line is where the railroad is going to go?"

"Yes."

"But it looks like you've already built three-quarters of the railroad. Why do you want investors now?"

"Laying track through the mountains will be six times as expensive as the flatlands. You have to blast away sides of the mountain, build tunnels in some places. . . . Chuck and I can't do it alone. The portion of the railroad that's already built is bringing in some revenue, but not enough to fund the final push over the mountains."

"Do you have another map that shows the other railroads in the area?"

She sounded genuinely interested, so Lucien rummaged around in the small stack of maps beside him on the settee. "Here," he said, and spread it open. As he did so, he slid a few inches closer to Emily, so that their hips were touching.

She didn't scoot away. She didn't look at him, either, but her cheeks appeared to be a little pinker.

Although the unbuilt portion of the Great Mountain wasn't marked on this map, Emily ran her finger west from Bramble Creek, through Dead Horse Pass, and down into the valley beyond, repeating the line she'd seen on the previous map. She'd clearly been paying close attention. "I can understand why you haven't had any problems gaining investors' interest. I'm surprised that no one has tried to buy you out entirely."

It was an astute observation, and Lucien almost asked her how she had come to know so much about business before he recalled Anna's comment that all the smart men liked to talk to Emily. He didn't want to bring that up again, so he only said, "You're quite clever. We've had a few offers, but none so large that Chuck and I want to give up on our dream of doing it ourselves."

Emily's eyebrows forked down in a V. "What do you mean?"

"Well . . ." He'd never had to put it into words, and he struggled for a few moments. "Chuck and I, together and separately, have made a lot of good investments."

"Like steamboats," Emily said.

"Yes, like steamboats, and land, and portions of other railroads. But we've never created anything. When we finish the Great Mountain, we'll have built something from scratch, and we'll be able to point to it and say, 'We did that.' If we sell it now, we won't be able to say that. And we won't sell it unless we can't afford not to."

Just then, a puzzle piece fell into place. Ever since receiving the telegram—and actually ever since he and Chuck had had the first conversation about sabotage— Lucien couldn't understand what Highfill would gain from sabotaging the Great Mountain. Revenge? But there was too much risk involved simply to gain emotional satisfaction.

However, everyone knew that Highfill had his eye on rail lines in the West, either to build them or to own them. No one wanted to sell—if you could build it without going bankrupt, a railroad would spill untold riches in your pocket. And Highfill didn't have the right connections to build his own. So that left a third option: buy a railroad in trouble and finish building it with the old owners still aboard and in charge of the rail laying.

And if you couldn't find a railroad in trouble, well, then you could always make trouble for it.

Lucien scowled. They wouldn't lose against Highfill this time. There was too much at stake. He and Chuck had sweated for ten years to get here. One crooked eastern industrialist wasn't going to get in their way.

He swiveled his head to look at Emily, head still bent over the map as she examined the other rail lines, and her hip pressed against his. He shouldn't let a blond-haired mystery girl deflect him from his plans, either. He owed Susan a letter. It didn't take a genius to figure out why he was having so much trouble writing one to her.

Emily settled back against the settee. When Lucien inhaled deeply, their shoulders kissed each other.

"Tell me more about Bramble Creek," she said. "You live there, yes?"

"Yes, an hour outside of town. I have a nice patch of land, and I run cattle on it."

She didn't respond, and he realized she was expecting him to say more about his home. "I like it," he concluded.

She gave him a pitying look. "Let's try again. If I were going to your house for the first time, how would I get there, and what would I see?"

Right—she was used to conversing with *smart* men. Well, he was smart. He just wasn't a poet.

"All right. Let's see. When you come along the track and bend around the big elm tree that was hit by lightning two years ago, you'll first see the outbuildings: the stable, the springhouse, the henhouse, the granary . . ."

Eyes shining and her shoulder now tucked firmly against his upper arm, Emily listened to him talk about his ranch. She laughed when he described the rooster who strutted among his lady hens as if he were the handsomest fellow on earth, and grew misty-eyed when he told her about his old dog, Rose, who'd been killed by a mountain lion the winter before.

She was a wonderful listener—completely focused and sympathetic. (Not that he needed sympathy: He had a very good life.) That, plus her good cheer and her own wit, explained why men flocked to her.

Hell, he was flocking to her. He wanted to slide her onto his lap, bracket her face in his hands, and kiss her until she gasped his name against his mouth.

If her sister wasn't in the next room, and if he wasn't almost promised to Susan—

As if she'd picked the thought out of his head, Emily scooted a few inches away, and cool air filled the new gap between them. "Your wife?" she said.

"I'm not married," he said quickly. Nor properly engaged.

"I mean, what you told the conductor. About me."

Oh. That. "I thought it would sound more convincing."

"Why?"

Because he was an idiot, that's why. Because the words *my sister* had stuck like a chicken bone in his throat.

"We don't look very much alike," he said lamely.

"You're lucky I'm a good actress," she said. "What if I'd acted surprised? The conductor would have known you were lying."

"If you were a bad actress, you wouldn't have been able to pretend to be my sister, either," he said, but he recognized his argument for what it was. Hindsight justification of an impulsive, thoughtless decision.

He'd been doing that a lot lately, especially with himself.

Emily opened her mouth to say something more, so he added quickly, "I'm sorry."

The only thing he was really sorry for was that he hadn't met Emily sooner. Ideally, before he had met Susan.

He cleared his throat. "I need to get back to my letter writing. You, too."

She stood, and her skirts swished again as she returned to the desk. "I'm still a little mad about the 'wife' surprise," she threw over her shoulder, "so I might not be using my very best handwriting."

If she'd been using her best handwriting before, then he'd be lucky if this next batch of letters were legible. That would definitely be the wrong thing to say, though, so he just grunted, rearranged his ankle on the chair, and pulled a piece of stationery and a pen in front of him.

And then he stared at the blank paper for the next hour, searching his brain for the right words, the right phrases, to write to Susan. In the end, he tucked the unwritten letter away. For how could he write to her when he didn't know what he wanted to say?

After writing fifteen letters and eating a light lunch, Emily insisted that she take a break because her hand was starting to ache. In reality, she was having trouble concentrating. Lucien's words about her grandfather Charles Highfill kept crashing through her mind like runaway horses: *I would throw all my steel rails and locomotives into the darkest ravine before asking that whoreson for help.*

And then they had sat practically snuggled together on the settee as Lucien told her about his dreams and his home, tugging her heart down a path it had never traveled before.

It was a relief to finally hide herself in her small bedroom and collapse on the couch.

She didn't have very long of a reprieve. Annabelle knocked at the door and let herself in without waiting for permission.

"This dress is just awful," Annabelle complained as she plopped down next to Emily. "It's ugly. It itches. And it doesn't fit right."

Emily squinted at her sister. The bright colors or perhaps the looser-fitting style of the dress had changed Annabelle's appearance more than Emily had expected. For the first time in years, Annabelle did look younger than Emily. "Thank you for putting it on. The conductor was fooled."

Annabelle groaned. "Mother and Mr. Grant are looking for us?"

"Unfortunately, yes." And Emily realized she was disappointed in her parents. She and Annabelle were not five-year-olds. Immigrants who were younger than they and couldn't speak the language often traveled halfway across the continent in search of a new life. Why couldn't their parents let them—young women who had money and spoke English and, most important, weren't complete idiots—travel to San Francisco without raising an enormous fuss?

Now she almost wished that she and Annabelle had taken tickets for seats in the railcars with all the regular passengers. When they finally reunited with their parents, that would prove how capable she and Annabelle were. Traveling in a private Pullman car was in no way a challenge.

Aside from the ever-increasing challenge of trying to figure out what was going in Lucien's head.

Annabelle poked her. "I didn't realize you'd gotten married, Mrs. Delatour."

"What? Oh, that. It was a surprise to me, too."

"So, has he kissed you yet?"

"Annabelle!"

Annabelle giggled and then kept staring at her, waiting for an answer.

Confiding her seesawing thoughts in Annabelle was not something Emily normally would have done. Annabelle's judgment in most matters did not parallel Emily's, and in romantic situations Annabelle's decisions were downright dangerous. But she knew far more about men than Emily did. Maybe, just maybe, Annabelle could shed some light on what was going on.

"I'm not as confident as you are that he truly likes me," Emily started. "He—"

"He never takes his eyes off you."

"He—"

"He buttoned you up—which shocked even me."

"Yes, but he—"

"He told the conductor you were his *wife*."

Emily half shrieked, "Just let me finish! He likes me most of the time, and then there are times when I can tell that he wishes he didn't like me at all!" She then slammed her hand over her mouth. The walls between the rooms were not thick. Hopefully Lucien had only heard her yelling and not the actual words.

"Oh. Why didn't you say that in the first place? Well, that's happened to me several times. A gentleman is attracted to me but he doesn't want to be because he knows I have many admirers and he fears being seen a fool."

That was a remarkably perceptive comment, and Emily was impressed. However: "That is not my situation," Emily said dryly. "He is not one among a seething hive of admirers."

"Then what is it that he's afraid of?" Annabelle asked. "He likes you—I mean, you as a person. So it must be something else that worries him."

Emily shook her head. "You mean it's something about him and not me?" That was even more discouraging, because that put it outside her ability to change.

Annabelle settled back against the couch. "Let's put ourselves in his position. Two lovely, charming girls appear in his railroad car. One of them he finds especially attractive. But he knows nothing about them except how charming and lovely they are, and that they do not want their family to know where they are. Oh! That must be it! He's afraid of who our family is! If we are related to someone important—maybe even one of the people who he is seeking as an investor—and his other investors find out that he helped us sneak across the country, he could lose all the people who wanted to invest with him!"

The logic was somewhat convoluted but entirely possible. Whatever was worrying Lucien *had* to center on the railroad. "No one in our family was approached for an investment," Emily said. "I've seen the whole list."

"Then just tell him who we are. That should help settle his worries, and he won't struggle so much with liking you." Annabelle beamed. "He'll be so relieved."

Emily wished it were that easy. "I'm afraid he might have the opposite reaction." She repeated Lucien's words about their grandfather, substituting *fellow* for *whoreson*.

Annabelle frowned. "I wonder what happened."

"I don't know. I'm afraid to ask."

Tossing her head, Annabelle said, "Whatever happened, I'm sure Grandfather was in the right."

If only it were that cut-and-dried. While Annabelle had been kissing the young gentlemen of Boston, Emily had been talking to the more established and, yes, boring gentlemen, and their views of her grandfather, while politely veiled, were often not complimentary. At first she had attributed it to sour grapes or being on the losing end of a business deal. But after a few years of paying attention, she'd realized that there was more to their responses than that. While the gentlemen she spoke with acknowledged her grandfather's success, they did not trust him.

"Every story has two sides," she finally said to Annabelle. She really had nothing but the accumulation of small details to explain her unwillingness to put all her faith in her grandfather's good intentions.

"Does he dislike Grandfather so much that he'll throw us out?" Annabelle asked. She grinned at Emily. "That would make kissing him even harder."

"Are you *always* thinking about kissing?"

"Always," Annabelle said cheerfully. "With the right person, it's lovely. Unfortunately, you have to kiss a lot of frogs with slimy tongues to find a princely kisser."

"Ew."

"It's worth it. And I bet Lucien is a good kisser."

He'd certainly be a better kisser than Emily was. Less than a dozen kisses snatched during walks in the park at dusk or at country parties didn't give her a whole lot of experience to draw upon. And there had maybe been only one or two kisses out of those that had caused her toes to curl in her shoes. Probably because there had been only one or two gentlemen whom she'd actually been halfway interested in kissing.

She was *very* interested in kissing Lucien. Her toes curled in her shoes just when he smiled at her. But—

"It feels like we're deliberately lying to him, now

that we know he dislikes"—well, hates—"Grandfather."
Emily paused. "No, I'm wrong. We *are* deliberately lying
to him now."

"Lucien knows that we won't tell him our names. So
what difference does it make?"

"The possible repercussions have changed. I honestly
wouldn't be surprised if he dropped us off at the next
station if he found out. He was very adamant." Emily
wrapped her arms around herself to ward off a shiver.

"So you and Lucien have something to fear, and it
is holding you both back. He's afraid of what he doesn't
know. And you're afraid he'll find out about what he
doesn't know."

Emily nodded glumly. "I suppose that's the problem
in a nutshell."

Annabelle braced her hand on the wall for balance
as the train lurched into a slower gait. "It feels like we're
approaching the next station now."

Emily tried to forget her problems with Lucien and
inject some excitement into her blood. She had been
looking forward to seeing Grand Island with her own
eyes. It was a major stop on this railway, and she'd as-
sisted many immigrants in figuring out how to travel
here from Boston. Perhaps there would even be a Society
member on the train platform, helping newcomers to the
area.

Emily stood. "I promised Lucien I would send a telegram to his friend. And I need to stretch my legs and get
some fresh air. Coming?"

"No, I'm going to stay here. I don't find these provincial train stations to be as invigoratingly interesting as you do. How many more days until we reach San Francisco?"

"Three days, if all goes well."

"An eternity," Annabelle groaned, and headed back to her room.

Several minutes later the train crept to a stop. Emily could look down on bare heads and straw hats from her high window. Beyond the people stood a now recognizable squat station house where tickets were sold, two-story-tall hotels, and stores of all kinds. Grand Island was not the largest town they had stopped at, but she had never descended to the platform in any of those places. The buildings and houses here stretched out almost as far as her eye could see.

Taking a deep breath, Emily walked back to the salon.

Lucien was where she had left him. He immediately looked up and smiled when she entered, and on cue her toes curled in her shoes. Really, it was completely unfair how much an effect he had on her.

"I'll send that telegram for you," she said quickly. "Do you need anything else?"

"A new ankle would be nice. And a newspaper."

Emily pointed at the paper discarded on the seat beside him. "That wasn't good enough?"

"Grand Island is a busy town for the railroads. The paper here will have more news of the goings-on back east. And more railroad news in general."

"Ah. Then I will search for a newspaper."

He beckoned Emily closer. She walked toward him and stopped. He beckoned again. Her pulse kicking up, she took a few more steps and then stopped when her skirts brushed his knee.

Another slow, beckoning wave, and Emily leaned down, her breath tangling in her chest.

Was he going to kiss her? If he did, what was she supposed to do? Keep her eyes open? Close them? Worry about slimy tongues?

Lucien's voice whispered against her ear. "Are you taking Anna with you?"

*That* was why he'd coaxed her closer? To ask about Annabelle? Emily jerked away, scowling at him. "No; she's staying here."

"Then hurry back, please."

That made her feel a little better, but not a lot. Emily widened her eyes at him in mock surprise. "You can't handle my little sister?"

"I would rather not 'handle' her at all—hence my request."

There was no use pretending she didn't know what he was talking about or getting indignant on Annabelle's behalf. "She'll be good."

"Promise?"

Emily considered that. "No, sorry."

"You look like you're trying not to laugh at me," he accused.

She did laugh then. "You'll be fine."

He took a nickel from his pocket and placed it in

her palm, wrapping her fingers around it gently as if what he'd given her was more precious than five cents. "Hurry back," he said again, holding her gaze, and this time Emily thought he wasn't thinking about Annabelle anymore.

Was he trying to keep her confused about his intentions? If so, he was doing a fine job.

"Oh, and could you please mail the letters as well?" Lucien asked, gesturing to the stack on the desk.

"Of course." Emily picked up the letters and shuffled through them. All were letters that she had written this morning. "Shall I take your letter as well?"

Lucien frowned. "It's not quite ready."

He'd spent literally an hour bent over it before they had lunch, and it still wasn't done? "It sounds important." Maybe it was to the most important investor he was trying to woo, which was why he was writing it himself.

"Perhaps." He ran his hand through his dark hair and then gave it a frustrated tug. "That's the whole problem. It might be important, or it might not."

Then the mysterious recipient wasn't an investor— she knew he thought each and every one of them was important. "Who—" she started to ask, and then bit the question back. It was really none of her business.

The train trembled beneath her feet and then went still. They had stopped.

When Emily opened the railcar door, noise buffeted her. It sounded like hundreds of people were on the platform outside the train, either hollering good-byes at ascending passengers or hawking goods and services to descending passengers.

Stepping down onto the platform, Emily tucked her arms close to her side, dipped her chin like a charging bull, and bulleted through the crowd, aiming for the telegraph office. She delivered Lucien's message and got an approving smile from the telegram clerk. "Short and sweet," he said. "Quite professional."

The post office was directly next to the telegraph office, and after posting the letters she pushed into the crowd again, searching for someone who sold newspapers.

She was starting to get the hang of it, she decided. It was like swimming in a river: Paddle with the current of humanity as much as possible, and move fast when you hit an eddy or patch of calm, because it wouldn't last long.

Within a few moments she had three newspapers tucked under her arm. She glanced over at the Pullman car. Approximately a million people stood between her and it, but if she started back now, she'd be back on board with plenty of time before the train departed the station.

But halfway across the platform, she spotted a sign that made her smile, and she switched directions, finally coming to a breathless stop before a man in his fifties wearing the floppy hat of a farmer but the neat clothes of a man who lived in town. He held a big sign reading, BOSTON IMMIGRANT AID SOCIETY.

"Hello!" Emily said. "My name is Emily Highfill

Grant, and I've worked with the Boston Immigrant Aid Society for years." *Worked with* was a bit of an understatement. The Highfill family had started the Society twenty years ago, and Emily had been its vice president for the last eighteen months. "It's a pleasure to meet someone who is receiving the immigrants out west!"

Not smiling back, the man looked her up and down. "Are you here for the Society, then?"

"No, I'm on my way to San Francisco for personal reasons, but I saw your sign and wanted to say hello."

"That's all right, then," he said with a nod. "I can't abide people coming in from the east and telling me what to do. What you fancy ladies think is the reality out here and what *is* the reality are quite different."

Emily looked around to see if anyone was waiting to speak to the Society's agent. "Am I the only person from this train who has approached you? I thought that there were many opportunities here in Grand Island for new immigrants."

He snorted. "Sure, and there were . . . five years ago. Immigrants are needed where the land hasn't been thoroughly settled yet, not in areas that have matured like Grand Island has."

"But we're not sending only farmers out west. Merchants wish to move out here, too. Wouldn't they be better off in an established town?"

"Lady, this town already has ten German brewers, six Czech funeral homes, nine Italian grocers, and three Polish butchers. We don't need any more merchants of any kind."

That seemed like something incoming merchants should decide, not this fellow. On the other hand, she could see his point: It was easier to be successful without so much competition.

"If that's the case, what are you doing here with this sign?" she asked.

"I have an arrangement with a fellow up in North Loup. I tell newcomers to get on the train that goes to North Loup. It's only another ten cents for the ticket. When the immigrant shows up, that fellow in North Loup then gets five of those ten cents from the railroad, and he gives two of those cents to me."

"That's quite . . . entrepreneurial," Emily said finally. She wasn't sure it was legal, and she was very sure that the Society would frown upon it.

He chortled. "You're an innocent lass, aren't you? Everyone wins. The railroad gets a ticket sale. The immigrant still gets an opportunity to find his own patch of land. And I get two cents per head on top of my Society stipend, which isn't that much, let me tell you."

"Why not be the man in North Loup or another town and get three cents per head instead of two?"

Shrugging, he said, "I like it in Grand Island. The Society directed me out here six years ago, when I was new to this country, and I took to Grand Island right away. It's my home now. I moved homes once already—and I don't want to do it again."

Emily could understand his perspective, but the Boston Immigrant Aid Society wasn't paying him a stipend to greet immigrants and then send them farther down the line. He was being paid a stipend to help them get settled near Grand Island—show them good land, introduce them to civic leaders, assist them in setting up an account at the local bank, and all the other things new settlers would need to do to be successful. Undoubtedly the Society was paying the fellow in North Loup a stipend, too . . . unless the fellow in North Loup wasn't part of the Society. Emily hadn't even heard of North Loup until today.

Emily started to get a bad feeling. "And have you been to North Loup? To see if it is truly suitable for newcomers?"

"Now, where would I get the money to do that?"

Enough was enough. "From the two cents per head you're getting for sending people to a place you can't even vouch for yourself," Emily said tartly. "Sir, I strongly recommend that you travel to North Loup, and if you still believe after that trip that North Loup is a good location for new settlers, please do let the Society know."

He stepped into her face, giving her a nauseating whiff of onions on his breath, and growled, "You're putting me out of a job."

Emily glanced at the BOSTON IMMIGRANT AID SOCIETY sign quivering in his fist. It could be a weapon against her—but it was also her inspiration to do the right thing.

"Do you think that you are doing your job?" she countered.

The sign quivered again only a few inches from her face, and he breathed more onions at her. An attempt at intimidation? Well, if so, it was working.

She straightened her spine and glowered back at him. "Every penny the Society pays you for *not* doing your job is a penny that could help an immigrant find a new home." She tried to take a calming breath. "You yourself benefited from the Society's aid, so you know how important it can be."

"Not all immigrants are as worthy of help," he growled. "Those Swedes, for instance—"

Enough was enough. "Go to North Loup. Then send a letter to the Society letting them know if it is a good place for newcomers to go. Thank you."

The Society agent's face flushed beet red, and his fist tightened around the sign until his knuckles whitened.

That was her sign that it was time to go. Holding his gaze, she backed up a few steps and then turned and headed for the train.

She'd gone only a dozen feet before a hand roughly grabbed her upper arm. Gritting her teeth, she swung around to give the Society agent a piece of her mind and maybe a slap across the face.

One hand on her arm and one hand on his cane, Lucien stared down at her, his eyes darker than usual. He wasn't quite frowning, but he wasn't smoldering at her, either, alas. "I've decided to escort you," he said. It clearly wasn't an offer or a request but a statement of fact.

Emily let out the breath she'd been holding without realizing it. Suddenly her knees felt trembly. An aftereffect of her near altercation with the Society agent, she supposed, as well as her typical response to Lucien's nearness. She was lucky she was still upright.

"Your ankle is feeling better?" she asked.

"Much," Lucien said without hesitation. Then he glanced over his shoulder in the direction of the Society agent.

Ah. Lucien must have seen the conversation between her and the Society man start to deteriorate, and he'd limped over to investigate.

She eyed the distance between them and the Pullman car. Lucien must have limped *very* quickly. The still-roiling crowd surely had not helped, either.

A glow began to spread in her chest, and she smiled up at him. "Thank you."

He released her arm and jerked a thumb over his shoulder at the Society agent. "What was that about?"

She didn't miss the fact that, without one hand on her arm, Lucien was leaning very heavily on his cane. That race across the platform had done some damage. "I'll tell you once we're back inside. It's quite a good story."

"Does he know you somehow?" Lucien asked, not moving.

"He clearly didn't know my name before today, and no, we are not acquaintances."

Too late, Emily realized that she'd given Lucien dangerous information.

"He knows your name," Lucien said, eyes gleaming.

Oh, no. She had to get Lucien away from the Society agent. Emily dragged Lucien's free arm over her shoulders. The feeling of his long body pressed against the length of hers was becoming familiar but still caused her heartbeat to hitch. "Come on," she said firmly. "Let's go back before you fall over."

"I'm fine," he said, but he limped forward with her, unresisting, as she started walking toward the Pullman car. "Did you get my newspaper?"

"Hmm?" The electric friction of his hip against her side was fracturing her thoughts with every step. "Oh, yes. I got three for you, actually. But there's a newsboy. You can see if there's another paper you like." She steered them to the right and stopped a few moments later.

As Lucien reviewed the front pages of several different papers—some local and some a few days old but from larger cities—Emily stared sightlessly at the bustling crowd. The heat of his muscular arm across her shoulder felt both possessive and right. Now that they had stopped moving, she could step away, and he'd easily be able to keep his balance with his cane. But she stayed where she was, flush against him from thigh to shoulder, Lucien's deep tones sinking through her skin and into her bones as he casually conversed with the newsboy.

Lucien had rushed to her rescue. If she weren't the granddaughter of a man who he clearly hated with every cell of his body, she'd tell Lucien who she was. And then she would curl her body toward his, gently skim her palm up his chest and around the nape of his neck, and guide his mouth down to hers.

She quivered, imagining it.

"Do you have a preference?" Lucien asked, and Emily realized he was talking to her.

"Uh, no. Anything is fine." She glanced down at the stack of papers at their feet and froze. MISSING! BOSTON'S BEAUTY was the top headline of the Boston paper. Oh, no.

"I would like to read the New York paper, of course," she added quickly. *Please, please, please don't pick up the Boston paper.* "But I already purchased a copy. We should get back on the train now, I think."

Lucien smiled down at her, and her heart lurched sideways.

Darn it, why did this have to be so complicated?

"That, that, and that," Lucien said to the boy, pointing to three papers. One of them was the Boston paper. Trying to look like she didn't care, Emily tucked the papers under her arm with the three she had bought earlier. She'd have to read the Boston paper as quickly as possible to learn if Lucien was likely to connect the story with her and Annabelle.

The whistle blew, signaling the train's imminent departure. Impossibly, the crowd between them and the train seemed to thicken. Where had all these people come from?

"We're going to have to run for it," he murmured in her ear.

"With our sharp elbows poking out," she replied, and he laughed.

Limping, sometimes stumbling, they pushed through the throng of people. Lucien lost his smile within moments, and as their torturous progress through the sea of humanity continued, Emily could feel the weight on her shoulders increase until she, too, was stumbling with fatigue.

Finally they reached the steps to the Pullman car. The whistle blew again, its shrill demand echoing down the length of the train. "Quickly," Lucien panted, and gestured at the metal stairs.

"You first," Emily said, unwrapping his arm from around her. She seized the cane from his hand and tossed it through the open door, narrowly missing Annabelle. The newspapers followed, fluttering like doves freed from their pen. The train lunged a few inches forward before halting again. "Go!"

Face white with pain, Lucien grabbed the handrails and heaved himself up the steps and into the car.

The train lurched forward again but this time didn't stop. Emily yelped, made a frantic leap for the steps, and tumbled into the car, sprawling half on top of Lucien as he lay on his back on the rich carpet.

"Ow," Lucien said, but his arm came around Emily, gluing her against him. "That was exciting."

She grinned at him, exhilarated by their close call. *This is exciting, too*, she wanted to say.

His eyelids lowered a fraction, and all the breath vanished from her lungs. He was smoldering at her again.

The newspaper underneath Lucien crackled as he shifted his arms around her, pulling her even closer, his heat seeping through her clothes everywhere their bodies touched. His mouth looked both hard and deliciously soft at the same time, and Emily's fingers clenched the fabric of his shirt. She leaned forward, his lips her target.

She glimpsed movement out of the corner of her eye. Oh—Annabelle was right there in the salon, probably staring down at them in fascination. Although Annabelle had kissed probably a score of young men, she'd never done it while prone on a carpet and in full view of others.

Lucien's arms tightened as he tried to pull Emily's attention back to him, and again the newspaper beneath him rattled, reminding Emily that she had other problems as well.

She sighed and shoved herself up into a seated position. His lovely, delicious-looking mouth now angled down in a frown, Lucien let her go.

She wanted to brush her fingertip over those lips and coax them back into a smile. Maybe, if Annabelle left the salon right now—

Annabelle settled into one of the leather chairs. "I almost got this whole car to myself for the rest of the trip to San Francisco," she said. "What took you so long?"

"Your sister was arguing with a man from the Boston Immigrant Aid Society," Lucien answered. Using his cane for support, he levered himself to his feet and then almost instantly dropped down onto the settee. Now that the excitement of almost missing the train and their near kiss on the rug had passed, the strain of that long, painful walk across the hideously crowded platform was catching up with him.

Without asking, Emily took down the bottle of spirits, poured two fingers into a glass, and handed it to Lucien. He nodded his thanks and swallowed half the contents in one gulp. Face screwed up against the biting, fiery taste, he tossed the second half of the spirits down his throat as well.

Annabelle wisely didn't pursue Lucien's comment about the Society and instead began flipping through the newspapers still on the floor. She stopped at the Boston paper, blinked, and picked it up.

Emily scooped up the remaining newspapers and put them on the table in front of Lucien. While Lucien was busy reading, perhaps she could throw the Boston paper off the back of the train.

Unfortunately, Lucien was more interested in talking than reading. "What was that fellow saying to you?" he asked Emily.

Emily pretended confusion. "Who?"

"The man from the Boston Immigrant Aid Society. For a second I thought you were going to take a swipe at him." Lucien scowled at her. "Or him at you."

"Oh, was that why you rushed out the door?" Annabelle asked him.

"One reason," he said, and Emily realized that for Annabelle to know that Lucien had left the car, she must have been in the salon with him. Perhaps Lucien had considered Emily's altercation with the Society man a good excuse to leave. "Well?" he asked Emily. "What happened?"

The truth was easy enough to share. "I work often with the Society, and so I introduced myself to him and began to talk to him about his work here. I was shocked to learn that while the Society sends people here for his help in getting settled, he sends them to another place—and receives money from the railroad for doing so!"

Lucien nodded, apparently unsurprised. "The railroad is likely trying to sell plots of land that it owns alongside the rail line. Land sales are one way for a railroad to make money during the first few years while the railroad is building track but not hauling many passengers or much freight."

"I realize that"—and she did, for their social circle included many railroad investors—"but his job is to cut through bureaucracy and help get newcomers settled. It's not to be a signpost to another location."

"And you told him that?"

"Not in so many words, but yes."

"Brave," Lucien commented, and a warm glow spread inside Emily's chest. "Next time you try to remove a man from his job, though, please do it when I'm there with you."

Did his last comment mean that he expected her to be constantly trying to fire people on their journey to San Francisco, or that perhaps he expected their acquaintance to continue beyond San Francisco? They would reach that town in only three days, according to the train schedule.

No, they had fewer than three days. Lucien hadn't told her exactly when he would switch trains to take him up north, but he'd been clear that it would be before San Francisco. So maybe, just maybe, Lucien would never find out that she was the granddaughter of Charles Highfill.

Emily's eyes drifted back to Lucien's mouth.

Just one kiss. She wanted just a single memorable kiss before they parted ways.

And two would be even better. . . .

His mouth was moving now, and she shook herself out of her thoughts.

"Why do you work with the *Boston* Immigrant Aid Society?" Lucien asked her.

Annabelle jumped in with an answer. "They have branches everywhere. And we have some family in Boston."

Both true. Both also said in a way that was meant to deceive.

Emily sighed and rubbed her forehead. All this misinformation was becoming difficult to keep track of. More important, she didn't *want* to keep track of it. In her heart, she wanted to be honest and aboveboard with Lucien. Of all the men out there, why did it have to be her grandfather whom Lucien hated most?

"You look tired," Lucien said, and Emily realized he was talking to her.

"I'm exhausted," she said frankly. The nonstop lying, her argument with the Society man, and the struggle to get back to the train had sapped her strength.

"Then go lie down," he suggested. "We'll wake you for supper." Lips quirking, he added, "I know you wouldn't want to miss a meal."

"Ha ha," she retorted. But she left the salon anyway, crawled into bed, and dropped off to sleep immediately.

When Emily awoke, the compartment was as black as the inside of a mine, and rain beat against the windows with tiny fists. It was clearly well past sunset.

*Had* she missed supper?

Combing loose strands of her hair back from her face with her fingers, she walked into the salon.

It was empty, the lamps dimmed.

Was it so late that she had missed supper and everyone else had gone to bed? Lucien had promised to wake her. . . .

As she walked toward to the clock on the desk to check the time, a gust of rain-scented wind rattled the discarded newspapers on the settee, and the clatter of the wheels on the tracks sounded louder than usual. Following the noise, she continued past the desk and clock and entered the short hall at the tail end of the car. There were no lamps in the hall, and no light seeped in from the salon, so she could hear but not see that the door to the back platform was open.

Moving carefully in the dark, she took a few more steps forward and reached for where she hoped the door would be.

"Planning on locking me outside?" a familiar amused voice said from the back platform.

Lucien.

Although it was far cooler back here, with the door

open to the outdoors, Emily felt her skin heat. They were alone. A delicate, dangerous situation.

Her eyes adjusting, she could now see his tall shape as a darker blot against the rain- and night-blackened landscape. The shape shifted, and his warm hand wrapped around her upper arm and then slid slowly down, brushing his palm against every inch of skin until his fingers finally laced with hers. Her flesh goose pimpled in the wake of his touch.

"There's an overhang that will protect you from the rain," he said as he tugged her closer to the doorway, "as will the speed of the train. In fact, you could stand all the way out on the platform and likely not get wet."

Emily realized that she hadn't said a single thing to him since she'd stepped into the back hallway. All she could do was breathe in and out and do her best not to throw herself at him.

She wanted one kiss from him. That was all. One kiss.

Annabelle kissed boys at parties all the time. What harm could one kiss between her and Lucien do?

A few more steps and she was out on the platform, the wet night wind cutting around them but not touching them, instead forming a wild cocoon about their two bodies.

She could sense though not see him smiling. "Cat got your tongue?"

Emily couldn't wait any longer. She placed one hand on his cheek to guide her path in the dark, rose up on her toes, and pressed her lips to his.

He groaned, angled his mouth to increase the friction, and kissed her back with a barely leashed desperation that made her heart gallop in a mixture of exultation and panic.

He wanted her, and he wasn't bothering to hide it.

Panic quickly vanished. He wanted *her*. The real her, who had opinions and liked adventures. Not the sensible Highfill girl who made small talk at parties so that men felt comfortable, or Annabelle's sister who was a possible conduit to the fair Annabelle herself. No, Lucien wanted Emily as herself.

*If he did know she was that Highfill girl*, a small voice reminded her, *he wouldn't want her at all*.

Emily ruthlessly ignored the voice and kissed Lucien back for all she was worth. And as a Highfill, she was worth quite a lot.

She tangled both hands in his rain-damp hair and licked the corner of his mouth. He parted his lips, and their tongues danced, dueled, and then danced again.

This wasn't a kiss they would be able to shrug off tomorrow morning as a fun adventure, or a kiss that would get lost among the memories of dozens of other kisses. This was a kiss that bared souls and intentions, leaving nothing concealed.

A rogue spray of rain splashed across Emily's neck. She shivered and pressed herself into the heated shelter of Lucien's body, closing all remaining distance between them. She shivered again but with entirely different emotions as her breasts rubbed against his hard chest.

She'd been kissed before, and she'd kissed men while

standing so near to them. But with Lucien it was magical. Wild. Her whole being yearned to be even closer, to tear away everything separating them.

His hand slipped farther down to rest against her lower back, and one of his hips nudged hers. No—not his hip but a fierce erection.

Emily gave her own hips an experimental swirl against his hardness. "Emily," he breathed against her cheek. His hand on her back forced her tight against his shaft, and she sighed her pleasure even as her whole lower body went taut.

A little alarm bell began to ring in her head. This went far beyond acceptable behavior. A kiss could be excused, even a passionate one. But to rub sensually against each other as their senses spun and common sense grew dizzy . . .

Well, at least they still had their clothes on.

At that moment Lucien drew his hand from her back and touched his fingers to the top button at her throat. When she didn't protest, he slipped the button free. Another button followed. Then another. Inch by inch, her sensitized skin was exposed.

When he undid the button just above her waist, Emily shrugged her shoulders and arms free of the dress sleeves, allowing it to fall completely open, baring her breasts to the night air. She couldn't see Lucien's expression in the dark but she could tell by the way his whole body went rock-still that his entire attention was focused on her and what she offered.

Well, at least they still had *most* of their clothes on.

His free hand skimmed up over her naked belly, and his breath hissed out in surprise.

"No camisole?" he said.

"It was dirty. I didn't want to wear a dirty camisole under a clean dress."

"I'm not complaining, you realize." His hand angled up and to the right, cupping one breast in a confident hand, and his fingers brushed her nipple.

She exhaled and tried to sound like she wasn't shattering to pieces under his caresses. "I'm not, either."

From his low chuckle, she guessed he hadn't been deceived by her attempt at calm sophistication. And when he again sealed his mouth to hers in a hotly devouring kiss, she realized that she wasn't the only one who was rapidly unraveling inside.

His fingers shaped and teased her breast. Emily's breath caught in her throat with every stroke of his hand. When she imagined the havoc he could wreak if he had both hands available instead of keeping one firmly on the handrail, her knees threatened to give way.

He would have both hands free if they were lying on a bed. Or maybe the settee in the salon—that was closer.

The wind gusted, and the cold night rain again sprayed across their bodies. Emily yelped as her bare chest and back were peppered with chilly drops.

Another gust attacked them, and then another. This adventure was quickly changing from exciting to miserable.

Emily sighed unhappily and broke free of his embrace. "I think the wind has turned," she said. She threaded her arms into her sleeves and tugged her top up. Her buttons still unhooked, she took Lucien's hand and pulled him into the back passageway of the car. He slid the outside door shut behind them with a heavy click, muting the sound of the wind, the pounding raindrops, and the endless clacking of the train's wheels on the rails.

There was still the settee in the salon. . . .

She took a deep breath and pushed the delicious thought aside. Now that they were inside, out of the wild weather, she couldn't pretend that to sprawl half-naked across Lucien's hard body on the settee wouldn't send them deeper into the dangerous territory they had already eagerly entered.

She wasn't an idiot or naïve. If they lay down with each other, her dress would soon vanish entirely. Then his shirt and trousers. Every step of the way her body would pant for Lucien to be on top of her . . . inside her—

She shuddered and hauled her thoughts back to a safe place.

Silently standing in the darkness of the back passageway, his hand still clasped in hers, Lucien seemed to be waiting for her to come to a decision.

"This is where we should say good night," Emily finally said.

"I'd give you a good-night kiss but I'm not sure I'd be able to stop," Lucien said, his deep voice thrumming across her skin.

She wasn't sure she would be able to, either. She also knew that to voice that thought would fan the flames between them again, so she just nodded.

He lifted their still-joined hands to his mouth. He gently bit down on one of her knuckles, soothed the spot with a flick of his tongue, and then kissed the back of her hand like a courtly gentleman.

"Go," he said, and released her hand. "While I'm still thinking straight."

Turning her back on him, she entered the salon, where the low light from the dimmed lamps wrapped the room in a cozy glow. Avoiding looking at the settee, Emily strode on to her room and shut the door behind her.

As she began to remove her clothes, she realized that she'd walked half the length of the train car with the front of her dress gaping wide open.

Emily clapped her hand over her mouth to cover her gasp. Then she started to giggle. She smashed her other hand over her mouth to try to stifle the sound, then finally gave up, wrapped her arms around her waist, and let herself laugh with abandon as the rainy night sped by outside.

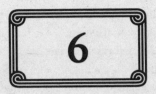

**6**

L UCIEN TOOK A LOOK at the investor list one last
time and then handed it back to Emily, being
careful not to let their fingers touch. If they did, they
were likely to singe the paper. "That's it," he said. "Almost done."

"If you had let me help," Anna said in an aggravated
tone from where she was reclining gracefully against the
settee, yesterday's newspapers spread around her like the
makings of a bird's nest, "we could have finished the letters yesterday, or even the day before."

Lucien flexed his ankle under the cover of the card
table's tablecloth. When he'd woken up this morning, the
ankle had felt much better, cool to the touch and able to
take more of his weight without pain. Probably a twist
rather than a sprain, which meant he would need the
cane for only a few days more.

Looking back, his bargain to take the mystery sisters

with him to assist him while he was lame had been an unnecessary one.

Watching Emily pick up her pen and accidentally splatter some ink on the paper, Lucien mentally shook his head at himself. The sprained ankle, the letter writing to the railroad investors . . . they were merely excuses he had concocted to keep Emily with him. Sure, he'd tried to do the right thing by putting them on a train back east—but he'd seized the first opportunity to take her with him all the way to San Francisco.

He'd seized other opportunities, too, like peeling Emily's dress off her shoulders last night and cupping her lovely breasts in his hand.

If he did any more "seizing" like that, by his own code of honor he would have to propose to Emily. As an orphan, he'd known a lot of innocent, unprotected girls who were coaxed into intimacy with whispers of love and future security and then discarded like trash. He wasn't going to be one of those men.

Emily had blushed this morning when she'd walked into the salon with a breakfast tray, and then she'd sent him a sunbeam smile that had smote him in the chest. Because while he hadn't mentioned love or future security last night, he also hadn't mentioned that there was another girl back east who expected similar things from him.

Lucien sighed. He prided himself on making good, thoughtful decisions. So how had he ended up in both a loveless near engagement and a passionate embrace with an incognito girl of good family? Chuck would laugh so hard at his predicament, he'd bust a gut.

Well, it wasn't really a predicament. If he could keep his hands off Emily until he switched trains at Cheyenne and removed himself from temptation, then everything would be fine.

One more day. No problem.

Right?

Emily nibbled on the end of her pen, and Lucien wondered what if would feel like if she nibbled on his lower lip while he smoothed his hands over her waist, hips, luscious bottom—

"You didn't answer me," Anna complained, and Lucien blinked at her.

"What?"

"You didn't answer me about the letter writing. Why didn't you ask me to do it, too?"

He shrugged. "I didn't know you were interested."

"I can write, you know."

Lucien blinked again. "I assumed so."

"Did you think I was vapid?"

Whoa, something had gotten Anna riled up. He slid a glance at Emily. Had Emily told Anna about their encounter on the back platform last night, and was Anna now defending her sister in a roundabout way by attacking him? But Emily looked equally perplexed by Anna's aggressiveness.

"I don't think you're vapid," Lucien said. Anna was beautiful as hell and way too enamored with her sensual allure and the powers of persuasion that accompanied it, but she was not vapid. "I don't know you very well, but I'm sure you're quite clever." In a sneaky way he didn't trust at all.

"What has you so upset?" Emily asked.

Anna gestured at the paper. "I'm not upset for *me*. I'm upset on behalf of that poor girl that the newspaper is slandering. She's probably not vapid, either—they just don't know her very well."

Willing to seize on any distraction that would keep him from staring at Emily, Lucien leaned over and snagged the Boston newssheet Anna had been pointing at. He murmured, "I must've skipped over this article." On purpose. Society news rarely interested him. It was too often about how Mr. So-and-so's fabulously rich and beautiful daughter had met Mr. This-and-that's handsome and successful son at a boating party, and they had immediately realized how much they had in common. . . . Such as having a pampered life. He rolled his eyes and started to read.

Behind him, Emily laughed. It didn't quite sound like her normal laugh—maybe her throat was dry. "No wonder you skipped it. Who reads that sort of thing?"

Anna scowled at her. "I did."

"Yes, but *Lucien* doesn't need to read it," Emily said. She reached for the paper in Lucien's hands, and her fingers closed over a corner of the newspaper. "If this is causing so much distress, let's just throw it out."

Lucien twitched the paper out of her grasp. "Give me a chance to make up my own mind about the amount of distress I'm experiencing. So far, it's actually entertaining." If you liked seeing the rich and powerful humbled publicly, which he did on occasion. He'd been poor long enough that it still felt odd to think of himself as part of the wealthy echelon.

**One of Boston's renowned beauties is missing! A young lady famous for being fair of face and form—and now perhaps for lacking in common sense—was last seen more than a week ago in the arms of a young man at an exclusive dinner party. Rumors abound of a surprise elopement, yet the young man in question is still in town and without a new wife, while the girl is nowhere to be found. Is the vapid Grant girl in the arms of another man? Or the victim of more dangerous adventures? The girl's father, William Silas Grant, has refused to speak with reporters, and the family has retreated from their house in the city to their summer home in order to avoid embarrassing questions. Perhaps our fair Grant girl is already there, enjoying rural pleasures such as animal husbandry and the turning of the seasons.**

Lucien folded up the paper and handed it to Emily, careful again not to let skin brush against skin. "I don't want to ruin it for you, but it's the usual sad story about a 'nice' girl getting pregnant and her family trying to conceal it."

Anna shook her head furiously. "Pregnant! That's not what it said."

"You need to read between the lines. Why mention animal husbandry and the turning of the seasons? It's a code, telling the readers that the girl will be in the country home for several months because she's pregnant."

Anna jumped to her feet. "Then it makes me even angrier!"

Emily, her eyes scanning the article, nodded. "I agree with Anna. This is terrible. The paper has ruined this girl's reputation based on only rumors alone."

Lucien shrugged. "That's what reputation is: the ability to withstand poisonous rumors. I don't know the girl, but where there's smoke, there's fire. Her reputation was probably shaky before she disappeared." He scratched his chin. "Grant. The name is familiar. . . ."

"He's not on the list," Emily said quickly. "He can't be very important."

"Yes, he's not on the list," Lucien agreed. "So where have I heard— Oh." William Silas Grant was Charles Highfill's son-in-law.

"'Oh,' what?" Emily said. She also jumped to her feet, the newspaper crackling in her hands.

The mystery sisters were strangely agitated this morning. Perhaps being cooped up on a train for so long was making them stir-crazy. If he took Emily out again onto the back platform—

*"Do you know him?"* Emily demanded.

What was she so upset about? Was she regretting last night? Idiotically, the thought hadn't even occurred to him before now, but maybe what he was remembering as an axis-tilting encounter was merely an acidic regret for her.

"Know who? Oh, William Grant. No, never met the fellow. Or this daughter of his. He knows someone I know," Lucien said, being deliberately vague. He didn't want to speak about Highfill—it left a bad taste in his mouth.

"I need some fresh air," Emily said abruptly, and half ran out the salon, skirts swishing furiously. She was heading to the back platform, most likely.

Lucien stared after her and then turned to Anna. "Did I miss something important?"

Anna tossed her head and didn't answer.

Lucien grabbed his cane and levered himself to his feet. He'd said something to upset Emily, but for the life of him he couldn't figure out what.

Perhaps the newspaper article had sparked the fear that, by dallying with him on the back platform last night, she'd placed her own reputation in similar jeopardy as the Grant girl's. He'd reassure her that he didn't kiss and tell. Besides, who would he tell? He still had no idea who the hell she was.

He didn't want her to regret last night, or to fear uncertain repercussions. He would calmly and reasonably tell her that while he'd enjoyed—greatly enjoyed—what she'd so generously given him last night, they should consider it a onetime private adventure not to be repeated between them nor spoken of with others. And he'd remind her that he would be leaving them tomorrow, changing trains to go north. That should reassure her as well.

Cane thumping alongside his twisted ankle, but not as hard as it had yesterday, Lucien left the salon, turned the corner, and slammed full tilt into Emily, losing his grip on his cane. The cane banged against the floor like a thunderclap as he staggered and grabbed her to regain his balance.

"Sorry—" he started to say, and then Emily stepped closer and stopped his words with her mouth.

Without waiting for his mind's permission, he wrapped both his arms around Emily in the way he'd wanted to last night. Like he was never planning to let go.

He wondered if she could sense the overwhelming relief he was feeling. She had no regrets or fears—of that he was now certain.

Whispering, "Lucien," Emily nibbled on his jaw. Lucien ducked a bit to put her mouth back where it belonged—smack on top of his—and was immensely satisfied when she wound her arms around his neck and kissed him with an honest fierceness he hadn't experienced since he was a young man first learning the ways of passionate women.

He kissed her back, licking the inside of her mouth, sucking on her bottom lip, and doing just about everything in his kissing repertoire to ensure that she didn't move her delicious mouth away from his.

His hands started to slide down her slim back, aiming for Emily's lovely behind.

Another body crashed into him, making Lucien's next kiss miss its mark and graze Emily's ear instead, and Anna squeaked, "Sorry! Oh, I'm so sorry!"

"No problem," Lucien muttered, deciding that Emily's ears were also delicious. He didn't know why he'd neglected them before.

Emily sighed and tilted her head, allowing him to slide his kisses down the side of her neck.

"Emily!" Anna said from the salon, her voice a bit muffled but still carrying plenty well. "I really need to talk to you!" Another two seconds passed. "Now!"

Emily groaned and braced her hands against Lucien's chest, dislodging his mouth in the process. Lucien lifted his head, knowing what she'd say before she said it. Emily apologized, saying, "She sounds upset."

"What about me? *I'll* be upset if you leave." He was joking—sort of—and she smiled at him. Then she ducked out of the circle of his arms and entered the salon. Anna and Emily spoke a few words too softly for him to hear, and then their voices disappeared. They'd left the main room, probably going to Emily's or Anna's room to speak with more privacy.

Lucien braced himself against the doorframe and took a deep breath, trying to slow his heartbeat, which was thumping like a jackrabbit escaping a bobcat.

How had he lost complete and utter control of his life?

Had she really just thrown herself at Lucien?

Emily could hear Annabelle's voice, but she wasn't

really listening to the words as she slid her bedroom door shut behind them.

Yes. Yes, she had just thrown herself at Lucien.

And he'd caught her, embraced her, and kissed her in a way that proved he was entirely willing to restart what they'd stopped last night.

"You're not paying attention!" Annabelle howled, and Emily snapped her eyes to her sister's face.

Goodness, Annabelle was *crying*. Emily hadn't seen Annabelle cry since she was eight and had fallen out of an apple tree. "Oh, sweetie, what's wrong?"

"What's *wrong*? I can never go back to Boston now!"

The newspaper article—Emily had almost completely forgotten it. Shame ate a hole in her stomach as she stared at Annabelle's tear-streaked face. While she'd been mindlessly kissing Lucien in the back hallway, Annabelle's life had been crashing down around her.

Emily nudged her younger sister into a seat and then sat down next to her, taking her hand. "We'll figure out something. And Mr. Grant and Grandfather will have that reporter's head, you know."

"Even if he's run out of town on a rail and the paper publishes a retraction, it won't change anything."

"Maybe not immediately, but it will take only a few months for people to realize you aren't carrying a child."

"Well, I don't think I am," Annabelle muttered.

Emily briefly shut her eyes. Strangling Annabelle would not improve the situation. "Could you be?" Emily asked evenly.

"I— Well, it's possible. It's never happened before . . ."

Emily literally had to bite her own tongue.

". . . but I suppose I could be unlucky this time."

"How many— Oh, never mind. It doesn't matter." Though it did, in a way. Lucien's comment about there being no smoke without fire when it came to reputation was making far more sense now. Even if Annabelle could prove she wasn't pregnant and never had been, Emily guessed that there were at least one or two gentlemen out there who knew from experience that Annabelle was not chaste.

A piece of conversation they had had a few days ago resurfaced in Emily's memory. "You said that you thought Judson Bacon had arranged for you to be caught together so that you two would have to get engaged. Would he be so low as to talk to a reporter about it as well to make sure your reputation was ruined and you couldn't back out?"

"I wouldn't be surprised. He has a mean streak a mile wide."

"Then . . . why were you kissing him?" Or doing more than kissing, as Annabelle had just admitted.

"Well, Judson might have been a cad, but he was also a wonderful kisser."

Impatience steamed under her skin. "And that was enough of a reason to throw away common sense entirely?"

Annabelle snorted. "From someone who I just caught kissing a man in a dark hallway, that's a funny thing to say."

"Perhaps, but it is still a legitimate question."

"Just because you're older doesn't mean that you can act high and mighty with me."

"I'm not trying to act high and mighty." In fact, she was doing everything in her power to tamp down that impulse. "I'm trying to point out that there is a lesson to be learned here if you want to rebuild your reputation." A lesson such as: *Stop sleeping with men you aren't married to.*

Annabelle folded her arms across her chest. "Lessons are tedious. Let's talk about what we're going to do to get me back to Boston so I can prove I'm not pregnant. That is, assuming I am not. Emily, we need to get off at the next stop and take the first train back east."

No. Oh, no. She was not going to head back east now. She might have at least one more day of kissing Lucien to look forward to, and she still wanted to see the Pacific Ocean.

Emily's brain scrambled for a better excuse than that—an excuse that also wouldn't sound so self-centered. "I suggest that we wait another few weeks or so to find out if you *are* pregnant before we return east." Inspiration struck. "And perhaps the longer you stay away, the less likely Mother and Mr. Grant are to push for an engagement to Mr. Bacon. He might find someone else to marry in the meantime."

"I doubt it. Although I didn't see it at the time, he's clearly a fortune hunter."

Dodging fortune hunters was something she and Annabelle had been doing since they turned fourteen, and Emily liked to think that she could spot one a mile away. Sadly, it wasn't that hard: Any young man who looked past Annabelle and focused on Emily generally could be tagged as a fortune hunter. With Annabelle, it had always been more difficult to determine. Men so often fell under her spell that Emily could rarely tell who was taking advantage of whom.

A queasy feeling stole over Emily. From the very beginning, Lucien had ignored Annabelle in favor of Emily. He'd teased her, flirted with her, kissed her, unbuttoned her . . .

But Lucien wasn't a fortune hunter—she *knew* he wasn't. He was a self-made, successful businessman who was trying to find investors for a very large railroad project. And he didn't even know who she was.

Unless . . . he did know who she really was. But seizing her fortune wouldn't be his goal. Ruining her reputation, and therefore shaming Grandfather, would be his goal.

Emily placed a hand on her stomach as the queasiness there doubled and then redoubled.

"Everyone is ignoring me today," Annabelle complained. "Honestly, Emily, have you no compassion for my plight?"

"Indeed I do. And it made me wonder whether Lucien knows who I—who we are. And he's trying to hurt Grandfather through us."

"How could he possibly know who we are?"

"The newspaper article. He knows the connection between the girl in the article and Grandfather—I could see it in his expression. And if Lucien knows Grandfather well enough to hate him, he might know that there are two Grant girls who exist, not just one. And Lucien might figure out that the reason why we snuck into Grandfather's private car—of all the available cars to sneak into—is because we knew the car already."

Tilting her head, Annabelle looked thoughtful. "I'm not sure he realizes this is Grandfather's Pullman car. If he did, wouldn't he have mentioned it at some point?"

A shred of hope quivered to life in Emily's chest. "Perhaps," she allowed. "If he was trying to conceal that he knows our identities, he might be careful to not mention it, though."

"Emily." Annabelle waited until Emily lifted her eyes and met hers. "Do you really, truly think that Lucien has been lying to us this whole time? Do you think he tried to buy us tickets at the train station and pretended to get mad and then fell off the platform in order to sprain his ankle—all as a very devious plan to keep us here with him?"

Well, put that way, it didn't make a lot of sense.

Emily started to squirm, but Annabelle took no mercy on her. "Does he tease you about how much you eat because he knows this is a tried-and-true technique of fortune hunters? Does he pretend apathy toward me even when you aren't in the room—or on the train at all—so that he can sink his hooks deeper in you? Does he stare at you even when you aren't looking at him on the off chance that I'll mention it to you?"

"Like you did just now," Emily pointed out, but her heart wasn't in it.

"Emily Highfill Grant, do you really, truly think that Lucien has been lying to us the whole time?"

"No," Emily said. Then she said it again, stronger, and the word reverberated through her bones. "No!"

"Then stop acting like a ninny and start thinking about how we're going to fix my reputation." And with that, Annabelle swept regally out of the room.

She stuck her head back in a moment later. "As a lesson learned, though: You might want to think twice about going to bed with him."

Emily made a face at her. "Thanks for the advice."

"It's from hard-won experience, and more the valuable for it. So do consider it."

Emily propped her chin on her hand and stared at the closed door. Perhaps her little sister was finally growing up.

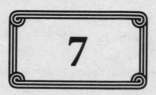

7

Lucien woke up and lay perfectly still, eyes closed, listening.

It was a habit left over from the orphanage, where the smart kids did everything possible to escape attention, even to the smallest detail of faking sleep as the headmistress peered in through the doorway.

The train wasn't moving, and the air in his room was as hot and heavy as the hand of death. Lucien flung the finely woven bed linens off his body and sat up. He could see through his windows the faint glow of candlelight from hotels hunkered hard up against the station platform.

They must be in Lornaville. More passengers would board the train in the early morning, and he knew from experience that almost every seat would be filled.

After they departed Lornaville, the train would make one more stop a few hours later, where he would change trains to shoot north to Bramble Creek. The Mystery

Sisters would continue on in the Pullman Palace car, slowly climbing over the Rocky Mountains and then pushing on to San Francisco.

Once dawn came, he would have only two or three hours left with Emily.

Only two or three hours to figure out what he was going to do with her.

Well, the first thing he'd do is take her off the train in the morning so that she could get her first good look at the Rockies in daylight. Much as he liked the back platform of the Pullman car, it limited their sightseeing to where they'd been instead of where they were going.

A firm click came from the salon. Had someone just slid shut the outer door that led from the salon out to the platform?

Lucien swung his legs off the bed and silently stood. It was most likely Anna or Emily shutting the door after they'd leaned out to get a better view of the town, so he took a few extra seconds to step into a pair of trousers and button up the fly. He didn't trust Anna enough to be around her without pants on, and he didn't trust himself enough to be around Emily in the same state of nakedness.

Then he grabbed the revolver he kept under his pillow. While Anna or Emily was the most likely reason for that door shutting, they weren't the only possibility.

Not a speck of light guided his steps down the interior hall that led from the bedrooms to the salon. Trailing his fingers along the wall to his right to keep him centered in the passageway, Lucien glided forward. After six steps he paused. His fingers had discovered that Anna's door was open.

Good thing he'd put his pants on, then.

Not bothering to be as quiet as before but still touching the wall, Lucien continued down the passageway. And learned that Emily's door was open, too.

Were both girls in the salon? If they were, why weren't they talking?

His hand tightened on the revolver's smooth grip. Something wasn't right. It didn't sound like the girls were in the car. But they were smart enough not to exit the car in a strange town in the small hours of the night.

Weren't they?

Swearing under his breath, Lucien strode into the salon and, by touch and memory, lit one of the kerosene lamps on the desk. The salon was empty, as he'd expected it would be.

Hesitating for only a heartbeat, he took the lamp back to Emily's doorway and stared into her room.

Her top sheet spilled off the bed and onto the floor in a riotous avalanche, and the bottom sheet was scraped away from a corner, revealing the tan mattress below.

Her shoes—her only shoes—rested neatly under the room's single chair, which also had a pair of stockings draped over its arm. Wherever Emily was, she was barefoot.

A quick glance showed Anna's room was in a similar disheveled state.

Stalking back to his room, Lucien strapped his gun

belt around his hips and then tucked a second revolver into an empty holster. Chuck always teased him about wearing two guns when one worked just fine—said it was a dead giveaway that Lucien was a city boy trying to play gunslinger.

Well, he wasn't playing at anything now.

He grabbed a double handful of bullets and shoved them into his pockets. Throwing a shirt on but not bothering to button it, he ran back to the salon, wrenched open the door to the station platform, and stuck his head out.

Nothing. Most of the platform lay in deep shadow, the half roof of the station blocking out the faint light from the stars and the quarter moon.

Lucien gritted his teeth and closed his eyes. If he couldn't see anything, maybe he could hear—

A scraping of boot heels on wood and a faint whimper came from the right. Lucien's eyes popped open. Far down the platform, almost at the locomotive, five figures stepped out from the concealment of the station's shadow, walked through a patch of starlight, and then vanished again.

Moving quickly and quietly—or at least as quickly and quietly as he could with a twisted ankle that was already grumbling with pain—Lucien dashed across the starlit platform to the station's shadow. Then he mentally crossed his fingers that he was making the right decision and cut through the station and out to the street that ran parallel to the track.

There—on the same street but several blocks away.

The five figures again. Two of them looked small enough to be women.

Lucien smiled. Maybe Chuck thought Lucien was a city boy playing gunslinger, but being a city boy was going to come in handy tonight. One thing Lucien excelled at was slipping through dark streets without being seen.

Stalking his prey, Lucien kept to the shadows, picked up his pace, and began to close the distance between them.

He was still half a block away, though, when the five people disappeared down an alley between a hotel and a general store. Going to a back door, most likely, to smuggle the girls into the hotel without being seen.

Or they'd seen him and were trying to lose him. None of the kidnappers had looked back once, though. So he'd keep up his speed and gamble they weren't waiting in ambush.

Lucien reached the alley mouth and without hesitation entered the near blackness between the two buildings. A doorway only a shade darker than the night lay to his right, leading into the general store. No doors led to the hotel. He wasn't looking for a door now, though—he wanted windows.

The alley spit him out into a small backyard, where he took two steps forward and nearly garroted himself on an invisible clothesline. Brilliant. If he killed himself, who was going to rescue the girls? Their family? Their family had last heard from Emily about a thousand miles back.

Moving more cautiously—the damn clothesline was like a massive spiderweb—Lucien reached a spot where he could see the back side of the hotel. He stopped, waited, and hoped he'd made the right decision.

And . . . yes. There, up on the second floor, in the corner room. A match flared in a tight pinprick of gold that bloomed into a larger flame as a lamp was lit.

Maybe it was the kidnappers. Or maybe it was someone disturbed by the sound of three large men hauling two women through the hallways. Either way, he now had a decent idea of where the girls were.

Lucien checked that both revolvers were fully loaded and then pushed open the hotel's back door.

Creeping silently up the stairs was as easy as breathing. Another skill learned during his years at the orphanage. And another thing a gunslinger didn't do as well as a city boy.

The doors did not fit tightly to the doorframes, and light shone out through the cracks of a single door on the second floor. Lucien didn't even have to press his ear to the door to hear what was going on inside. Muttered voices seeped out into the hallway along with the lamplight.

"We know it's you," a man growled. "We have a sketch—see? And who else would be with you but your sister?"

A lighter, feminine voice answered: Anna's. "You are entirely mistaken. Look at these dresses. Do we really look like who you think we are? You'll not get any ransom for us."

Why wasn't Emily saying anything? Was she in there? Anna kept saying *we* and *us* but surely Emily would have spoken up by now.

"We're not kidnappers, miss," said another man with a deep, persuasive voice. "We're from the Pinkerton Agency. That should help you rest easy."

Pinkertons? Tougher than federal marshals and renowned for their loyalty—to those who paid them. No one tangled with Pinkerton operatives.

"Mrph mmm rmph!"

Lucien couldn't understand what she was saying, but he knew it was Emily, and relief shuddered down his spine. Good. Both girls were in there and alive. Now he just needed a distraction. . . .

"Can't you take the gag off her?" Anna pleaded.

The deeper-voiced man said, "And have her try to scream for help again? No, miss. You're lucky you're more practical."

*Practical*? Not the first word Lucien would use to describe—

Anna let out a scream like an Indian on the warpath.

That was the distraction he needed. Lucien shouldered the door open and charged into the room, both guns drawn and seeking targets.

Four men were in the room, not three. All turned to stare at him. The man closest to him, skinny and with a thin beard, began to draw his weapon but Lucien snapped out, "One more move and I'll put a bullet in your chest." The skinny Pinkerton froze.

Lucien sized up the other operatives. A big, bulky fellow had his arms around Anna and was caught in the middle of stuffing a rag in her mouth. A third, younger man lounged in a corner near the bed, and the fourth, a man older than the rest and with an air of being in charge, sat in a chair by the lamp that had guided Lucien to this room. No one made a move for their weapons. See? Having two guns sometimes *was* better than having one.

Emily sat on the bed, gagged and with her hands bound in front of her. Her bare feet were brown and dusty, but her eyes shone with clear relief.

The head Pinkerton spoke, and Lucien wasn't surprised to hear he was the deep-voiced operative. "We don't have anything of value for you to rob."

"I'm afraid that's not true. You've stolen two extremely valuable items from me tonight." Lucien nodded toward Emily and Anna. "And I want them back."

The Pinkerton holding Anna said, "No one said they had a man with them." He was a fat fellow who probably couldn't move fast, but he looked strong. Strong enough to do damage to Anna if he wanted to.

Two of Lucien's guns against four armed men, one of whom had a hostage. Not great odds.

But he'd spent his life working against the odds.

"I don't know who you are, sir," said the head Pinkerton, looking relaxed and confident, "but these ladies' family also wants them back. And I'm afraid the family has priority over you, whoever you are."

"Really?" Lucien arched an eyebrow. "When did a husband become so unimportant? I believe the law says otherwise."

"A husband?" the leader repeated. "She already has a husband—or at least a fiancé—waiting for her at home. It's one reason why we're bringing her back."

Lucien shot an outraged look at Emily. "Fiancé?" he bellowed.

Hell, no. She might not know it yet, but Emily was marrying no one but him.

"Oh," the Pinkerton leader said. "Not that one. That one's yours?"

"Yes, she's mine." Lucien didn't have to fake the possessiveness in his tone. "And I'm taking her back."

Emily's eyes were wide-open above the gag. He gave her a little nod and hoped she could read the *play along* message in his gaze.

The Pinkerton leader scratched his chin. He was a trim fellow with salt-and-pepper hair; based on how neatly pressed his clothes were, Lucien guessed that he had waited in this room for the other operatives to bring the girls to him. Even though he might not want to get his hands dirty, there was a look in his glacial blue eyes that signaled he'd had plenty of practice doing just that. "Hmm. Seems we have a problem, then, because I have orders to bring the girls—both of them—back to their father and mother. And no one mentioned a husband." He gave Lucien's rough clothing a skeptical look. "You don't look like someone she'd be likely to marry."

"Opposites attract, you know. We're newlyweds." Lucien hoped none of the Pinkertons who'd taken Emily started to wonder why, if they were newlyweds, Lucien hadn't been in Emily's bed when they'd seized her. "My name is Lucien Delatour. What's yours?"

"Michael McGrath, of Chicago."

"Mr. McGrath, you and your boys are standing between me and my bride. Our train leaves in two hours, and I have letters I want to post before it departs. So I suggest that we come to an arrangement right damn now before I become even more impatient than I already am." He narrowed his eyes at Michael McGrath, who gazed back, unflustered. "I say again: You have my bride. I want her back."

Without taking his eyes from Lucien, McGrath nodded at the younger Pinkerton standing next to Emily. "Let the bride go."

It was a test—Lucien could hear that in the faintly incredulous way McGrath said *the bride*. He just hoped Emily heard it, too.

Once the Pinkerton removed the ropes from her wrists and stepped back, Emily plucked the gag from her mouth, flew to Lucien, and threw her arms around him. She briefly got in the way of his guns, and for a horrifying second Lucien wondered if Emily's freedom was meant to distract *him*, but McGrath and his men didn't move.

Lucien took a chance and folded one of his arms around Emily, leaving only one gun trained on a Pinkerton: McGrath. He dropped a quick kiss on the top of Emily's head. "Hello, sweetheart. Miss me?"

She nodded fiercely and buried her face in his neck.

Lucien nodded at McGrath. "All right. That's one. Now I need the other girl, too."

"O-ho. Married to both of them, are you? Didn't take you for a bigamist."

"Listen, McGrath, I don't know who the hell you are except that you're from Chicago. Why would I leave my sister-in-law with you?" Lucien unwrapped Emily's arms from around his waist and shifted her behind him. He raised his second gun again. "Anna comes with me."

McGrath smiled at Lucien the way one might at an unruly but beloved child. "I'm from the Pinkerton National Detective Agency, Mr. Delatour. Does that help ease your mind? But I don't really care either way. Annabelle is returning east with me to her family."

Annabelle? Lucien stiffened. Was Anna a false name? But never mind—he'd figure that out after they all got out of this mess.

Lucien blew out a breath and assessed the situation: McGrath sitting with an unconcerned expression on his face, the fat Pinkerton with his arms wrapped around Anna like an anaconda, the skinny Pinkerton guarding the door, and the fourth, younger Pinkerton lounging against the wall by the bed, his hands tucked in an unthreatening way under his armpits. The fourth Pinkerton had a bit of McGrath's look about him, but Lucien couldn't stop and stare long enough to decide if the resemblance was in their features or their self-confident posture.

"Anyone can say they're a Pinkerton," Lucien said, stalling for time as his mind raced to find a solution.

"Indeed. But I also have paperwork." McGrath slowly slid his hand inside his vest and even more slowly pulled out a few documents and laid them on the table. "Maybe Miss Emily would take a look?"

It seemed unlikely that they would relinquish Emily to him and then try to grab her back as she came closer to read the documents. Lucien took another hard look at McGrath and made up his mind. "No. I believe you. All right: You're Pinkertons. And their family wants them back. Problem is, they don't want to go back."

Anna rolled her eyes frantically above Fat Pinkerton's hand clamped over her mouth. McGrath noticed. "Annabelle, if you promise not to holler anymore, I'm happy to hear what you have to say. Do we have a deal?"

Anna nodded.

McGrath gestured at Fat Pinkerton, who cautiously moved his hand away—but not too far away.

"I want to go back east but not yet," Anna said breathlessly. "Please, let me go on to San Francisco, and let me stay there a few months. Then I'll go back home. I promise."

"If you go back on your own, we don't get our fee," McGrath pointed out. "And since we've already let one of you girls go, I need some way to recoup my expenses."

"Please!" Anna gave him a wide-eyed, beseeching look designed to melt the hardest heart. "You have my word of honor."

McGrath snorted. "I'll be needing more than that from a girl who bolts from an engagement. Seems like you already have a lot of practice at breaking promises and running away."

The fourth Pinkerton—the younger one, who'd

stayed silent until now—said, "You know why she wants more time, boss. To clean up her reputation."

Reputation? That tickled a memory at the back of Lucien's mind, but he shoved it away. When they were back on the train, he'd get the whole story. Now he had to concentrate on getting the three of them out of here.

"I'm sympathetic and all, miss, but that doesn't change the job we have," McGrath told Anna. "We'll take the next train back east, and you'll be with us."

"No!"

"Boss," the fourth Pinkerton said. He pushed off from the wall and took a step deeper into the room. Closer now to the lamplight, he appeared to be in his mid-twenties but his dark brown eyes looked a decade older. "Listen. Give her three months in San Fran to patch up her reputation and buy some Chinese silks. I'll pick her up then and bring her back to her family, so we'll still get paid just fine."

"What if she runs for it?"

The fourth Pinkerton shrugged. "Then I find her. It's what I'm good at. And with that face of hers, she won't be able to hide for long."

"Kittridge, you've been hoodwinked by a pair of pretty eyes," McGrath accused him.

"Boss," Kittridge said patiently, "it's not about me. It's about the family. If we can clear up this problem by returning Miss Annabelle to them with her reputation intact, then we'll be doing them a greater service than they even asked us for. And they have big mouths—they can send a lot more jobs our way if we do this one right.

Plus, you have some other things on your plate right now, and this isn't the best use of our time."

McGrath, amazingly, seemed to be thinking about it. "And what if a few months doesn't patch up her reputation?" His eyes seemed to drop to Anna's stomach.

Mouth trembling, Anna managed to say in a brave tone, "I should know soon enough—won't I?—whether a few months will help or I should return home immediately."

Huh. So Anna might be in the family way, but didn't know yet? It didn't shock Lucien, but he was surprised by the tug of disappointment to his heart. He'd been hoping, he realized, that Anna's budding-seductress performance was just an act.

Kittridge said confidently, "I'll go with them to San Francisco. As soon as Miss Annabelle knows for sure what her, uh, status is, I'll either take her home or I'll give her a few months of reputation patching and then take her home. Her fiancé can hold his horses." He paused and then said, "Think of Catherine, boss."

McGrath shot him a dirty look. "You're pushing your luck, Kitt."

"I don't like it," the skinny agent by the door said petulantly. "Who cares what happens to her or the family? We got both girls, and we should turn 'em over for the cash they promised us."

"Well," McGrath said, "that settles it. You never did have good sense, Walt, and if you think we should keep them, then my decision is to let them go. For now." He fixed his eyes on Anna. "Annabelle, Kittridge here will be as close to you as a shadow for the next few weeks. Assuming all goes well, he'll then leave you to your 'reputation patching.' On the morning of March first, meet him at the local Pinkerton office so he can take you back home to your loving parents." He pointed at Emily. "And you: If I find out that you aren't the bride of this Lucien Delatour, you both are in a whole mess of trouble, and I'm happy to be the one to bring it raining down on your heads."

With an unhappy sigh, the fat agent let go of Anna. Head held high, she walked straight toward the door. At the last moment Walt the skinny Pinkerton moved aside, and Anna vanished into the hallway.

Lucien didn't lower his guns. "I appreciate it," he told McGrath. He also gave a nod to Kittridge, who'd settled back to lean against the wall again. "If you have any trouble getting your expenses paid by, uh, the family because they don't agree with your decision, just let me know. You can track me down in Bramble Creek, in Wyoming Territory."

"And I appreciate that. Now get yourself and your pistols out of here, Mr. Delatour, before I change my mind."

Keeping one gun trained on Walt, Lucien lowered the other gun a bit to show, as much as one could while fully armed, that he didn't mean to be overly aggressive. Nudging Emily before him, he walked backward out into the hall and then shut the door behind them.

He swung around on Emily, almost invisible in the dark hallway. He grabbed her hand. "Run," he told her, and sprinted for the stairs.

*They were safe*, Emily chanted to herself. *Safe safe safe safe safe.*

Lucien's hand was still tightly wrapped around hers, providing reassurance and strength as they tore through the predawn streets of town.

It didn't stop the pain of the stitch in her side, though, and as they turned the fourth corner, presumably heading away from the hotel and toward the train, she couldn't stop the whimper that sawed in the back of her throat.

Annabelle heard. "We're almost there," she gasped. "Just two more blocks after this church. I remember passing it—"

"Church?" Lucien said, and yanked Emily to a stop. "Good. Just what I needed." He let go of Emily's hand, crossed the street, and pounded with his fist on the whitewashed wooden door.

"We're going to have to wait to pray," Annabelle hissed at Lucien.

"This can't wait," he threw over his shoulder.

A man in a nightshirt and holding a candle opened the church door. "Yes? Is someone dying?"

"Better than that," Lucien said. "Someone is getting married. Right now. By you."

"Now?" the minister said.

"Now?" Emily said. She repeated it even more loudly. *"Now?"*

Lucien hurried back to Emily's side. He was limping, and she realized that he didn't have his cane. How had he—

Dropping to his knees in the middle of the night street, Lucien seized Emily's hand again and stared up at her. "Emily, will you marry me?"

Was he serious? She stared down at him, afraid to believe that his proposal was real.

But of course it would have to be. She hadn't thought it through while in the small, stuffy hotel room too full of men balancing on the knife edge of violence, but if Kittridge was coming with them to San Francisco, he would find out soon enough that Lucien and she weren't really married, and then McGrath and his agents would be after them again. McGrath wouldn't give them a second chance to fool him.

So they had to get married to keep up the charade.

Well, that was probably Lucien's motivation for proposing—or at least part of it.

Holding her eyes with his, Lucien brought her hand to his mouth and pressed a kiss to her palm. As if the kiss had been a key springing a lock, Emily felt her heart open in an almost painful burst of joy.

She was going to marry Lucien. Lucien, who encouraged her adventurousness. Lucien, who made her laugh every day. Lucien, who looked at her and saw *her*. He didn't see Annabelle's less attractive older sister, or William Silas Grant's middle adopted daughter. He saw *her*. And he liked her.

Enough to propose to her and tie himself to her for the rest of his life.

"Yes," she said.

He staggered to his feet, clearly favoring his right ankle. "You won't regret it," he said.

Emily wrinkled her nose. It wasn't the romantic response she'd hoped for.

A horrible thought hit her. Would Lucien regret it? She hadn't told him who she was: the granddaughter of Charles Highfill.

She should tell him. But the words wouldn't come out.

And really, should she deny herself a chance at lifelong happiness just because of a fact of ancestry that she had no control over?

The minister cleared his throat. "I'm not in favor of hasty marriages. Why don't you have breakfast, wash up, and return here if you are still inclined to go through with the ceremony? I won't be going anywhere." He chuckled at his own wit.

"Our train leaves shortly, and we're of a mind to get married now," Lucien said. Pulling Emily with him, he limped back to the church door. "So let's do this."

The minister shrugged and led them deeper into the church, holding his single candle aloft.

The ceremony went quickly. Barely able to see Lucien's face in the light of the minister's one candle, Emily repeated the minister's words, pledging herself to Lucien. Lucien, his expression unreadable, also spoke the lines fed to him. He stood stiffly, keeping his eyes on the minister.

Emily felt her arms and hands grow chilly. Even though the reason for their marriage was practical, was this how their marriage was going to start? In near darkness, with terse words and no loving warmth?

Before, when she'd imagined her wedding, this was not what she'd dreamed of. A sunny church, white flowers, a smiling groom—

Had she made a terrible mistake?

The minister said, "You may kiss the bride."

Lucien said, "Thank God," hauled Emily up against his mostly bare chest, and slammed his mouth down on hers.

Heat arrowed through her entire body, and she arched into him. He wrapped his arms around her, compressing to nothing every bit of space between their bodies, and she fisted her hands in his hair and kissed him back like these were the last kisses they would ever exchange instead of the first of many while they were man and wife.

*The first of hundreds of kisses*, she thought vaguely as she dared to tangle her tongue with his. Lucien groaned and tightened his embrace. *Maybe the first of thousands. Or tens of thousands . . .*

Annabelle's nervous giggle and the minister clearing his throat reminded Emily where they were. She broke off the kiss but, after a single glance at Lucien's hungry expression, pressed her lips to his again. A girl didn't get married every day. She would savor the moment instead of rushing—

A now familiar train whistle pierced the wooden walls of the church, and she yanked herself away. "The train! We're going to have to run for it!"

Glancing down, Lucien swore, and she remembered his damaged ankle.

"Annabelle, we need your help," Emily said. After running through town in her bare feet—twice—she didn't couldn't support all of Lucien's weight on her own.

"Annabelle," Lucien repeated, his mouth twisting like he tasted something bitter.

Emily threw him an exasperated look. "I'll apologize after we are on the train."

"Wait! You need to sign these." The minister had a bulky book under one arm and a piece of paper in the other hand. "The church register and your marriage certificate."

Lucien grabbed the wedding certificate from the minister and scribbled his signature on it. While her heartbeat was chanting, *Faster faster faster*, Emily signed the certificate, writing "Emily Highfill Grant" as legibly as she could. She didn't want the Pinkertons—or her family—to have any cause to doubt the legality of the marriage.

Without looking at the paper, Lucien stuffed it in his trousers pocket as indelicately as if it were a used handkerchief. Emily winced. She'd smooth it out . . . after they were on the train.

Oh, and after she revealed who she was to her new husband.

"We'll sign the register the next time we travel back through town," Lucien told the minister, and casually dropped one of his hands on his guns. "We have to go now."

Emily scowled at him. Not only had her dream wedding not included all this, it had never been a shotgun wedding . . . with the minister being the one threatened with violence!

Lucien wrapped one arm around Emily and braced his other arm across Annabelle's shoulders. The three of them hobbled out the church front door looking like they were trying, unsuccessfully, to win a four-legged race. Hmm, having her bridegroom leave the church while half embracing another woman hadn't been in her dream wedding, either.

Dawn peeked past the town's buildings, laughed at them, and then bloomed across the sky in a crazy quilt of pinks, purples, and oranges. Their train whistle hollered again, and Emily gritted her teeth and picked up her pace.

"This is," she panted, "the only time I wished . . . we weren't . . . the last car on the . . . train."

"Ungh," Annabelle said, too winded to reply. Lucien kept his mouth shut. Emily guessed from the expression on his face that if he opened his lips, only curses would come shooting out.

The people on the platform took one look at the three

of them, dusty and grim-faced, and parted before them, one little girl squeaking in terror. They hauled themselves up into the Pullman car, and Lucien and Emily collapsed next to each other on the settee, where Emily tilted sideways and half crashed into Lucien's side. She started to apologize and sit up straight—but they were married now. Surely she could do something so wild as rest against him.

Married.

Married?

How could she possibly be married? She felt just the same as she had when she'd laid her head on her pillow last night, except for some dozen splinters in her feet and a huge astonishment that she'd been kidnapped, rescued, and married within the past hour.

"I don't feel married," she told Lucien. "I feel like I've been run over by a locomotive."

As if in response, the engine's whistle let out a final long, loud yowl that shook the station's windows in its frames, and then the whole train lurched forward. Emily slid more thoroughly against Lucien, and he wrapped his arm around her shoulder to anchor her against him.

"So far, marriage doesn't have much to recommend it," he agreed.

A hole opened up in the pit of Emily's stomach. Had he really felt forced to marry her to keep her out of the Pinkertons' clutches? Perhaps she'd been silly to assume that just because he liked to kiss her, he actually *wanted* to marry her—

Ducking his dark head, Lucien kissed her again, his

lips moving on hers with a magic that was intrinsically his. "But it's getting better minute by minute," he murmured wickedly, and her worries broke free and sailed out of her head.

"I wonder if that Pinkerton made it on the train," Annabelle said, pacing the salon.

"Probably," Lucien said. "He looked determined. Anna—or Annabelle, or whoever you are—we'll see you in the morning."

"It *is* morning!" Annabelle objected.

"Then good morning, and we'll see you in a few hours." He climbed to his feet, flinched at the pressure on his ankle, but moved toward the bedroom hallway with determination, towing Emily behind him.

She wasn't an idiot. His intentions were as clear as day even to her, who'd never done more than kissing.

He'd do more than kiss her this time. She was sure of it, and her heart was racing like a wild mustang at full gallop. She had to say it, though: "Maybe, ah, we should wait."

He hauled her into his room, turned, and blinked at her. "Why? Oh. Because your sister is nearby? We can be quiet . . . I think."

She felt her skin grow pink. "No. I mean, you don't even know who I am."

"Of course I know who you are."

What? He *knew?* She'd been suffering anxiety for the past few days over his reaction—for no reason?

Relief swamped her, and she could no longer stand. She dropped down on the edge of his bed and tried to breathe and bring her pulse rate under control. "Really?"

"Yep." He undid the single button that was holding his shirt closed and then tossed the shirt aside. Emily's inhalation caught halfway down her throat, and an embarrassingly loud gasp came out. Lucien grinned, braced his hands on the bed next to her hips, and whispered, "You're Emily Delatour," before capturing her lips with his again.

*Emily Delatour*. Yes, she supposed she was now Emily Delatour, at least in name. And soon to be in reality, too.

He leaned into her, and she followed his body's silent instructions until they were both lying on the bed, legs tangled together. As she kissed him, she rubbed one foot up his calf, and he smiled against her mouth before redoubling his efforts to kiss her senseless.

However, two thoughts managed to poke through:

She'd tried to tell him who she was—sort of.

And he didn't want to know.

8

THE KNOWLEDGE THAT THEY had their whole lives to do this—kiss, peel each other's clothes off, and have sex—should have been a brake slowing Lucien down, but all he wanted to do was get Emily out of her dress *right now*. He'd make love to her slowly . . . next time. Because this time slow wasn't possible.

That was part of their pattern, wasn't it? They hadn't gone slow at any time in the past three days. Why should tonight—or this morning, rather—be any different?

Well, it was their wedding morning. So he took a deep breath and tried to undo her dress's buttons as slowly as possible.

His plan backfired. Emily, blond eyebrows arrowing down in a frown, pushed his hands out of the way so that she could deal with the buttons faster.

"No, you find something else to do," Lucien said, taking mastery over her buttons again. "I've been thinking about this for days."

"Fine." It didn't take her long to find a new target. Her fingers fumbled at his pants, and he inched back to give her better access. He wanted to look down to see what she was doing, because the thought of her stripping him out of his pants had also been a constant fantasy over the past few days, but his fingers suddenly became difficult to maneuver, and he had to pull all his concentration to undoing her dress.

Just as he managed to pop the last of her buttons free and pull her dress down over her shoulders, his pants loosened. Lucien yanked his gaze down her near-naked body just as her hand closed around him. God, it was one of the best scenic views of his entire life.

He flexed his hips slightly. Emily let out a tiny hiccupping noise somewhere between a squeak and a gasp, and let go.

Lucien reached down between them and replaced her hand where it belonged, keeping his hand over hers to encourage her to stay put. "You had it right the first time."

"I don't know what you want me to do," she whispered, and he looked up into her worried brown eyes.

"Don't think about it too much," he said. "Thinking is going to get in the way. Just act."

She let out a half laugh. "I'm very good at not thinking and just acting."

Now was the last moment that he wanted his bride to have second thoughts about the wisdom of their rushed wedding. "Oh? You're *very* good at not thinking and just acting? So you've done this before, then?" He licked the corner of her mouth even as he pushed himself against her hand still intimately cupping him.

"No, not that," she breathed, and tilted her face to kiss him fully. Their tongues slowly waltzed together, and for a few minutes, as he lay there skin to skin with Emily, his shaft in her hand and his tongue in her mouth, he forgot what he had been saying.

Right. He was trying to remind Emily that getting married—even hastily—had its benefits.

He kissed her a few more times before he dipped his head and sucked the tip of one of her breasts into his mouth. She yelped and arched against him. She lost her grip on him in the process, but that was all right; he would survive. "Then you've done this before?" he murmured. He tangled his tongue around her nipple, mimicking the kissing they'd been doing only moments before.

To her credit, she managed to answer, "No."

"Seems to me, then, that you're good at not thinking and just acting only with me. Which is the way I want it."

He could have added that he was good at not thinking and just acting only with her, but he had more important things to do.

Breaking away, he kicked off his pants and then peeled off Emily's dress and underclothes. Amazing girl: As soon as they were both completely naked, she pulled him down beside her again on the bed, where he quickly resumed where he'd left off.

As he teased her nipple with his tongue, he brushed

his palm over her other nipple in light, tight circles. Emily twisted against him, and he levered himself above her and settled between her thighs. Hand still on one breast, he kissed a trail up to her neck. She squirmed as he licked the spot beneath her ear.

"Are you still thinking?" he whispered.

"Well, not much," she said hesitantly. "Maybe just a little here and there."

Hmm, she did sound a bit too clearheaded. "Then I'm doing this wrong."

"Oh, no, I'm sure you're— Oh!"

His penis wedged against her clitoris, Lucien swirled his hips. Her eyelids drifted half shut and her thighs dropped open farther, allowing him greater access.

He gave her one more circle with his hips and then tried a long, straight stroke, careful to keep himself outside of her body.

God, that felt good. Way too good. He bunched his fists in the covers as he paused and breathed and tried to force back the tide that was building up inside him.

Emily's hands slipped down his rib cage and skimmed over his waist, coming to rest not quite on his ass but close enough that his exhale shuddered out of him. She pressed her hands against his skin, silently coaxing him to repeat the movement, and he did so, gritting his teeth against the wave that wanted to sweep him away.

"Again," she whispered, and this time the glide of his shaft against her was hot and wet. He pulled back for another thrust, and the head of his penis nudged against her opening.

*Slow down, damn it,* he commanded himself. She was a virgin, and he wanted this part to be as easy as possible for her. But she was also gloriously naked underneath him, her body open and quivering for his touch, and his own body fought the order. He sank an inch inside her before he got control again.

*Go slow.*

He didn't realize he'd said it out loud until Emily said, "I don't think I can," and rocked up against him.

The tide that he'd been trying to contain rolled over him and sent his senses in a spin. He sank deep, pulled back, and then sank deep again. He managed three, four, five more thrusts, and then reached down to tease Emily's most sensitive spot. She whimpered and then said quite clearly, "Oh, God," and trembled beneath him.

Lucien pumped into her until his arms suddenly began to shudder. He half rolled away and collapsed next to her.

Her hand fluttered up to land on his shoulder, and he twisted his head to dab a kiss on her knuckles. Her hand flexed, her nails biting gently into his skin, and his exhaustion of a moment before vanished like fog hit by the noonday sun.

They would change trains to shoot north in only an hour, and the trains on that line didn't have private cars or even sleeping compartments. This was their last chance for more lovemaking over the next few days.

But then he felt Emily's hand relax on his shoulder. Opening his eyes, he saw that her lashes lay still and her breathing was soft. She had fallen asleep.

Well, that was the natural aftereffect of being kidnapped, getting married, and making love with your new husband.

Married.

He was *married.*

He was married to a girl he hadn't met more than four days ago—someone whose last name was still a mystery to him.

He rolled onto his back and stared at the ceiling.

And then a grin pulled at his mouth. Who was he trying to fool? Right now, at this very moment, he was probably the happiest man alive.

Maybe he should have spent more of his life being impulsive. Because now that he'd experienced the results, it had an awful lot to recommend it.

He turned his head to look at Emily again. He'd spent enough time imagining her in his bed, both on top of him and underneath him. But he'd never imagined how her presence would sink into his bones and infuse every inhalation he took, even when she was sleeping.

He should grab the chance at sleep, too, but he was now wide-awake. His stomach, also awake, rumbled. Moving carefully so as not to wake Emily, Lucien sat up and swung his legs over the edge of the mattress. He would surprise his always-hungry bride with breakfast in bed before they switched trains to go north.

Someone who would not be pleased with his spontaneous wedding was his business partner, Chuck. The end of Lucien's much-rumored though never finalized engagement to Senator Hutchins's daughter might cause some investors to leave. Hopefully it would be only the ones who had been angling for another way to please or gain access to Senator Hutchins. But if Susan or Senator Hutchins made their displeasure at Lucien's marriage publicly known, the negative ripples could widen.

On the other hand . . .

Lucien glanced over his shoulder at Emily as he stepped into his pants and pulled on his shirt. Her fancy gown, her ability to pay a ridiculous cross-country train fare, and her knowledge of most of his investors proved Emily was from a well-to-do family with extensive connections. Her social standing had nothing to do with his proposal, but it might be convenient or even beneficial. If her parents got over the shock of Emily marrying a near stranger almost as soon as she left their sight, Emily's family connections might open up doors Lucien had never even tried to knock on.

Depending on who she actually was.

Lucien dug into his pants pocket and retrieved the crumpled-up marriage certificate. He smoothed it out on the bed next to the bump that was Emily's hip and read the name carefully penned by his bride just before dawn.

*Emily Highfill Grant.*

He squinted and read it again. A roaring pressure in his head was blurring the words, making them almost impossible to see. His vision narrowed to a pinpoint, as if he were deep in a black tunnel, with only Emily's name visible at the other end.

*Emily Highfill Grant.*

Still unable to see beyond the handwritten scrawl on

the certificate, he reached out blindly and his hand closed over a hip that he'd so lovingly stroked only a few minutes ago. A few minutes ago, when he was a complete and utter idiot but hadn't realized it yet.

His lungs unfroze in his chest, and he hissed out a breath and a curse. He gave the hip a sharp shake, and suddenly his vision snapped wide-open again.

Emily sighed sleepily and rolled toward him. "Good morning," she murmured, and gave him a shy but happy smile.

Lucien held up the marriage certificate. "Good morning, Miss Highfill."

*Oh, no.* Emily wriggled into a seated position, blinking the cobwebs away and keeping the covers up to her chin. She had fallen asleep with the lovely image in her head of waking up snuggled in Lucien's arms—not with him staring at her like she was a poisonous scorpion he'd found curled up on his pillow.

"I can explain. . . ." Her voice came out shaky and small.

His eyes didn't waver. "Then go ahead."

How had she not planned for this conversation? Had she imagined that, once wed, he would chuckle about her deception and then forget about it?

If so, she had been gravely mistaken.

No—she'd known his reaction wouldn't be amiable. The curling, withering feeling in her stomach was one hundred percent guilt.

She swallowed against the acidic burn in her throat

and tried to give him the story of her trickery, from her point of view.

"I was born Emily Highfill. After my father died and my mother married William Silas Grant, I became Emily Highfill Grant." Maybe, just maybe, if she tried to explain herself as being more Grant than Highfill, the condemnation in Lucien's dark eyes would lessen. "I live in Boston and I work with the Boston Immigrant Aid Society."

"You're not from New York." He seemed to be mentally tallying up all the ways she had lied to him.

"No. From Boston. Last week Annabelle, my mother, and I took the train down to New York. We went shopping for a few days, and then my mother planned to travel on to San Francisco to visit my sister Lily, who is having a baby in a few months. I begged to go along, but Mother wouldn't let me. So I snuck aboard the train, intending to surprise her. I surprised you instead. Mother must have canceled her trip because she has a phobia of train travel. Because I still wanted to go west, and because I was afraid you would send me back home if you knew who I was, I kept my name a secret . . . *before* I realized how much you disliked my grandfather," she pointed out.

The cold expression on Lucien's face didn't flicker. The subtleties of why or when she'd lied to him were apparently immaterial. "And when did you decide to make a fool of me?" he said in such a calm voice that it took her a moment to recognize the depth of fury behind his words.

Emily drew away as far as she could, but the outer wall of the little bedroom let her go only so far. "That was never my intention."

"No? I shudder to imagine what you're capable of when you do act with intention, then."

Emily's spine stiffened. Enough was enough. She was his wife, not his enemy. "I'm sorry I lied. And I'm sorry I didn't tell you who I was before we got married. That doesn't mean I'm going to listen to insults from you all day long until you're over your anger."

"There's another option," he said, and held up the marriage certificate as if he were going to tear it in two.

A chill sank into Emily's heart and lodged there like a rough stone, hurting her chest every time she breathed. "You wouldn't," she whispered. "We're married, Lucien! Ripping that up won't change anything."

"You're right. There's another option, though. The train stops in one hour. I'm getting off—I need to take the first train up to Bramble Creek. If you like, you can continue to San Francisco with Anna—I mean, Annabelle—and wait to see if you're pregnant. If you're not pregnant, then we can get a divorce."

Emily shook her head as if she could dislodge those hideous words from her ears. "We've been married less than a day and you already want a divorce?"

"It might be a good idea."

Staring at Lucien, she wasn't sure whether to smack him or weep. This was the man she had fallen in love with in less than a week? How had she been so utterly wrong?

He stared back, his face like granite, and then something she couldn't identify flickered in his eyes, and he dropped his gaze.

Hope? Was that hope that she had seen in his eyes?

Hope that she would stay with him?

She drew in a deep breath. She was at a crossroads: continue west and perhaps be unwed in a few months, or strike out north with a husband who may or may not want her.

She wished she could ask Lucien what he wanted her to do, but at the same time the hard set of his mouth and shoulders told her she might not get the answer she wished to hear.

She reached out, took the marriage certificate from his fingers, and neatly folded it up. "I'll go north with you," she said, infusing every word with a confidence she wasn't entirely sure she felt. She held up the certificate and strove for a lighthearted tone. "And I'll keep this, if you don't mind."

She'd hoped his expression would lighten a bit at the last remark, but it remained inflexible as stone. "All right. We get off the train in an hour. Pack up."

He stood, obviously preparing to leave even though all his belongings were in this room, and his order to pack up must have applied to himself as well.

Pausing at the door, he turned back. "Just one question," he said.

"Yes?" Emily found herself leaning forward. Perhaps he would ask *why* she had married him. Her reasons for lying had been cleared up—but not her reasons for marrying him. Did he realize that she had only been following her heart?

"Are you the Grant girl in that Boston newspaper article?" he asked.

The Grant girl— Oh. The "renowned beauty" whose reputation had been ripped to shreds with sly innuendos of being bedded before being wedded. It was so unlike her that the question should have been truly funny— except that it was her *husband* who was asking the question.

Emily wrapped her arms around herself and laughed. It grated in her ears and bowed her shoulders. "Mr. Delatour, I'm going to let you figure that out for yourself." Then she turned away and stared out the window until she heard the door click shut behind him.

In the salon, waiting for Lucien to appear, Emily gave Annabelle a hug. "Be good and stay out of trouble," Emily said. She handed Annabelle a small bag made plump by twenty gold double eagle coins. "But if trouble finds you, this should help."

She had kept the rest of the coins for herself. If worse came to worst—and she had the sinking feeling that worst was entirely likely—Emily could buy her own train fare back to Boston with plenty to spare.

"I'm not the one who got married without our family's permission last night," Annabelle pointed out. "Nor the one who had the grand idea of sneaking onto the train. You are officially now the more reckless sister."

"Reckless indeed," Emily murmured. She glanced at the card table and winced. "Looking back, it was rather dumb."

"I have no regrets," Annabelle said firmly.

Emily turned to her in surprise. "Really?"

"Really. In the beginning, I thought it was silly to venture across the country simply to do something different."

"That wasn't—"

"Yes, that was most of your motivation, Emily, as you'll realize if you'll just be honest with yourself."

Emily pressed her lips together. Boredom wasn't what had driven her. A little bit, yes. But mostly she'd wanted to see more of the country—to see what she had been missing by remaining in her rarefied bubble in Boston.

It was hard to explain the difference, though, and with only a few minutes left before she would say goodbye to her sister, whom she'd never been parted from for more than a few days, Emily didn't want to waste their time squabbling.

"But now," Annabelle continued, "I'm glad we became stowaways on Grandfather's train car. It's been quite exciting. We got kidnapped. You got married. I'm going to travel *by myself* for the next few days to San Francisco while being tailed by a Pinkerton agent. These are adventures we would not have had if you had decided to passively stay behind in New York."

Uh-oh. An Annabelle with a thirst for adventure

might be more than the world could handle. And definitely more than Annabelle's already-tattered reputation could survive.

Emily took Annabelle by the shoulders and looked her in the eye. "Be good," she repeated.

Annabelle grinned. "I'll try," she said so insincerely that Emily shuddered.

Lucien limped into the salon, a leather bag in each hand. The stationery and pens were gone from the desk, so presumably he had packed them up along with his clothing.

He glanced around. "Where are your things?" he asked.

"You're getting me with just the clothes on my back—and one or two dresses to spare," Emily replied, nodding to the two ready-made dresses lying over the back of the desk chair. She had changed into her one nice gown and its matching jacket for the trip north, hoping it would help sustain her spirits.

Lucien frowned, and irritation spurted through Emily. Did he think that she'd somehow magically transform into an heiress with all the trappings now that he knew she was a rich Highfill? No, wait: She had *been* a rich Highfill. She was now a Delatour, whatever that meant. A Delatour with a dozen gold coins she'd sewn back into her skirt hem.

But he said, "It will be a journey of several days because the train stops at almost every town on the route, and we won't be traveling in such luxurious accommodations. We'll likely be in seats, without even sleeping bunks. Do you want to bring a novel to help pass the time?"

"I just finished a book you'll like," Annabelle declared, and darted from the salon.

Emily finally dared to look Lucien in the eye.

He'd apparently been waiting for just that, for he said immediately, "Last chance to change your mind."

Emily desperately hoped Annabelle wouldn't find the book immediately and reappear in the middle of this awful conversation. "I'm not the one who wants to back out of this marriage. That's you."

"I didn't say that."

"You've said everything but that."

"Look, I don't think you'll be happy where I live. It's a ranch that's practically in the middle of nowhere. Town is an hour or so away, and town has maybe sixty people in it. Not exactly a flourishing hub of culture. And I'll be gone for weeks at a time, overseeing progress on the railroad, leaving you alone."

It was a little late to be worrying about details like this. Before the marriage ceremony, she hadn't spent much time considering where he lived, and he hadn't asked whether she thought she'd be happy there.

She rubbed her forehead and sighed. Maybe even if she wasn't a Highfill, this marriage would hit the rocks within only a few weeks. She'd never lived on a ranch. Was he expecting her to cook him dinner? Probably, if he lived alone. She'd never cooked even a single meal, and the rest of her homemaking abilities were just as paltry as her cooking skills.

Disaster loomed.

But unless she tried, she'd never know if she could be married. Be a . . . ranch wife.

She tried on an optimistic smile. It didn't quite fit— but hopefully she'd learn to grow into that as well. "It sounds like an adventure," she said.

Lucien shook his head, but she couldn't tell if he was disagreeing with her or resigned to her presence.

"And let's take these on the train," she said, scooping up a deck of cards from the card table. "This will help pass the time."

Lucien frowned. "You shouldn't steal a book and a deck of cards just because you're bored."

Oh, Lord—she had forgotten that Lucien didn't know that this was her grandfather's private car. This didn't seem like a good time to correct him. "Um, Annabelle will make sure everything is settled when she arrives in San Francisco."

"I found it," Annabelle said, coming through the door with perfect timing and holding up a book. She gave Emily a sharp look. "Write often, won't you?" Annabelle said, and Emily realized that Annabelle's timing had not been perfect by accident.

"Yes, I'll write to you at Lily's house at least once a week until you return east, and then of course I'll write to you in Boston. And you will write to me as well."

Emily had her own problems—an angry, stubborn husband and her almost certain impending failure as a pioneer wife—but Annabelle's problems might be larger. If Annabelle was pregnant, Agent Kittridge would return her to that cad Judson Bacon. "Write me," she repeated. If Annabelle was with child, maybe Emily could spirit her up to the ranch to hide from Kittridge—assuming Lucien would let her.

Annabelle nodded and then frowned. "Where, again, are you living?"

Bramble Creek, Wyoming Territory.

Not an auspicious name, unless there were a lot of blackberries there. Emily loved blackberries.

"An hour outside Bramble Creek, to be exact," Lucien reminded her as they walked down the train platform toward the ticket book. "Riding."

"At least it's not an hour by boat. I'm a terrible rower," Emily said, hoping to coax a smile.

It worked—for a moment. Lucien's eyes crinkled up as he gazed down at her. Then he seemed to remember that he was mad at her for being related—through no fault of her own, mind you—to his nemesis. And his eyes got cool again.

When they got closer to the ticket window, he asked her to stand on the platform with their luggage while he bought their tickets. Rather, his luggage plus two of her dresses, a novel, and a deck of cards. Not exactly an impressive trousseau.

Lucien stepped away, and Emily really and truly looked around for the first time since they'd descended from the Pullman Palace car.

And found at least a dozen eyes looking back at her with frank curiosity.

Emily dropped her gaze, giving everyone else a chance to politely look away, and then glanced up again.

No, everyone was still staring at her.

She dropped her eyes again, this time to look at herself. Her dress was not in its finest shape—only quality time with an iron would return it to its glory, and using an iron was yet another of the many basic household skills that Emily lacked.

She should start a list of her shortcomings so that she could keep track of what she'd need to learn. Cooking, laundering, and ironing, for starters. Rowing—in case she truly did need to navigate the waterway that presumably ran near Bramble Creek.

Regardless of the wrinkles and a few spots she had been unable to remove (again: no laundering skills), she was wearing by far the most elegant dress of all the ladies on the platform.

Oh. Maybe that was why everyone was staring.

Well, she had had plenty of experience in awkward social situations, and her most successful technique was to tackle them head-on.

Emily caught the eye of the nearest lady and gave her a friendly smile. "A fine day, isn't it?" Emily said. "The air is lovely and crisp."

The woman looked startled at being addressed directly, and then her expression turned downright hostile. "Fancy ladies aren't welcome here in Gladistone. So pick up your bags and keep moving."

"I beg your pardon?" Emily said automatically even as her brain scrambled to make sense of this unwar-

ranted aggressiveness based on her choice of fine clothing. Was this town, Gladistone, a hotbed of Socialists?

She twisted to see if Lucien was on his way back to
her, but the line for tickets was long, and he had several
people in front of him. He was staring straight ahead,
unaware of the new drama his bride was embroiled in.

The woman took a step toward her. Emily planted
her feet and stared her down. Honestly, she'd set foot in
only four towns since leaving New York, and she'd been
kidnapped, nearly whacked by a sign, and verbally attacked. Maybe there was a reason why people wore guns
on their hips out here.

Shooting people: another skill she didn't have and,
until now, hadn't realized she would need.

The woman hissed, "Fancy ladies bring the worst elements to a town. Drinking, gambling, fighting . . . We
got rid of our last whore only two months ago, and there
ain't room here for a new one. Just keep traveling down
the line."

A *whore*?

"How dare you?" Emily said. "I'm not a whore."

The woman sneered. "I've heard that before."

"Well, if you accuse every woman who is wearing
fashionable clothes of being a whore, then I'm quite
certain you have. I'm a newly married woman traveling to Wyoming, and I'll have you know that until just
a few hours ago I was as virginal as—" A proper simile
wouldn't pop to mind, so Emily concluded a bit lamely,
"As a virgin. Which I was."

"Easy enough to say," the woman replied, but she

looked and sounded less confident in the blackness of Emily's morals.

Did everyone here think she was a whore? Was that why everyone had been staring at her dress?

Emily walked over to stand in front of another woman who had been eyeing her clothing. "Pardon me, but do you think I'm a whore?" Emily asked as pleasantly as she could.

"It crossed my mind," the second woman admitted, "but I've seen real nice clothing in *The Delineator*, and your dress reminded me of those outfits. Is that silk?"

"Yes." Emily held out her arm so the second woman could feel the sleeve of her jacket.

"The *whole dress* is made of silk," she whispered, impressed, and Emily moved on to the next closest person, a man with a potbelly and a graying beard.

He held up his hands and backed away before she could even speak. "Didn't even cross my mind that you could be a whore," he said quickly. "Clearly you're a woman of good character."

Emily bent her gaze on the man next to him. He turned and briskly walked away so as not to even have to deal with her.

"Is there a problem?" Lucien asked from behind her. She turned, gratitude streaming through her. But he wasn't shooting his patented arrogant stare at any of the other people on the platform. He had his eyes fixed on her.

"I'll explain on the train," she said in a low voice she

hoped the others couldn't hear. She didn't want to tell the story until they were far away from here. "I need you to do something for me right now, though. Kiss my hand."

His eyebrows flew up. Then, shaking his head again, he bent over and picked up his bags in one hand. Taking her hand with his other, he started to lead her farther down the platform. "We're in luck. The train we want will come through here today, but not for another five hours. Let's get something to eat and also purchase food for the train," he said. "It's going to be very different from what you're accustomed to."

Emily sighed. One little thing was all she'd asked of him. Just. One. Little. Thing. And he'd ignored her, hadn't even asked her why. Annoyed, she started to edge away so they had more space between them as they walked.

With a quick tug, he brought her a half step closer to him and then raised to his lips the hand that was clasped in his.

Ha! She wanted to look back to see if any of those mean people on the platform had caught Lucien's sign of affection, but that might have undermined the effect she was hoping for.

"All right?" he said, allowing their hands to swing between them again.

"Yes, thank you," she said, giving him a wholehearted smile. The first wholehearted smile she'd felt since he'd realized this morning who she was.

"Sounds like it will be an interesting story," he commented.

"You have no idea."

"It's not funny," Emily said crossly five hours later.

Lucien was holding his sides and bent over as far as he could go—which wasn't very far. The cowboy in the seat in front of Lucien half turned and gave him an irritated look.

"I'm dying," Lucien gasped between howls of laughter. "I think you broke something somewhere under my ribs."

"Don't blame this on me."

"For the record, ma'am," said the cowboy, twisting around in the seat, "I didn't think you were a fancy lady when you came on board. I've seen my share, and they aren't as fancy as you might think. Why, there was a whore down in—"

"Thank you," Emily said quickly. "I'm sure I'll see my own share of, uh, fancy ladies soon enough."

"I'm surprised you didn't wave our marriage certificate in her face," Lucien said, finally leaning back in his seat with a thump.

The seats were not padded. That was Emily's first unpleasant discovery. She'd expected, of course, that they would be sitting on benches and riding with many other passengers in the same car, but she'd visualized some sort of cushion. Given the varying levels of cleanliness of the passengers, she could understand why the railroad hadn't wished to provide cushions. Or perhaps they had . . . and they had since thrown them out.

Her second unpleasant discovery was linked to the first and had her breathing through her mouth as much as possible. Baths, apparently, were quite expensive, otherwise wouldn't more of their fellow passengers have partaken? Or perhaps some still believed that taking a bath was just asking to catch the ague.

She wasn't going to complain. She had the feeling that Lucien was just waiting for her to do so and would take excessive satisfaction in it.

Another thing she wasn't going to do was ask when they would arrive at Bramble Creek. Whenever it happened, it would simply be a lovely surprise. The fact that Lucien had purchased at Gladistone what looked like three days' worth of food was a bit distressing, but she wasn't going to dwell on it.

Whether she had one day, two days, or three days on this uncomfortable train with Lucien, she would make the most of that time by convincing him to give her a chance. If they arrived at his ranch home with their relationship patched up, perhaps he wouldn't be as annoyed when he discovered her lack of practical skills.

"You know a bit about my family," Emily said. "Tell me about your family." It would help take her mind off the less-than-ideal traveling circumstances, and it was also information she should know. Most brides did.

"They're dead. As far as I know."

Emily blinked at Lucien's matter-of-fact tone. "Pardon me?"

"I was left at a Chicago orphanage when I was two with a note that listed my name and my parents' names.

The orphanage tried to track my parents down, but they were listed as having died in a scarlet fever epidemic in the city a few weeks earlier. No one knows how I got to the orphanage."

"And you had no brothers or sisters, nor grand-mother or grandfather?"

He shook his head.

No family. . . . Emily had on occasion wished for it when she was a callow young girl, but now she couldn't imagine it. Her mother, her stepfather, and Annabelle were all interwoven into who she was: Emily Highfill Grant.

*Emily Highfill Grant Delatour*, she reminded herself.

"So you truly are a self-made man," she said, remembering their conversation from when they first met.

He shrugged. "In some ways. I didn't have family with money or connections to get me started. The early years were . . . rough. But I couldn't have gotten where I am now without some good friends. One of those friends is Chuck Winthrop. He's my business partner on the railroad, too."

"Is he at Bramble Creek?"

"Yes, and our nearest neighbor."

"A one-hour ride away?" Emily asked dryly.

Lucien chuckled. After his laughing fit, he seemed to be more comfortable resuming the banter they'd always had between them. A good sign that she might not be venturing into the wilderness for naught.

"No, he and Jacqueline live a mere fifteen minutes from us. Walking."

Emily perked up. "He's married?" Thank goodness. She would have someone to ask questions of. Lots and lots and lots of questions.

Which reminded her: "Should I get my own gun?" She nodded at the two guns resting on Lucien's hips. He'd belted them on before they descended from the Pullman Palace car, and she'd thought at the time that it made him seem even more unapproachable. But now, with him relaxed in the seat next to her, she realized the guns hadn't made the difference.

"You should only if you know how to shoot one."

"Not yet."

"Then you shouldn't get one yet."

Oh, well. "Can Jacqueline shoot a gun?"

Lucien shrugged. "I have no idea. I don't think she carries one with her, but then again she doesn't venture far from her ranch."

"I want to learn," Emily stated. She wasn't entirely sure that she really did want to—guns were awfully loud, weren't they?—but she wanted to demonstrate that she wasn't afraid of her new life.

"Fine."

"Tell me more about how you grew up."

"Cold and hungry and desperate," he said, looking out the window instead of at her. "The opposite of your childhood."

"You don't know anything about my childhood," Emily replied, a bit stung. Why was he constantly trying to drive a wedge between them?

"Oh?" He did look at her then, and she didn't like the

smirk on his face. "You were hungry, cold, and desperate, too?"

Well, put that way . . . "I was certainly always hungry," she said. "Though not desperately so. Isn't every child?"

"You are still always hungry. Why do you think I bought so much food?" He gestured at the sack between his feet.

She would take that as a gesture that he was being attentive to her needs. "Thank you," she said.

"I don't want you starving and grumpy," he said. "Grumpy people are the worst traveling companions."

She couldn't keep the indignant words back. "I'm a bit more than a traveling companion. I'm your wife."

He shrugged.

Emily gritted her teeth. Then she took a deep breath and tried to steer the conversation back where it had begun. "When did you leave the orphanage?"

"When I was thirteen. I made my way over to St. Louis, where I picked up work on the Mississippi. After a few years of that, I fell into the railroad business, and that's what I've been doing since then."

"At what point did you stop being cold, hungry, and desperate?" she asked.

"When I was fifteen—the first time I set foot in New Orleans. Hot as blazes, wonderful food"—he grinned fondly, then shook his head—"and chock-full of human misery unlike anything I'd experienced. It put things in perspective for me."

"Oh." The food part sounded nice. The rest she could live without.

They didn't speak for a moment, and Emily started to feel lethargy glaze over her. She'd gotten maybe two hours of sleep the night before, coupled with a boatload of excitement. Nothing—not even these hard seats—was going to keep sleep away for long.

Then, looking straight ahead, Lucien said, "That Pullman railcar was Highfill's, wasn't it?"

Emily winced. "Yes." Another thing she'd been untruthful about.

"It was awfully convenient that it was available when I needed it."

Something in his voice made her squint at him. What was he trying to say? "It wasn't very convenient for *me*," she pointed out. "At least in the beginning."

Of course, if Lucien hadn't been on the train, they wouldn't be married to each other right now and heading north into the wilderness.

"You told me that you stowed away in the Pullman car because you were escaping to a new destiny," Lucien said.

"I said that?" Funny how correct she had been.

"Yes; it was quite memorable," he said. He paused. "This morning, I, uh . . . well, I do realize you aren't the Grant girl in the newspaper."

She should probably accept the apology gracefully—not that he'd really apologized—but she pointed out instead, "Yes, you should know that better than most."

He huffed out a breath. "I said I was sorry."

"No, you didn't." Whereas she had said she was sorry about a million times—and felt it in every inch of her body—for deliberately concealing her identity. Not that their offenses against each other were in any way similar in scope. She still held a wide edge over him in damage done. Would he always hold it against her, though?

She sighed, rested her head on the back of the horribly uncomfortable seat, and closed her eyes. "Wake me when we reach the next station, please," she said, and let the swaying of the train lull her to sleep.

When his new wife's head bobbed against his shoulder for the third time, Lucien sighed and put his arm around Emily, tucking her close so that her head was on his shoulder and her body resting against his. She mumbled something he couldn't catch and remained asleep.

What was he going to do with her?

The enormity of his impetuous mistake had clobbered him this morning when he realized who she was. But as the train drew them closer and closer to his ranch at Bramble Creek, the horrible details began to sting him like hornets.

Jacqueline would not befriend Emily. Not in a million years. Still grieving for her brother, Jacqueline would never be able to see past Emily's family name to who she was.

And Chuck . . . Chuck would be hopping mad, but for entirely different reasons. Highfill was behind the saboteur, and Lucien had gone off and married Highfill's granddaughter? Plus their investors could flee, and, still reeling from two major accidents, their credit at the bank was nearly tapped out.

Make that three "accidents."

Two dead.

The cowboy in front of Lucien turned in his seat. "Pretty lady you got there, if you don't mind my sayin' so."

Lucien stiffened and sized the man up. In his fifties and leathery from a lot of years in the wind, sun, and saddle, he didn't seem like competition.

Lucien allowed himself to relax a fraction. "Thanks." But he added anyway, in case the fellow was getting any funny ideas, "We're just married."

"I've been married three times." The cowboy chuckled. "Never really took."

"I'd ask for advice," Lucien said dryly, "but it sounds like maybe you aren't an expert."

"Oh, I'm an expert on both getting married and getting *un*married. Getting married is better by far, I tell you. All about love and imagining the future and flowers and songs. But for me, getting unmarried is like removing a splinter. Sometimes it hurts like hell while you're doing it, but the pain goes away mighty fast, and then you wonder why it took you so long."

*Love and imagining the future and flowers and songs.* Lucien glanced down at Emily's blond head nestled against his shoulder. They hadn't had any of those things. Maybe that would make ending the marriage easier.

His arm tightened around her. She mumbled in her

sleep again. Realizing that he was squeezing her too hard, he took a deep breath and loosened his hold.

Clearly his mind was still not in charge of his body—which had been his problem all along.

She had *lied*. He needed to keep remembering that. Because if he didn't keep that at the front of his mind, he knew already—knew down deep in his bones—that he wouldn't be able to keep his hands off her when she was with him. When she was his wife.

He should have tried harder to make her leave.

*She lied to you. She lied to you. She lied to you.*

He chanted the words in his mind until his skin heated with anger and burned away the memories of her smooth softness in his arms.

The cowboy said, blue eyes twinkling, "Bet you can't guess how short my shortest marriage was."

Lucien tried to refocus. "Uh, one year?"

"Ha! Two weeks. We fought like cats and dogs before we got married but thought it was all part of the romance. Once we were hitched, we figured out purty darn quick that squabbling every minute for the rest of our lives was going to be hell on earth."

"How long was your longest marriage?" Lucien asked.

"Twenty-five years or thereabouts."

Lucien blinked. That wasn't the answer he'd been expecting. "What happened?"

"Oh, she left me."

That sounded like his wife had been the one to remove the splinter.

"She got tired of me always not being at home. We had a bunch of kids together, and once they grew up and moved out, she decided she would move out, too." The cowboy shook his head. "Too bad. She was the best of the three."

"I'm sure she'd be delighted to know that."

"Oh, I tell her that when I see her, and I ride through her new town fairly frequent. She still doesn't want to be married, though. And I don't want to stay in one place, so that's fair enough." The cowboy pointed his chin at Emily. "She's not a local gal. Where's she from?"

"Boston."

"Never been there."

And apparently that was all he had to say on the subject, for the cowboy turned around and faced forward again.

Lucien glanced down at Emily and realized his hold on her had tightened again. Damn it, he was snuggling her up against him like she was the girl of his dreams instead of the deceitful granddaughter of the man who was trying to ruin him.

Had Emily deliberately snuck aboard the train to entrap him?

It was an intriguing idea, and the best part about it was that if Emily had tried to ensnare him, then he could stop berating himself for falling for her. She had been the one who had instigated their kissing both times, hadn't she?

But the more he turned that hypothesis over in his mind, the more holes he found with it.

If Emily planned to trick him into marrying her, then why bring her younger, more beautiful sister along? Unless the plan had been for Annabelle to capture his interest, and the girls had decided to switch roles when he'd made his attraction to Emily more plain. But then why would Annabelle bring Emily along?

And what about the story in the Boston paper? Annabelle's pained indignation hadn't been feigned, and it was a puzzle piece that fit better with Emily's story that they were traveling west to visit their sister in San Francisco.

Had the Pinkertons been paid to pretend to kidnap the girls so Lucien could rescue them? If so, then why hadn't they been more obvious in their kidnapping and made sure he awoke? It had been only sheer luck that he had found the sisters gone and tracked the kidnappers to the hotel. And Emily hadn't suggested that he pretend to be married to her—that had been Lucien's own bright idea.

So as much as he wanted to blame Emily for tricking him into proposing to her, he couldn't find grounds for it.

Now, blaming her for not being honest to him, when she clearly knew how much he despised her grandfather . . . he could blame her for that.

The train ground to a shrieking, shuddering stop. Outside the window, a ramshackle town made up of three large buildings and a dozen smaller houses pressed up against the tracks.

Disturbed by the jolting of the train as it came to a

halt, Emily began to stir. As he watched, her eyes flickered slowly open like butterfly wings. She yawned without covering her mouth, and Lucien had to fight the urge to keep his arm around her. He dropped his embrace, and she slid back into her seat without comment but with a lighter, more hopeful expression on her face.

If she thought that the fact that he had been holding her in her sleep meant that all was forgiven, then she was mistaken.

"Your grandfather—" he started to say, but the cowboy turned and started speaking to them again.

"This is the last big stop. Best pick up any essentials here if you need them." Taking his own advice, he pushed to his feet and hopped down the steps, vanishing from sight.

"We're fine," Lucien said, intercepting Emily's inquiring look. He wanted to delve deeper into her awareness of her grandfather's low character.

"I would like to walk around, though." She set her chin in a way he was beginning to recognize and dread. "You can stay here if you like."

"And have you mistaken for a 'fancy lady' again? No, I'll come with you." His legs could use some stretching as well.

She rolled her eyes but didn't insist he stay behind.

They descended onto a rickety wooden platform that had seen better days. Half the platform was mossy and slick; the other half was well on its way to rotting into the mud.

Though it was certainly the largest town they would

see until they hit Bramble Creek, this wasn't one of the finer ones. Emily, however, was gazing about in wide-eyed delight. "Can we go into the general store?" she asked breathlessly.

"Sure," Lucien said, and they strolled across the rutted main street, dodging piles of dried-out horse dung. The horses tied up at the rail outside the general store barely flicked their ears at them, and Emily stopped to gently rub the nose of a paint horse that had captured her attention.

They crossed the threshold into the store, and the familiar smells of oiled leather, dried corn, and iron nails made Lucien take in a deep breath.

Emily immediately started for the labeled bins filled with everything from flour to boots to buckets. She had a rapturous expression on her face that reminded Lucien of a woman approaching a jewelry counter with unlimited money to spend.

"We have a general store in Bramble Creek, too," Lucien said, allowing himself to be dragged along behind her.

"How often would we go into town?"

"As often as you want to ride the distance." An hour there and an hour back was not a strenuous trip for him but he didn't know Emily's experience with riding.

There was an awful lot he didn't know about Emily.

What he did know was that when she turned away from the bolts of fabric stacked against the wall, her back straight and her chin firm, she was preparing to tell him something she didn't think he would like.

"I'd like to send a telegram to my parents."

She was right: He didn't like it. "Let's wait a few days." Or weeks.

"A few days or weeks isn't going to change the fact that we are married."

"It could, actually. What if you hate Bramble Creek?"

"I'll give Bramble Creek more than a few weeks for the chance to grow on me." She gave him a straight look. "Are *you* planning on giving me that much of a chance?"

"It's more complicated than that," Lucien said, knowing even as the words left his mouth that he wasn't being as brave and direct as she was. He was known for being a straight shooter in business. Maybe he should just pretend this was a business discussion. "Your relationship to Highfill, frankly, could ruin us."

"How?"

"He'll do anything to get his hands on the Great Mountain. He's already hired someone to sabotage it—"

"What?" she exclaimed loud enough to make several other shoppers' heads turn, and Lucien realized that he'd never told her about Chuck's accusation.

He summed up the three "accidents" and Chuck's telegram, and watched as Emily's face grew pale. He then braced himself for an impassioned declaration of her grandfather's innocence, but she surprised him by only saying, "I've never heard even a rumor of him going so far as killing someone. That must have been an accident."

"Accident or not, it happened," Lucien said harshly. "Two men are dead."

Emily began to pace between a box of coffee tins and a spool of rope. "What do you think my grandfather would gain from my marriage to you, though?"

"Access."

"Access?"

"Access to you and therefore to all our business plans. With that information he can directly or indirectly affect what we do." There was another way, too, that Highfill could influence the Great Mountain, but he didn't want to tell Emily what it was. If Highfill had forgotten about the clause in the original partnership agreement, and then Emily revealed it to Highfill and made him remember—

Emily stopped her pacing and shot him an indignant look. "Even if I don't entirely believe that Grandfather is behind the sabotage of your railroad, I wouldn't gossip with him about your business when I know full well how determined you are to keep him out of it."

"You might tell him things without realizing they are important. Or you might tell someone else in your family, and then they would tell him."

"Are you asking me to not talk or write to my family?"

"Yes," he said, seizing on that very easy solution. "Yes, that would do it."

"Well, I won't agree! While I understand your antipathy to my grandfather, I cannot cut myself off from my family because of it. You're going to have to trust me and my good judgment."

Incredulous, Lucien stared at her. "You lied to me," he said. "You lied to me and I married you, and now I'm related to a man I despise more than anyone else in the world. Why would I trust you?"

"Because I'm your wife," Emily whispered, her eyes big and her face white.

"I'm not going to trust you because you're my wife, Emily. Wifeliness isn't the same as saintliness. I've met plenty of cheating, lying wives. I'm going to trust you when you earn my trust."

She lifted her hand to her face and turned her back to him.

Oh, great—she was crying. He sighed and began to speak, but she quickly whirled around, interrupting him. "Have you never made a mistake?" she demanded, her eyes bright with unshed tears.

*I made a mistake when I married you*, he thought. But he knew that those words, if spoken, would be words that could never be taken back. So he stayed silent.

She must have read some of his thoughts on his face, though, for her shoulders slumped as if ten-pound sacks of flour had just been stacked on them, and she blinked furiously to keep the tears at bay.

Then she straightened up and gave him a defiant look. "I'm going to send a telegram to my parents to let them know I'm married," she said, and stalked out the door of the general store, skirts swishing furiously.

Lucien ran his hand through his hair. He had the feeling this wouldn't be the last time she walked out on him. But now everything was out in the open, and that was good.

Wasn't it?

If he was going to be honest with himself, not everything was out in the open. What he had desperately concealed was that hope burned like a bright needle in his chest that Emily would prove herself trustworthy, would prove that the one lie was an aberration instead of part of a pattern, and would prove that his asking her to marry him was not the biggest mistake of his life but possibly the best decision he'd ever made.

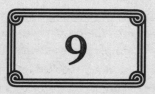

# 9

EMILY STUMBLED FOR THE second time on the almost nonexistent boardwalk between the general store and the tiny post office that also housed the telegraph operator. The problem wasn't the boardwalk that was rotting into the mud. The problem was the tears that were trembling in her eyes, affecting her vision.

She could list *crying several times during my wedding day* as yet another thing she'd never dreamed would happen, right after getting married without her parents' permission or presence, and taking vows in front of a minister who'd been practically threatened with violence by the groom.

Emily swiped at her eyes and scowled. This was it— the last time she would indulge in crying. If she cried again, then she might as well admit to herself that she had failed and her short marriage was over.

Her scowl deepened. She'd never failed at anything before when she really put her mind to it. She surely wasn't going to fail at something as important as *this*.

She stomped into the post office, and the clerk behind the desk—a simple plank of wood that looked like it could use more sanding—looked up and gave her and her dress an appraising look. "Can I help you, ah, miss?"

If he insinuated in any way that he thought she was a prostitute, she would smack him. She looked down her nose at him and said in her snootiest voice, "I wish to send a telegram."

"Certainly." He pulled out a pad of paper and looked at her expectantly.

"'Married Lucien Delatour. More soon. Emily.' No, wait. Make it: 'Wed Lucien Delatour. Em.' And that's it."

He read the telegram back to her and showed it to her as well to make sure his spelling of Lucien's name was correct. "Very terse," he said approvingly. He named the price just as Lucien walked through the door.

"Found you," he said genially, not looking at all disturbed by the fact that they'd just been fighting. The clerk repeated the price of the telegram, and Lucien paid him.

Good. She was starting to believe that she would be using her gold coins for her trip back east, and she'd need to keep them as intact as possible.

"Nice and short," Lucien said, reading the telegram upside down. "You've gotten better at this."

Did he think that a few words of praise were going

to erase all the sharp words between them? "Thank you," she said distantly, not meaning it at all.

"Time to get back on the train," Lucien said, and she followed him silently back to their hard seats in the passenger car.

What would her parents think when they received her telegram? She wished she had a pen and paper to write them a lengthy letter detailing how she had landed in this situation. Even better would be if her mother came strolling down the aisle of the train, her smile big, to give Emily a hug that would assure her that no matter how tough things were now, it would all work out fine. It was one of her mother's finest hugs.

Emily could understand why her mother had always been so confident that indeed everything would work out just fine. Emily was from a wealthy, socially important family, and she was well liked in their circles. The most troublesome thing Emily ever encountered was her disappointment that gentlemen seldom saw past Annabelle's showy beauty to her own qualities. Really, not a difficult life at all.

But now that she'd found that man who saw her and liked her, he disliked her family *and* was taking her to live far from her comfortable home.

A drastic change. One that, perhaps, even her mother's tightest hug could not solve.

The train shuddered and leaped forward, snapping Emily's neck back. It shimmied, slowed, and then accelerated quickly again, but this time Emily was ready, having braced herself with one hand on the seat of her chair and one hand on the seat back in front of her. "New engineer!" the cowboy said, twisting around. "Doesn't quite have the hang of this pony yet."

Emily felt Lucien's arm come around her and gently tug her up against his side, where she was mostly cocooned from the train's jerky progress. "I've got you," he said, his voice in her hair, and Emily slowly relaxed in his embrace.

Perhaps hugs that solved problems were now rare, but she had discovered a new kind: a hug that could patch things up.

The next evening the train galloped, bucked, shrieked, and then stopped at the Bramble Creek station.

When Lucien and Emily stood to depart, the cowboy said earnestly, "You lucky bastards," and then quickly added, "Beg your pardon, ma'am."

She just nodded her acceptance of his apology. It was too exhausting to do anything else.

As they stepped off the train, she looked around. Night was beginning to fall, enshrouding the town. One building with candles sparkling in its second-floor windows looked like a boardinghouse. Another two-story building appeared to be a general store. A little white church sat right beside it, then a livery stable, and then darkness veiled the rest of the town from her view.

They were the only ones getting off at Bramble Creek. About six men got on the train, heading north, and Lucien called to them facetiously, "Good luck!" Then he steered Emily down the street, stopping in front of the stable. "I'd like to get home tonight. Can you ride?"

"Yes, as long as the saddle isn't made of wood and flat." Her bottom was probably a completely different shape after sitting on those horrible seats for two days.

Lucien disappeared inside.

Down the street, laughter spilled out of a doorway or an open window. Emily took in a deep breath, smelling dust, the usual horse manure of a town (especially one with a livery), fresh-cut wooden boards, and the clear scent of running water.

Bramble Creek. Her new home. Or at least the nearest town to her new home.

She wished she could see it instead of only smelling it.

Lucien came out of the stable with two saddled horses, one that kept pushing its nose into his shoulder blade and another that was more aloof. Emily glanced down at her gown. There was no way she could get a leg over a horse in this dress. "I'm going to need to change my clothing."

"I thought you might. The first stall on the right is empty and clean. Mike said you could change in there if you needed to."

Inside the livery stable, the smell of manure was far more pronounced, and Emily wrinkled her nose. Horses and mules stuck their heads out to stare at her, but Mike—presumably the livery master—was nowhere to be found. Ducking into the empty stall and moving quickly, Emily wriggled out of her travel-crushed

Boston-made gown and into the cotton dress she'd bought as a disguise at the first town the Pullman car had stopped in.

That little adventure felt like it had taken place a year before, not merely days ago.

Silk gown draped over her arm, Emily stepped out of the livery stable and found Lucien and a short, squat man chatting in the glow of a lantern the man held in one hand. "Evening, ma'am," the man said, nodding to Emily. "Welcome to Bramble Creek, Mrs. Delatour."

*Mrs. Delatour.* This was the first time anyone had called her that, and the name felt strange, like a fancy new hat that didn't quite fit. "Thank you," Emily said. "I'm happy to be here finally. I just wish I could see more of it."

"Yep, it looks better in the daytime," Mike said, and chuckled at his own wit. "Well, I won't be keeping you. You've a bit of a ride ahead of you, and I admire your pluck for doing it in the dark your first time, Mrs. Delatour."

Emily simply nodded. She glanced up at Lucien. His face was only partly illuminated by the lantern, but she didn't need to see more to understand that he had no desire to stay the night in town.

"She might lack some things, but pluck certainly isn't one of them," Lucien said.

Emily stiffened. He'd made it clear in the last few days that he thought there was a key ingredient she lacked: honesty. Was Lucien intending to reveal to everyone they met that she had tricked him into marriage?

If Mike noticed the dry undertone in Lucien's voice, he didn't show it. "Gals with gumption are the only ones who thrive here, so that's good," he said, and chortled again. "Well, I'll see you when you're back in town."

Emily said, "Yes, and thank you again." She watched Mike disappear into the stable, taking the lantern with him, before whirling on Lucien, intending to call him out on his churlish behavior. "You—"

Lucien gently brushed his knuckles along her cheekbone, stopping her words. "I don't know anyone besides you who would have made that train ride without complaining," he said. "Pluck and backbone are your middle names."

She waited for him to take the obvious opportunity to remind her that her real middle name, unfortunately, was Highfill, but Lucien stayed silent.

Oh. So he hadn't been mocking her. "We'll see what my middle names are after the ride to your house," she said. "They might be Moan and Groan."

She couldn't see his smile in the darkness, but she heard it in his voice. "Mine, too. I'll be happy to be in a real bed again. And the sooner we get started, the sooner we'll get there."

He fastened his bags to his saddle, made sure Emily was mounted, and then swung up atop his horse and led the way out of town.

For about thirty minutes Emily managed to keep herself focused on trying to discern if they were passing fewer and fewer outlying houses in the dark, or if the road was getting more rugged, or if the woods were getting thicker—and all that indeed was happening—but finally her mind circled back to the one word Lucien had spoken that had seized her attention:

*Bed.*

Was he expecting her to share his bed? They were married, after all. And most of her yearned to again experience making love with Lucien. Whispers in the dark, kisses on hot skin, the delicious friction of his body against hers . . .

Yet it wasn't that easy a decision. She didn't want to fall into his arms and into his bed, and then in three months find herself pregnant and divorced. As much as she wished otherwise, a tender gesture here and a hug there didn't signal that Lucien now welcomed the idea of being married forever and ever. He had shot at her enough sharp comments about honesty and truthfulness to remind her that all was not forgiven.

On the other hand, one way for Lucien to truly embrace his marriage to her would be if they took advantage of all the pleasures of husband and wife.

And then on the other hand from that, if their marriage did end, it would be all the more painful if they had shared and delighted in such intimacies.

Emily suspected she wasn't the only wife in the history of wives to be stuck with this conundrum, but it didn't make the situation any better.

Ahead of her on the raggedy ribbon of a road, Lucien cleared his throat. It was so dark under the trees, Emily couldn't see even the shape of him and his horse. "Don't get scared, but I'm going to shoot off my gun."

"Why?"

"We're getting close to Chuck and Jacqueline's house. I want to let them know I'm back. I expect they'll show up at the house tomorrow morning."

To meet her, Emily supposed, and for Chuck and Lucien to plan a way to capture the saboteur, who they believed had been hired by her grandfather.

"All right," she said.

A few seconds later a gunshot ripped the night air, and Emily flinched. That had been *loud*.

Lucien fired another shot, and Emily let out a little scream.

"What?" Lucien said immediately.

"I didn't expect you to shoot twice," Emily explained. "It surprised me."

"Your screaming surprised *me*," he responded, but he didn't sound annoyed. "Maybe I'll call you Pluck and Scream."

"That makes me sound like a tortured chicken," she said, and he laughed.

He hadn't laughed much lately. She hadn't, either, for that matter.

He'd made her laugh while they were in bed together. . . .

Her mind circled round and round until Lucien stopped his horse and announced, "We're here."

She also halted. They were no longer beneath the trees, and nothing except a wispy cloud or two veiled the expanse of stars above her head. The large white shape of the house glimmered softly in the starlight.

Lucien dismounted and immediately came over to help her down. "I'm fine," she protested, and then yelped as her legs tried to collapse beneath her. When Lucien put his arm around her waist to support her, she pressed her lips together and decided remaining silent was the smartest choice. Still quiet, she allowed herself to be escorted into the dark house.

A match scraped, and Lucien lit an oil lamp that had been hanging by the door. He adjusted the wick and then handed the lamp to Emily. "Why don't you explore while I put the horses away?" he suggested, and vanished back into the night before she could explain that she wanted to see the house for the first time with him beside her.

She stood in the tiny hallway, unknown rooms branching off in all directions, and wondered if he'd left so quickly because he was unsure how she'd react. This wasn't a fine town house in Boston, after all, but a small house huddled on the edge of wilderness.

She took a deep breath, steeled her spine, and walked through the doorway to her left, lamp held high.

Then she stopped dead, her breath seizing in her throat.

Goodness gracious. The room was beautiful.

It must be the parlor. Two chairs and a settee handsomely upholstered in emerald and ebony fabric were the main furniture and clustered near a fireplace. A multi-hued woven rug covered the wide wooden floorboards, adding to the genteel coziness. Right now the windows were somber black eyes on the walls, but they were large and would let in a lot of light once the sun rose.

Emily stepped deeper into the room, turned, and gasped again. Three waist-high bookcases spanned the interior wall, and they were so full of books that many were piled on top of each other.

A small scarred desk in the corner looked a bit out of place among the lovely furniture and books, as did a large map literally nailed to the wall. She walked a few steps closer and realized it was a map of the Great Mountain Railroad.

"Here you are," Lucien said from the parlor doorway, then entered the room.

Emily peered at the map and the heavily inked lines on it that showed what had been constructed and what still needed to be built. "You're halfway there," she said as she turned around.

"Yes—the easy half." He frowned, and a familiar tension bracketed his eyes. "The rest of it is mountainous and will be an utter beast to build."

She didn't want to talk about the railroad. Talk of the railroad always turned into talk about her grandfather and then talk of her deceit. "This is the only room I've seen, and it's absolutely marvelous. Will you show me the rest?"

"You started with the best room, so don't get your hopes up." But the tension in his face disappeared, and he led her on a quick tour of the house.

She moved him through the kitchen quite quickly— now was not the best time to mention that a kitchen was as foreign to her as China—and lingered in the small dining room, which was indeed not quite as charming as the parlor but still quite suitable for feeding several people hospitably. The next room was a tiny bedroom with only a single sheet on the bed and no curtains in the window, and Emily's smile froze on her face. This bedroom looked barely more comfortable than the wooden seats on the train. "Chuck sometimes stays here if it's too late or he's too drunk," Lucien commented, and she realized this was a room for guests. Or, thinking ahead, for any children.

Lucien opened the next door without saying a word and stepped back so Emily could precede him.

This was another bedroom, and it was clearly the room Lucien used. There was a chair, a washbasin, a mirror on the wall, and curtains in the window, but Emily's eyes kept traveling back to the bed. The large bed clearly meant for two.

Emily felt Lucien step up close behind her. He wasn't touching her, but if she slid even a half inch backward, he would be pressed against her. "It's very late," he said, and delicious goose bumps prickled her skin at the husky note in his voice. "Let's—"

"Welcome back!" a man's voice shouted from the direction of the front door. More than one pair of footsteps banged against the hall floor, and the door slammed shut, presumably with the friendly intruders now inside the house.

"Are you here, Lucien?" a woman called, and Emily heard Lucien sigh.

"Later," he said to her in an undertone, and she felt a

light kiss on the nape of her neck. Then he turned away, leaving her jelly-legged, and said loudly, "Yes, I'm back."

He headed for the parlor, and Emily followed, trying to put on her face a welcoming smile that she was not feeling at all inside.

Emily saw the woman first. While not as fashionably gowned as ladies in New York or Boston would be while making evening calls, she was still wearing a dress fancy enough to have gotten her called a whore in Gladistone. Her long black hair was shiny and clean and elegantly coiffed, and she strolled around the parlor with an easy familiarity. This must be Jacqueline Winthrop.

Well, so what if Jacqueline walked around the house like it was hers, and that Emily's cotton dress was hideously unfashionable compared to Jacqueline's? There was nothing Emily could do about it now. And besides, she'd been outshone on almost every occasion ever since Annabelle turned thirteen. It was a familiar if unwelcome experience, and she'd learned long ago that if she dwelled on it, she'd only make herself grumpy. So Emily gritted her teeth and widened her happy, happy grin.

Jacqueline turned, displaying fine almond-shaped dark eyes that widened with happiness upon seeing Lucien. "There you are!" she cried out, starting to flash a smile.

Then she caught sight of Emily entering behind Lucien, and her smile froze and then dropped away entirely.

Emily kept her own smile fixed in place. Surely she didn't look *that* awful. And even if she did, she had quite a marvelous excuse of train and horse travel and no chance to wash her face before these people had burst in without even knocking.

Perhaps it was a good thing they had rushed over so quickly, though. If they had arrived even ten minutes later, Emily suspected they would have walked in on her and Lucien entangled in a far more socially awkward position. "Hello," Emily said, trying to sound hospitable.

Jacqueline continued to stare. A man walked in from the hallway and then stopped and stared, too.

Under the double-barreled onslaught of astonishment, Emily's smile faded around the edges.

"Jacqueline and Chuck, this is my wife, Emily," Lucien said, taking Emily's hand and tugging her a step closer to his side.

"Your wife?" Chuck said at the very same time that Jacqueline said, "Emily?"

Emily was starting to get annoyed, and not just for her own sake. She was annoyed on Lucien's behalf, too. Was it really so amazing that he had gotten married? Of course, marriages didn't usually spring out of a four-day acquaintance like theirs had, but still—

"But that's not Susan," Jacqueline said, her face still blank with bewilderment.

*Susan?* Emily snapped her head around to stare at her husband. Who was Susan?

"Um, no, this is Emily," Lucien repeated, not catching Emily's eye. "We had, ah, a whirlwind courtship."

"Apparently so," Jacqueline said, sinking down onto

the settee. Her bewilderment was metamorphosing into an expression Emily could only describe as one of betrayal.

"What happened to Susan?" Chuck asked. He was a tall man with a ramshackle way of moving but eyes that were quick as an eagle's. "We were expecting Susan," he said to Emily with a note of apology. "We're a bit surprised."

"Please pardon us for a moment," Emily said with a shiny, polite smile. Then she dragged Lucien backward out of the parlor and into the dim kitchen. "Indeed, what did happen to Susan?" she whispered at him furiously as she dropped his hand. "*Who is Susan?*"

Lucien rubbed his chin as he looked at her. Seconds ticked by, and Emily was about to shriek with sheer frustration when he said abruptly, "I was supposed to marry Susan. And then I met you."

Emily backed away in horror. "You were engaged to another woman?"

"No, not engaged. We had an unspoken understanding."

An iron band started to squeeze around Emily's torso, making it hard to breathe. "It must not have been entirely unspoken if your friends were expecting you to marry her."

He inclined his head and just watched her with steady eyes.

Emily pressed one hand to her stomach. "I'm not sure if I want to throw up or hit you." Maybe she'd hit him and then throw up.

"I'm not proud of my behavior," he said. "I know I shouldn't have asked you to marry me."

No, maybe she would hit him twice. And then shoot him. And then throw up.

But, by God, she would not cry.

Jerking her chin up, she strode past Lucien and back into the parlor, where Jacqueline and Chuck were speaking in low, concerned voices.

"I beg your pardon, but my husband forgot to introduce me properly." Emily smiled a smile she thought could probably cut glass. "My name is Emily Highfill Grant Delatour, of the Boston Highfills. I believe you've heard of my family if not of me."

Both Chuck and Jacqueline stiffened.

Emily continued sweetly, "I'm afraid I'm not prepared to entertain at the moment, but I will leave you in my husband's capable hands. Good night."

And she left the room and a rising hiss of furious, shocked whispers behind her.

Lucien, standing just outside the door, didn't look as angry as she'd expected him to after she'd deliberately and rudely provoked his friends.

"Pluck and backbone" was all he said in a resigned voice as she whisked past him.

Not quite sure how to respond, she sniffed in her best aristocratic Boston manner, entered the bedroom, and clicked the door shut behind her.

Lucien stood for another few moments in the hallway listening to Emily muttering under her breath and stomping around in his bedroom. No, *their* bedroom now. Unless she jammed the chair under the knob and kept him out.

A heavy scraping noise came from the other side of the door, and the knob jiggled.

Yep—she'd just locked him out.

Could Jacqueline and Chuck's introduction to Emily have gone any worse? Probably not. In retrospect, he should have sent a telegram to Chuck warning him that he was returning with a bride who wasn't Susan. But really, couldn't his friends have been a tiny bit more discreet upon meeting Emily for the first time?

Eyebrows tucking down in a frown, he walked back into the parlor.

Chuck was now seated next to Jacqueline, holding her hand but not saying anything. Jacqueline looked even more shell-shocked than she had when Lucien had first sprung Emily on her.

"You married Emily Highfill?" Jacqueline cried as Lucien seated himself across from them.

"Yes," he said calmly. "Do you know of her?" He himself hadn't—not until after the wedding—but that was something he wanted to keep between himself and Emily for now. Maybe in five years, if they all survived this, he'd tell his friends the true story of their courtship and marriage.

"Her name has been in all the papers ever since she and her sister 'disappeared.' It's common knowledge, Lucien, that they are not nice girls. More important, though, is that she is a Highfill. Her grandfather killed my brother!"

"And he has killed more men than that, too," Chuck said grimly. "A fellow who was hurt in the last accident died only last night. That makes three of our men dead."

Lucien rubbed his forehead and tried to figure out which attack to answer first. Lead with *She was a virgin?* The fact that he was even considering saying it was proof that he needed sanity-restoring sleep, and lots of it. Too bad he wasn't going to get that sleep while lying next to Emily tonight. "Emily is my wife now. Any insult to her is an insult to me, too."

Shaking his head, Chuck said, "That's all fine and good, but we're your friends, Lucien. And good friends don't stand silently by, allowing a friend to make a terrible mistake."

Jacqueline shot to her feet. "It's too late! He's already made a terrible mistake!" She pointed in the direction of the bedroom. "Hear me now: Emily Highfill is not welcome in my home."

Lucien grabbed onto his temper with both hands and tried to speak calmly. "Don't draw a line in the sand that you'll regret, Jacqueline." He slid Chuck a look.

Chuck stood, too. "As you're defending your wife, Lucien, I need to defend mine."

Frankly, Lucien thought he had done a piss-poor job of defending Emily. He should have tossed Jacqueline out when she'd insinuated that Emily had slept around. But he'd always been the calm and cool one in his partnership with Chuck, and that partnership included dealing with Jacqueline and Chuck at their most dramatic.

"I'll see you down at the track tomorrow," Lucien

said to Chuck, ignoring his challenge, "and I'll fill you in on the details from New York and Washington. Good night."

Heads held high, Jacqueline and Chuck stalked out.

After his friends left, Lucien walked back to his bedroom and contemplated the closed door.

He could climb in through one of the windows—none had latches. Or he could holler until she gave in and moved the chair away. But to what end? To argue with Emily while both of them were running on very little sleep and raw from Chuck and Jacqueline's visit? That seemed like the very definition of poor decision making.

He turned instead into the smaller bedroom that Chuck sometimes used and stretched out on the mattress.

Tomorrow he and Chuck would talk and get back on their usual footing.

Tomorrow he and Emily would talk and figure out what kind of marriage they could cobble together.

But when Lucien woke up the next morning, the house was empty.

Emily was gone.

**10**

BEFORE HE COMPLETELY GAVE in to panic, Lucien ran to the stable. Both his horse and the horse Emily had ridden last night were still there, dozing on their feet.

Spinning in a slow circle, he surveyed his property. Unless she had decided to set out for Bramble Creek on foot—and he couldn't imagine she'd be so impractical that she'd do that—she was still around. Somewhere.

Mentally, he was reassured. But his stupid heart kept *thump-thump*ing like he'd just outrun a mountain lion.

"Emily!" he shouted.

Nothing but a gust of hot late-summer wind answered him.

Swearing under his breath, he quickly saddled his horse and mounted. Maybe she was exploring. He'd start at the house and then extend his search in expanding circles. He'd find her for sure.

And if he didn't . . .

Well, that's when friends were supposed to help out. He'd roust Chuck up and into a saddle and force him to beat the bushes with him.

Worse came to worst, he'd take a piece of Emily's clothing to Mike Vant, the livery master. Mike could touch a piece of someone's clothes and tell you where that person's body was if the person was dead. It came in handy when a settler went missing, and Mike had helped locate more than one poor soul after the spring thaw.

But Emily couldn't be dead. He'd been talking to her only a few hours ago.

"Emily!" he shouted again, and trotted his horse around the back of the house, making the first tight circle of his search. "Emily!"

A flash of color caught his eye, and Emily popped up from behind the small springhouse, clearly still alive. Alive and disgruntled, based on the expression on her face.

"I'm having trouble with the well," she said as he reined his horse in beside her. She stuck her hands on her hips and glowered. "It's not working."

"Not working?" he repeated inanely. He wanted to grab her and squeeze her and yell at her for scaring him, not talk about the damn well.

"Or maybe I don't know how to work it," she said, a defensive tone now in her words.

Swinging down off his horse, he said, "I'll take a look." His legs wobbled as he hit the ground, reminding him that while his scare might be over, his body still hadn't absorbed the message. Muttering a curse under his breath hopefully soft enough for Emily not to hear, he followed her into the tiny, dim springhouse. "All right, show me what you were doing," he said.

Emily shook her head quite firmly. "No, you show me what to do."

He squinted at her. Something wasn't right here. "Is this the first time you've pumped water?"

"Wellllllll . . . yes." She glared at him. "Yes, it is. And today will be the day when I first start a fire, use a stove, and cook a meal. Three more reasons why you shouldn't have asked me to marry you."

Her phrasing tickled something in his memory, but he couldn't pin down what. "You can't cook?"

"Nor do laundry. Nor scrub floors. Nor gather eggs from chickens—or do anything else involving chickens, for that matter." With every word she spoke, her chin lifted a little higher and her voice got a little louder.

Lucien searched through her words to find something positive to say. "You're trying, though. Here we are, in the springhouse."

She sighed, and her shoulders slumped, all the fight suddenly wicked out of her. "I'm always trying, Lucien. At this very moment, though, I am questioning why."

The answer was so obvious, he didn't bother saying it. He showed her instead. Tilting her face up to his in the shadowy springhouse, he brushed his lips against her tight, unhappy mouth and continued to repeat the motion until her own lips softened in a sweet gasp and she allowed him to kiss her the way he'd wanted to ever since they'd crossed the threshold of his home and he realized that he wanted Emily back in his bed, where she belonged.

"You taste so delicious," he murmured. "I can't wait to taste the rest of you again." He hadn't told Chuck exactly when he'd meet up with him, so if he spent another hour in bed with Emily—

Emily's small hands stopped tugging him closer and reversed their motion, pushing him back a half step. "I've been thinking about this, and we shouldn't make love to each other while we still think our marriage might not last."

That was the worst idea he'd ever heard. "You came to this decision while you were mad at me about Susan, didn't you?"

"Yes—but before that, too."

He leaned close and nibbled on the corner of her mouth. "But now that you're not mad at me—"

She huffed, "Just because I'm kissing you doesn't mean I'm not mad at you, Lucien. Does it mean that you're not mad at me?"

"I'm not *actively* mad at you right now," he said, but just talking about being mad or not being mad had dimmed his fantasies of carrying her off to bed.

Next time he kissed her, he wouldn't make the mistake of talking to her in the middle of it.

"Were you on the way to the railroad?" she asked, stepping back and gesturing in the direction of his horse.

He didn't want to admit that he'd been rushing around like a madman, trying to find her when she hadn't really been lost in the first place, so he didn't answer directly. "I have to talk to Chuck about business." Last night, before dropping off to sleep, he'd decided that he would also invite Chuck over for supper tonight so that Chuck could get to know Emily. But if Emily couldn't cook, that wasn't likely to be a successful plan.

Well, now that Lucien thought about it, Susan probably wouldn't have come to Bramble Creek knowing how to draw water, cook, do laundry, and shoot critters. Susan came from the same rarefied, privileged social circles as Emily did. And now that he spent even more time thinking about it, Jacqueline still probably didn't do any of those things even though she'd been married to Chuck and living away from the gentle life of Washington, D.C., for five years now. Chuck had a housekeeper who probably doubled as a cook.

"I'll be back around sunset," he told Emily.

"Before you go, you need to show me how to work the pump."

He pumped water into a waiting bucket, and Emily watched him carefully. When he made her draw water herself so he could be sure she knew what to do, she imitated him perfectly.

He carried the bucket into the kitchen and set it by the stove.

"Could you also start the stove?" Emily asked. "I'd like to heat water and wash while you're gone."

He preferred that she wash while he was there to help make sure she didn't miss any spots. But they still needed to achieve kissing for more than two minutes without arguing. Unfortunately, soaping each other all over was at least a few days away.

So he started the stove and showed her where he'd put the food they had left over from the train ride as well as the jarred goods. She followed his every move with concentration, and he was confident he wouldn't have to repeat his instructions.

She was catching on mighty quickly for a soft, protected girl from Boston.

Opening the back door, he gave her one more instruction. "Don't wander far from the house." He didn't want to again go through the scare he'd had that morning. He probably had ten more gray hairs on his head than he'd woken up with.

She said disgustedly, "How far could I go? I can't even saddle a horse myself."

"Good," he answered without thinking, and she tried to slay him with a scowl. "I mean, I'll show you tomorrow." Before she could reply, he tugged her to him and dropped a kiss on her mouth. "See you at sundown."

"Wait! What happens if you don't come back?"

He blinked. "I'll come back. Do you think I'd just up and disappear on you? That's a coward's way out."

"No, no—I don't mean that. What if you're killed? Aren't there mountain lions and bears and things out there, waiting to eat you?"

"Sure, but it's unlikely to happen."

She still didn't look reassured, so he said, "Just follow the track back to town," and he pointed to the little road that ran due east from their house. "You'll find other houses within a half hour, and someone there will help you."

She sighed and said, "All right."

She was looking so demoralized that he decided to kiss her one more time before leaving. She pushed up on her toes and kissed him back, murmuring against his mouth, "Stay safe," before pulling away.

Just before he disappeared around the bend of the trail that led in the direction of the tracks, he twisted in his saddle and looked back. Emily had shut the back door behind him, and from his vantage point the house looked exactly as it always had every time he had rode away from it. But something about his home was different, even if it wasn't visibly different.

His *home*. Ah, that was the difference. Before, it had been a house. A nice house—in fact, the nicest house in the county, aside from Chuck's. But for all the books and fancy furniture, it had been just a house.

Without cooking a single meal or darning a sock— probably another thing she couldn't do—Emily had made his house a home.

Lucien grinned and heeled his horse into a trot. The sooner he got his business with Chuck done, the sooner he'd be home.

"I still can't believe you're such an idiot" was Chuck's greeting as Lucien walked over to where his partner was standing on a bluff, watching the men lay rail below.

"It perplexed me at the time, too," Lucien answered frankly. He and Chuck had always been honest with each other, even when honesty came equipped with some sharp edges. It was one reason why their partnership had been so successful. "But it's done, and—"

"It can always be undone," Chuck said, spinning to face Lucien directly. "Out here marriages don't always last very long, and separations can be amicable. She's got a powerful family, so I don't suppose it will be that easy to end, and you know that Highfill will take this chance to lay a boot across our neck. But it's an option that you should think about."

Lucien wanted to ask Chuck if he'd cast aside his marriage to Jacqueline if he thought it would help the Great Mountain, but he didn't want to travel too far down that road. For one thing, Chuck and Jacqueline had made a love match and seemed to have no regrets. Lucien had followed his very poor instincts and his very strong libido, and regrets pounced on him every moment he let down his guard.

But that was for him and Emily to work out—not him, Emily, and Chuck. "Tell me about the sabotage," Lucien said instead.

"As I said last night, we lost another man. There are now rumors on the line of sabotage, and some workers have left. Those who haven't left are twitchy, and Griffin has complained to me that the men are too rowdy at his saloon."

"It's a saloon," Lucien said. "That's what happens."

"He's said to me that if he can't wring the price of

a broken chair or table out of the fellows who've been fighting, he's going to come to us for compensation."

"Next time I'm in town, I'll talk to Griffin about the wisdom of pouring rotgut into men until they fight and see if we can find a different solution. What else?"

"We're overdrawn at the bank, but they'll be fine as long as we can show more money coming in from either investments or land sales." He gave Lucien a level look. "Those investments had better come, my friend, or you and I owe people a lot of money."

"They're coming. Almost everyone I talked to was eager to jump on the Great Mountain. A bank in New York will issue stock certificates to those who want shares. I sent the bank a list of investors to approach, so we should know within a few weeks exactly who is buying in."

"Good, good." The drawn look around Chuck's eyes faded. "That will keep our bank here happy. Jacqueline, too." He shook his head. "The accidents have been hard on her. She's restarted talking about giving up on the Great Mountain and going back east, and she's been quite insistent. I won't consider it, of course."

Even if sticking with the Great Mountain meant derailing his marriage? Lucien swallowed back the question. With success so close but failure still lurking like a wolf in the darkness, Lucien didn't want to know the answer.

"The saboteur," Lucien said. "What's the progress on finding him?"

"Zero. No one saw anything. I checked back on the

other two incidents and nothing seemed screwy there, either. We know the saboteur can use blasting powder, but so can half the men here."

"Who knows that we believe it's sabotage?"

"Just you, me, and Hendrick."

Good. Lucien trusted the foreman almost as much as he did Chuck. "And what about Highfill's involvement? Anything there?"

Chuck started to pace. "Nothing definitive. I hired a Pinkerton to follow him, and I got a telegram yesterday from the agent that Highfill had gotten on a train heading west."

It was ironic that Emily's family, who had used Pinkertons to find her, were now being hounded by the same company of agents. "From Boston, almost everything is west. You fall into the harbor if you go east."

Throwing him a furious look, Chuck said, "Don't start defending him because you're part of his family now."

"I'm not defending him. I'm giving you a geography lesson."

"Don't put on blinkers, Lucien. Why else would he jump on a train except to capitalize on his granddaughter's marriage to the owner of the one railroad he wants and hasn't been able to get his hands on?"

Unfortunately, Chuck was probably right. Emily had sent her family the news of her wedding only a few days ago, and it appeared that Highfill had boarded a train almost immediately afterward.

"There's nothing Highfill can do even though Emily

is married to me," Lucien said. "If anything, it should make the sabotage stop."

"Nothing he can do? Then you don't remember our partnership agreement very well."

Oh, he remembered. He had been hoping Chuck might not have, though.

Chuck went on relentlessly, "If any partner wishes to sell his stake, or if the partnership issues shares to non-majority investors, *family members* have the first opportunity to purchase all or a portion of what is being offered." Chuck pushed both hands through his hair and then yanked. "Why the hell did we do that? When we partnered, neither one of us had family or even a sweetheart. What were we thinking?"

"It was Highfill who thought that was a good idea. As for you and me . . . maybe we thought that someday we wouldn't be alone any longer."

Chuck snorted. "Then we were romantic fools. You more than me, though. Could you have picked a worse woman to marry?"

Chuck didn't mean that Emily herself was bad—at least, Lucien was willing to give him the benefit of the doubt. This time. Trying to inject some levity into the conversation, Lucien joked, "You should have met her sister. That one would have turned your hair white."

"My hair is turning white already," Chuck said, refusing to smile. "How did she ensnare you? Just tell me that."

Enough was enough. "I'm going to say this once, and

I expect you to believe it and then let it go. She didn't ensnare me. I ensnared her."

And it was true. As much as he wanted to blame Emily because it was easier than accepting the blame himself, he knew that he could have found out easily enough who she was before they married if he had bent his will to it. Even after he'd rescued her from the Pinkerton agents, he hadn't tried to find out her family name. Hell, he could have asked her right before he proposed, and he had no doubt that she would have honestly replied.

But he hadn't wanted to know. He had just wanted Emily bound to him, and so he'd proposed marriage as soon as he realized that she could be taken from him.

Chuck stared. "I refuse to believe it. You were to marry Susan, and instead you chose a Highfill trollop!"

It had been at least six months since Lucien had punched a man in the face. He'd forgotten that it hurt like hell.

Shaking his throbbing hand, he told his partner—who was writhing on the ground, palm to his nose and moaning—"I'm going to check out the progress of the track and talk to Hendrick about the saboteur. Best give me some space."

Then he stalked away, heading for the clump of men who were leveling the ground in preparation for laying the railroad.

"You're a goddamned fool!" Chuck shouted after him.

Of that, Lucien thought as he half walked, half slid down the rocky hill, he had no doubt. And as far as he was concerned, the most foolish thing he'd done all day was come out here to argue with his best friend instead of staying home and making love to his new wife.

Hands on her hips, Emily stared at the stove.

It looked quite capable of doing many wonderful, practical things. But Emily couldn't think of a single wonderful, practical thing that she herself could do with the stove.

Well, she could boil water, couldn't she? There was the bucket of water. There was a kettle. Easy enough.

Ten minutes later, sucking on burned fingers, Emily stared at the kettle that she had stupidly picked up without using a cloth to protect her fingers. The kettle was now lying on its side on the ground, dribbling hot water onto the floorboards and silently laughing at her.

Lovely. She was too inept to even boil water.

Wrapping her hand in a clean cloth, she picked up the kettle and managed to splash a few cups of steaming water into a basin. Adding cool water from the bucket, she swirled the cloth in the basin and then wiped three days of dust and soot from her face.

Ah, heavenly.

Maybe if she hadn't looked like a dirty, bedraggled fright last night, Jacqueline and Chuck Winthrop would have welcomed her more warmly.

Then again, probably not. Every time she thought of their rudeness, she wished she could have said something more clever and biting to them before she retired to bed. In any case, Lucien almost certainly wasted a lot of breath afterward, apologizing to his friends for her discourtesy.

Emily finished washing her face, but she still had the rest of herself to clean. She added more water to the kettle, placed it back on the stove, and then wandered into the parlor while the water heated up.

The sheer number of books startled her, as it did every time she saw them. William Grant, her stepfather, owned dozens of books and encouraged book buying in his family—but even his library was only half the size of Lucien's. Lucien hadn't read much on the train, though. Was this all for show, designed to demonstrate the intellectual breadth of Lucien Delatour for the mysterious, much lamented Susan? Or perhaps Susan herself was a voracious reader, and this library had been built for her.

Or maybe not. As Emily stepped closer to the bookshelves, the titles on the spines came into focus: *Cattle Ranching in Nebraska: One Man's Tale*; *An Olde Tyme but Good Tyme on the Union Pacific*; and *United States Land Grant Rules and Regulations* were a good representation of the literature there. Not Susan books, almost certainly. Not Emily books, either, for there wasn't a single novel on the shelves.

Why was she making herself crazy like this? She was here. Susan—whoever she was—was not.

Susan probably knew how to boil water without singeing her fingers.

The kettle screeched from the kitchen. Careful to protect her hand this time when she lifted the kettle from the stove, Emily again mixed hot water with cool in the basin. Then, stripping down to absolutely nothing, she gifted herself with the first complete sponge bath she'd had since sneaking out of New York.

There was even enough warm water left over to allow her to wash her hair.

Emily stepped into one of the dresses that she'd bought and buttoned up the front, leaving a few buttons undone at the top. Late summer in Bramble Creek wasn't as humid as Boston, but it was still warm enough that being completely buttoned up was not a desirable option.

She walked back into the parlor and began to scan the bookshelves in earnest. Maybe there was a book on pioneer housekeeping in there that could tell her all she needed to know, and in a few short days she would be able to cook, launder, saddle a horse, chase away Indians, and all that other necessary stuff.

But there wasn't a book like that on the sagging shelves. Her own shoulders starting to sag, Emily picked up the novel she'd brought with her to Lucien's home and squashed it between a treatise on community building and a book about pigs. There. At least they would have one fun book to read.

She should write a letter to Annabelle telling her what a disaster of a new bride she was, stuck in the middle of nowhere and only learning how to boil water. Annabelle would find it hilarious. All Emily's friends back in Boston would giggle at her predicament, too.

Going to the scruffy-looking desk in the corner, Emily found some paper and ink and a pen and started to write a letter to Annabelle. And as she wrote more and more of the hardships of a Boston lady turned hapless housewife, she began to smile.

Hendrick scratched his head, then his grizzled chin, and then his right earlobe. When they first met, Lucien had wondered if the fellow had lice. After four years, though, Lucien recognized the symptoms of deep thought.

He hadn't asked an easy question, but he assumed it was a question that Hendrick and Chuck had been posing to each other almost daily. Surely Hendrick had some kind of response.

"Couldn't say for sure," Hendrick finally replied.

"I'm not looking for a for-sure answer. I'm asking for your educated opinion. Look, we're here now." Lucien pointed to a spot on the map that was tacked to the inside of the tent he and Hendrick were in. This small tent could barely accommodate four men standing, but it served as the headquarters for this portion of the rail line. Closer to Bramble Creek proper was a sturdy two-room house from which they issued payroll and treated injuries received on the job. The only housing of similar permanence out here was the small tin shed that housed the blasting power, keeping it dry and safe from flame. "Assuming we have no more 'accidents,' where do you think we'll be by first snowfall? Over the pass?"

"Assuming we have no more accidents and can fill the empty spots with able-bodied men, yes." Hendrick scratched his forearm and then his nose. "But the accidents have the workers spooked, and there are mutters of sabotage in the saloons and in the tents. More men are fleeing Bramble Creek than are coming in."

Lucien remembered being surprised that he and Emily had been the only passengers disembarking at the Bramble Creek station, while nearly a dozen men had gotten on the train to leave.

"So we need more men," Lucien said.

"No—we need to have no more 'accidents.' The teams out front are at half the strength they should be, and even raising their wages won't work for long. I tried it last week, and then we had the avalanche. The men who'd come up from the back decided to return to their earlier spots."

"Even if those spots go away because the forward progress is slowed and we don't need as many men at the back end?"

"Well, no job at all is better than no life or losing an arm like Johnny Perkins did."

This was why Hendrick was invaluable. He understood what motivated the men, he gave them his ear, he had fifteen years' experience laying track, and, most important, he pointed out to Lucien when his thinking was wrongheaded.

"All right. Tell me about the avalanche."

Hendrick gave him an appraising look. "Would have thought that Chuck had filled you in about that."

That was Hendrick's subtle way of telling him that something about him or Chuck or both was now grist for the rumor mill.

Lucien scowled. "What's the scuttlebutt?"

"Your hand looks a little swollen, you know. You should put it in the creek, cool it down."

"Out with it, Hendrick. I've already punched one friend today—don't make me punch another."

Hendrick chuckled. "Wish I had seen it myself. Anyway, next time you two decide to battle it out, try to do it someplace other than on a bluff overlooking three crews where they can see you just as easy as you can see them. Plus Chuck wasn't smart enough to wipe all the blood off when he rejoined the forward crew."

This wasn't good. "Are the men now thinking that we're having a falling-out over the railroad? Will this drain even more workers away?"

"Nah. It's common knowledge that Chuck ain't wild about your new bride."

What? He'd returned with Emily only yesterday. Lucien said disgustedly, "Does everyone have nothing better to do than gossip with each other like old hens?"

"Bring in a half dozen whores and the crews will stop paying attention to your love life," Hendrick said cheerfully. "So, when do we get to meet her?"

He'd have to remember to ask Emily to wear one of her less fancy dresses when she came to visit the crews. The last thing he wanted was for his wife to be gossiped about *and* mistaken for a whore. "I'll see if she wants to stop by tomorrow. We arrived only last night, you know."

"Mike Vant says she's easy on the eyes."

"I like her," Lucien said, and tried to change the subject. "Have you and Chuck talked about the possibility that the saboteur could be one of the men?"

"Oh, sure. That makes the most sense. And it explains how quickly the rumors of sabotage have started. He's apparently smart enough to work at us from both ends—physical destruction and the eroding of morale."

Great. A smart saboteur. "What if we—" Lucien started to say, and then he cocked his head.

The sounds of explosions and crashes weren't unusual. Hillsides needed to be carved away, land flattened. But this new low, snarling noise rippling through the air sounded wrong.

And far too close.

Lucien ran to the tent opening, Hendrick on his heels. Hoarse shouts leaped up, and, following the gestures of the men, Lucien immediately saw the focus of their horror.

The blasting powder shed was on fire, flames licking at the bottom edges and roaring up at least two sides.

"Move out!" Hendrick hollered to the men. "Get the hell away!"

If the blasting powder exploded, everything close to it would be either destroyed or turned into missiles. The pile of gravel twenty feet in front of the shed would spray out like buckshot—but buckshot an inch across and deadly. The dozen railroad ties laid beside the track would turn into spears that could tear off a man's head or gut a horse.

Then Lucien saw what he was looking for. There, next to the corral: buckets.

Lucien sprinted forward, ignoring Hendrick's shout of dismay. As he grabbed a bucket and scooped water out of the horses' trough, another hand reached out and seized a bucket as well. Chuck, his mouth tight and grim.

They each filled another bucket and staggered toward the keening flames.

"At least if we die, it'll be quick," Chuck hollered at Lucien.

Right. If the shed exploded, they wouldn't even know what hit them.

Grunting with effort, they got close and threw the water on the burning shed. On one wall the fire whimpered and drew back, though didn't die entirely. The flames on the other wall hissed at them and continued to feed.

Lucien spun back toward the corral, Chuck only a few steps behind him.

Then Hendrick appeared, loaded down with two full buckets and red-faced and puffing. "Douse the south wall!" Lucien shouted, and Hendrick jerked a nod.

Lucien filled his buckets again. As he turned to run back toward the shed, his stupid damaged ankle buckled and he dropped to one knee.

Chuck grabbed the full buckets out of Lucien's hands and dashed to the shed, passing Hendrick on his way back.

Lucien filled two more buckets that had been lying near the trough and handed them off to Hendrick. Then he filled two more and limped toward the crackling flames.

The fire had diminished, but it still wasn't under

control. As Lucien approached, he saw one flame reach a fiery finger around the corner of the shed, aiming for a wall that had been so far untouched. Lucien splashed one bucket of water on the greedy flame, fighting it back, and then threw his remaining water against the unscathed wall to protect it from other incursions.

A huge clod of soil flew past his knee and thumped against the flaming wall, and Lucien turned to see one of the rail workers wielding a shovel. Two others had followed his example, and more wet dirt dampened the flames at the bases of the shed walls while Hendrick and Chuck tossed water at the tops of the walls.

Within a minute the fire was out, and wisps of smoke curling from the scorched walls were the only sign that danger had been roaring full-throated at them only moments before.

Breathing hard, Lucien stared at the blackened building. And something that Emily had asked him before he left resounded in his mind: *What if you don't come back?*

Lucien flopped down on the ground and winced as he jounced his ankle too hard.

"God, that was close," Chuck gasped as he collapsed next to Lucien.

Hendrick crouched down nearby and nodded, too winded to even speak.

"It has to be the work of the saboteur," Chuck said. "He's not even trying to disguise his actions as accidents anymore."

And that, aside from the near cataclysm that they had barely managed to escape, was the scariest part. If the saboteur wasn't afraid of calling attention to himself, the damage he could do was almost unstoppable.

On the other hand, now that the saboteur was out in the open, that gave him and Chuck a significant advantage, too.

"We have to catch that bastard," Lucien said.

"How?" Chuck demanded. "No one's seen anything strange before. Why would this time be different?"

"Before, they were accidents. Or at least everyone thought so. Now we can have two hundred men keeping an eye out for anything suspicious. With everyone looking for him, the saboteur will find it harder to maneuver."

"Maybe," Chuck said. "It's worth a shot, anyway. What do we have to lose?"

"More men will leave," Hendrick predicted.

Lucien nodded. "But they might leave anyway. If we're forthright about what we suspect, more might stay." He staggered to his feet and was relieved that his ankle held. "Let's go find out if anyone saw anything."

"And I'll put an armed guard on the powder shed," Hendrick added. "I have two boys who would be perfect."

Hendrick's "boys" were often as hard as horseshoe nails and looked like they'd just tussled with a grizzly bear—and won. Lucien gave Hendrick a nod, and then, side by side, Lucien and Chuck headed over to the men to confirm the presence of a saboteur and enlist their help in finding him.

**11**

*But lo, the springhouse was as fantastical and mysterious a place as famed Xanadu. Water was essential to happy survival, but the means of retrieving that water were utterly unfathomable. I tugged on one—*

A knock at the door cut off Emily in midsentence, and she lifted her attention from her letter to Annabelle.

Visitors! Well, at least she could offer them a cool drink of water.

Smoothing her damp hair with a nervous hand, she tugged open the front door. Jacqueline Winthrop stood there, looking as unruffled and clean as if she'd just stepped out of a carriage.

Emily peered past her. Oh. Jacqueline *had* stepped out of a carriage. It was more of a buckboard than a carriage, as it was exposed to the elements and a bit rough around the edges, but it still reminded Emily of how much she didn't know about living out here. She'd assumed—perhaps from reading too many dime novels or from Lucien's questions—that the only legitimate way of getting around out here was on horseback or powered by her own two legs.

Why was Jacqueline here? To make amends for her boorish behavior last night?

One glimpse of Jacqueline's flint-hard eyes made Emily reconsider that possibility.

But while Emily didn't have a clue about how to be a good frontier housewife, she was an expert on the ins and outs of polite behavior. "Good morning. Would you like to come in?" Emily asked with a false smile, stepping back so that Jacqueline could enter.

"I haven't come here to apologize," Jacqueline said bluntly.

Emily managed to keep her smile in place. "I wouldn't dream of insisting on it. Apologies wrung out of someone who has little genuine regret are worthless, don't you think?" She again gestured Jacqueline to come inside. "But do come in anyway. Would you like a drink of water?"

Spine as stiff as a porcupine's spines, Jacqueline glided into the house. "I won't stay long," she said over her shoulder.

*Boo-hoo*, Emily thought, not losing her smile, and followed Jacqueline into the parlor.

In the light of day, Emily could see details about Jacqueline that she'd missed last night. While Jacqueline's hair was black as the midnight sky, a dozen silver strands glinted like stars. Pinched brackets around her eyes and mouth signaled that a frown was her habitual expression, and her clothes, though quite fashionable, looked frayed at the cuffs. Emily suspected that Jacqueline had perhaps five or six lovely dresses that she wore, a different one each day, so they all got hard use.

At least Jacqueline had a few dresses to wear to boost her self-confidence. Emily's one beautiful dress looked like she'd dragged it behind a wagon for five hundred miles.

"Water?" Emily asked again.

Jacqueline shook her head. "No."

Apparently life out here wasn't hard only on clothes; it was hard on basic manners. Emily perched on the edge of a chair and gestured for Jacqueline to sit down as well. Then she waited.

She didn't have to wait long.

"If you care anything at all for Lucien, you will leave," Jacqueline said, and pointed in the direction of town. "Today."

She'd have to remember to write a letter about the myth of the hospitable frontier neighbor. "Why? I like it here."

"Really?" Jacqueline made a show of gazing around her. "This is your dream? Living in a five-room house so far away from civilization that you need to take a train to get here? I know the Highfills. Upper-crust Boston family with wealth and power. And you're *here*? What did Lucien tell you to convince you to move here with him?"

"Um . . ." Lucien hadn't told her anything at all. She'd closed her eyes and leaped forward into this marriage. "Well, he told me that he liked his house. And his friends." Emily raised her eyebrows at Jacqueline. "I think he meant you."

"Of course I'm his friend! Why do you think I'm here? He belongs here. You don't."

Well, yes, she didn't belong here *yet*. But once she knew how to shoot varmints, saddle a horse, and cook a meal, she would at least have a toehold on belonging. "Water?" Emily suggested again. *That* she could do.

Jacqueline threw her hands in the air. "Fine. I'll tell you the truth, then. If you stay here, you will destroy all of Lucien's dreams. He and Chuck have built this railroad with their bare hands. Others have helped, of course"—she gave a careless shrug—"but it is Lucien and Chuck who run it all and make it happen. Without them, it will die."

"I'm not planning on keeping Lucien from the railroad," Emily protested.

"That's not what I'm concerned about. What do you think the men leveling the ground and laying the track will do when they learn that Lucien has married the granddaughter of the man who is literally trying to blow up the railroad? They will desert in droves."

Emily had been wondering when this would come up. Lucien himself had never addressed it directly with her, no matter how angry he got. To Jacqueline she said steadily, "I understand there is no proof my grandfather is involved—only strong suspicion. And I would put to the men the question of which of them would want to be judged by their grandfather's actions, over which they have no control. I doubt many would raise their hands."

Jacqueline sniffed. "Perhaps that expectation is based on your own experience with your scoundrel of a grandfather. *My* expectation is that nearly all would be proud of their forefathers."

Emily didn't know whether her grandfather was guilty or innocent, but she did know that anyone with principles didn't passively sit by and let a family member get slandered. "Thank you for visiting," Emily said, standing.

Would Jacqueline go? She'd shown an astonishing lack of good breeding so far. But the other woman also rose to her feet and started for the front door.

Before she left, she turned back to Emily, her expression haughty.

Emily mentally braced herself.

"I was so looking forward to being neighbors with Susan," Jacqueline said, shaking her head. "*Her* family, at least, is quite beyond reproach."

"They sound terribly boring, then. Good-bye." And without waiting for Jacqueline to turn away, Emily shut the door.

Honestly! Would she herself become so ragged-mannered after a year or so out here? Though she *had* almost slammed the door in a visitor's face just now, so perhaps it wouldn't even take a year. She had been here less than a day and already wasn't living up to her own standards of proper behavior.

And why did Jacqueline have to bring up Susan

again—whoever she was? Emily had gotten past her initial anger about Lucien's silence about Susan . . . or at least she thought she had, until now.

She started to pace.

A sound from the kitchen made her whirl. Varmints in the house?

But it was only Lucien coming in the back door.

A long black smudge slashed across his cheek, and he reeked so strongly of smoke that Emily could smell him from fifteen feet away.

"What happened?" she almost screeched. She froze, not sure what to do, and then rushed past him into the kitchen and grabbed a glass of water.

"Thanks," Lucien said, drinking it down in three swallows. "That was exactly what I needed."

"But why do you smell like you've been fighting a forest fire?" she asked.

"Your grandfather struck again." He told her about the fire at the blasting shed and how he, Chuck, and some fellow named Hendrick had put it out. Emily could feel the blood draining from her face, and she put out a hand to grab the back of a chair.

"You were nearly blown up?" she whispered.

"That's a little dramatic, but— No: You're right. I *was* nearly blown up." He scowled. "And it was unpleasant."

Unpleasant. *Unpleasant?* "If being nearly blown up is 'unpleasant,' what on earth would you consider 'awful'?" Emily demanded. "Because I think it's awful."

"Actually being blown up would be awful. It occurred to me afterward that I'd be leaving you a widow—a widow unable to even get back to town without walking her shoes to pieces, assuming she could find town in the first place." He grabbed her hand. "Come on. I'm going to teach you how to saddle a horse."

She dug in her heels as he tried to pull her toward the back door. "I don't want a stupid lesson on saddling a horse."

"You need it."

"But not now. I don't need that now. I need this now." And she launched herself at him, grabbing his sooty hair and pulling his mouth down to hers.

He responded instantly, closing his arms around her like a vise and yanking her against his body so that every inch of space between them evaporated. "Thank God," she thought she heard him say, but a buzzing in her ears and her focus on his iron-hot kisses were interfering with her hearing. And it didn't matter much anyway— she could tell from his reaction that a saddling lesson was no longer the number one thing on his mind.

He walked her backward, and a few minutes later the edge of the settee banged against the backs of her knees. He lowered her down full-length on the settee and then followed after her, covering her whole body with his.

Emily dug her hands deeper into Lucien's smoky hair and sighed against his mouth. This was heaven. Forget about nasty neighbors, exploding sheds, and living in untamed wilderness. If Lucien would just kiss her like this every day, as if she were the only thing in his world, she would manage to get by.

"Dress . . . off," he growled, and started plucking at buttons.

She wasn't going to argue. "Shirt . . . off," she said back at him, and he grinned, his eyes sparking with a humor she'd missed and that gave her heart such a hard yank that she gasped.

Lucien peeled away the collar of her dress and started kissing her bare shoulder. "You taste wonderful," he murmured.

"No, don't talk," Emily said, suddenly panicking. "You always say the wrong thing."

"I know," he replied, then shut up and went back to kissing her skin.

Emily was tugging his shirt out of his waistband— difficult to do while prostrate and with little arm movement, but she was trying her darnedest—when a knocking reverberated through the house.

"Not again," Lucien groaned, touching his forehead to hers. "Weeks at a time can go by without anyone stopping by, and now two visitors in two days, both with terrible timing . . . ?"

Three visits, counting Jacqueline's awful social call, which Emily hadn't had time to mention yet. If this was Jacqueline again, Emily would insist that Lucien give her some shooting-varmints lessons before she got saddling-horse lessons.

Lucien stood, and Emily sprang to her feet, too, stuffing buttons back into their buttonholes and then smoothing her hair.

"Anyone home?" a male voice hollered. Not Jacqueline, then.

Lucien walked to the front door and opened it. "Mike, good to see you. Come on in."

The livery owner walked into the parlor, giving Emily a nod. "Afternoon to you, ma'am. You're looking fine today."

"Clean, you mean," Emily replied with a smile, and he laughed.

He then turned to Lucien and held out a piece of paper. "This came for you, and I offered to bring it, as I was heading out in this direction anyway."

Lucien took the paper and read it. His expression froze, and then he glanced at Emily and away again quickly.

"What?" she asked, tensing.

"Just a telegram," he said, shaking his head. "It's nothing."

She knew firsthand how expensive a telegram was. No one would send one simply on impulse. So Lucien was either lying to her for his own sake or for hers. But she didn't want to be lied to for any reason. "May I?" she asked, reaching out, palm open.

He handed the paper to her and she unfolded it with a snap.

HIGHFILL IN? WE ARE OUT. PARKER.

Macauley Parker was a loud, self-important industrialist Emily had met a few times during his visits from

New York to Boston. Her stepfather, William Grant, was an acquaintance bordering on friend, and he had invested with Parker in several schemes in the past half dozen years. While traveling west, Emily herself had written a letter to Parker from Lucien, thanking Parker for his pledge to invest in the Great Mountain.

Given Grant and Parker's relationship, why would Parker pull out of investing in Lucien's railroad if he thought Emily's grandfather was now involved?

And who was "we"?

Eyebrows tugged down in a frown, she gave the telegram back to Lucien. "I don't understand."

"Parker's telling me that he won't support the railroad, and his cronies in New York and Washington won't, either. If your grandfather is thought to be an investor in the Great Mountain, this railroad is now soiled goods."

Emily flinched. "That's strong language."

Lucien ran his hand through his hair, and flakes of ash fell on his shoulders. "And true. Unfortunately. Your grandfather has made his fortune in less than respectable ways. Plus, Parker and Highfill have been in competition for years. Parker is going to try to undermine anything Highfill is investing in—not invest in it as well."

"But my grandfather isn't investing. You said you wouldn't let him invest in the Great Mountain."

"That was before." *Before they got married*, he meant. "Now, as a member of my family, Highfill can buy some or all of the stock we're offering. And if I know him, he'll want all of it."

A surge of optimism lifted her chin. "You must be

mistaken, Lucien. I know that you and Chuck have to sell shares in order to keep the Great Mountain operating, but the law doesn't work like that. Family doesn't automatically get to buy stock." She might not know how to cook supper, but a dozen years of listening to her stepfather's conversations with his friends and business partners had taught her a thing or two about investing.

"Not usually, but the partnership agreement that Chuck and I wrote gives family the option to buy stock before anyone else."

Of all the ridiculous things to put in a partnership agreement—

"I know," Lucien said, correctly interpreting the expression that must've been on her face. "Looking back, it was a dumb thing to do. The worst of it is, your grandfather, as one of the original partners in the partnership, is well aware of that clause. As soon as he learned that we were wed, he must have sent a gloating telegram off to Parker."

"But what about the sabotage? How does that fit?"

Flicking a glance at Mike Vant, who was still standing awkwardly in the doorway, Lucien dropped his voice and stepped closer. "The sabotage started more than a month ago—long before we met each other. Highfill's plan must have been to drain our resources and scare away our men, then swoop in and buy the failing Great Mountain for a song. Now that we're married, Highfill can buy into the Great Mountain without having to damage it any more."

Touching the smudge on Lucien's cheek, Emily said, "The saboteur must not know that he can stop now."

"Or he's a bloodthirsty bastard."

Mike cleared his throat and started backing away. "Well, I'll be going. See you next time you're in town, Delatour." He tipped his hat to Emily. "Ma'am."

Emily's thoughts were churning as fast as a locomotive's pistons, and a clear realization fell into place.

Jacqueline had said that Emily would ruin Lucien's dreams, and Jacqueline was right—though not for the reason she'd thought. Lucien's main worry wasn't that the men would desert the Great Mountain because Emily was related to the man who was trying to bring it down. Because of Lucien's marriage to her, Lucien had to worry about his investors deserting him.

Behind Lucien's ash-dusted shoulder, she could see the map of the Great Mountain nailed to the parlor wall. From what he'd told her during their short time together, she knew the Great Mountain was Lucien's life.

If he had to watch it collapse because of her—

"Please wait," she told Mike, and he paused just outside the front door, head cocked.

She turned to Lucien and said before she could lose her nerve, "I'm leaving."

He stared. "The hell you are."

Luckily she'd grown accustomed to his swearing in the past couple of weeks, so that didn't even rattle her. "I think it's for the best. Mike can escort me back to town and then I'll take the train to San Francisco."

Lucien said incredulously, "And . . . that's it? We're married for four days and you're giving up already?"

Mike, cheeks reddening, strode out of earshot but stayed within sight of the house. Emily blew out a quick breath of relief; if Mike left her, she didn't know how she'd get back to Bramble Creek. Walk?

"I don't belong here." She could tell from just a glance at him that he wasn't buying it, so she peeled open her deepest vulnerabilities and prayed he'd believe that it was her shortcomings that were driving her away—not her need to keep his dreams whole. "I can't use the stove. I'm scared of big, wild animals. The idea of winter here terrifies me. I hate being so isolated, and I think I hate our closest neighbors, too, who happen to be your closest friends. *I don't belong here.*"

Lucien stepped close, and his eyes burned down into her. "I never figured you for someone who gave up so easily, Emily."

She swallowed her immediate defense and lifted her chin so that she could look straight back at him. "Well, we don't know each other very well, do we?"

He slowly leaned in, and she wavered. If she was leaving him, surely she could take just one kiss to remember him by?

One final kiss, and then she wouldn't ever see him again. Their marriage could be dissolved through legal correspondence, and then he'd be busy convincing Parker and his friends that Highfill was not part of the Great Mountain. And he'd avoid her like poison if he happened to be in Boston.

But if she kissed him, she wasn't sure she could leave.

*Think of the varmints*, she told herself harshly. *And how terrible your neighbors are. You don't know how to cook even a single meal. And if you stay, you will destroy everything Lucien values. What you told him is true: You don't belong here.*

Her mind was telling her one thing, but her heart had plugged its ears and was refusing to listen.

Lucien's dark eyes filled her vision, and she swayed toward him.

The reek of smoke in his clothes and hair slapped her like a giant hand. That throat-closing smell was the smell of his dreams dying, and unless she left him, Lucien would find himself with nothing.

Heaving a sigh dredged up from the soles of her feet, she stepped out of reach. Without a word, she entered their bedroom and retrieved her belongings, then came back into the hall. Lucien's eyes narrowed as he recognized the dresses in her arms, but before he could say anything more, she whispered, "Good-bye, Lucien," and slipped past him to where Mike was waiting outside.

Unfortunately, the next train heading south wouldn't come through Bramble Creek for another six days. "There's a train traveling north that should arrive four days from now," the stationmaster said, trying to be helpful.

Maybe escaping two days earlier would be a better choice than waiting for the southbound train, even if it meant she'd be heading in a completely different direction from where she wanted to go. But after poring over the various railroad maps that the stationmaster pulled out for her, she decided to wait. Two extra days in Bramble Creek wouldn't make that much of a difference, and it would save her about a week of train travel. Thinking about the hard wooden seats on the last train, she shuddered.

Mike Vant, who had become her new—and only—friend in Bramble Creek, helped her secure a private bedroom at the only boardinghouse in town. "Most everyone else bunks together," the proprietor, Henry Clark, said sourly as Emily handed over one of her double eagles. Her extravagance appeared to annoy him even though she was paying triple the usual rate for the room, plus meals, for six days. As Mr. Clark had empty rooms and no other female guests, she would not have shared a room anyway even if she had not insisted on her privacy.

"You can take my money or you can complain, but I'd prefer it if you do not do both while in my presence," Emily said sweetly, and Mr. Clark sniffed again but shut up.

Mike, standing behind Mr. Clark, grinned at Emily and gave her a thumbs-up.

After that, there was nothing much to do. Mike had to tend his horses, Mr. Clark clearly wouldn't be good company, and the rest of the boarders were out and about somewhere. So, after a few moments of thought, Emily returned to the stationmaster's office, where she settled into the only chair for guests and they discussed the expansion of the rail lines and where immigrants were settling. At the very least, she would return from her adventure and resume her work at the Boston Immigrant Aid Society with more thorough knowledge of the places they were suggesting people go to get a foothold on their new lives.

"And, of course, Bramble Creek could use more settlers," the stationmaster said. "As I'm sure you know, Mrs. Delatour, the railroads are always seeking people to buy and live on the land near the tracks—land that the railroad had to purchase to gain right of way. That's how railroads make money in the early years, before the line is complete and they can charge significant money for hauling goods along their line."

Hmm, the Great Mountain needed settlers. And the aid society needed places to send newcomers. It sounded like the perfect match . . . assuming that the railroad survived. Otherwise new settlers would find themselves living next to a dead railroad.

Knowing that she could help save the Great Mountain *and* find new homes for immigrants helped ease her pain a little. She'd made her choice and she refused to regret it, but every time she thought of Lucien, she felt like a dull knife was sawing a hole around her heart. And she thought of Lucien on every inhale and every exhale.

Maybe she *should* take the next train to come through Bramble Creek, no matter where it was going. If distance could serve as an opiate to her heart's agony, she could live through the agony that would be inflicted on her spine and backside.

The door to the stationmaster's office was propped open to let in a breeze, so no little bell signaled the arrival of a visitor, and Emily was so consumed by her thoughts that she didn't realize they had company until she caught a whiff of smoke and a shirtsleeve slid into her view.

She jerked her eyes up, half hoping and half dreading that Lucien had managed to track her down and was planning to drag her back to his home, but the man standing beside her was a complete stranger.

He was a very handsome complete stranger, though, and as his blue eyes settled on her, she sat up a bit straighter. Yes, she was a married lady, at least for now, but that didn't mean she didn't want other men—especially attractive ones—to not notice her.

"Afternoon, ma'am," he said, touching his fingertips to the brim of his cowboy hat, and then he paused and squinted at her. "Are you Mrs. Delatour, by any chance?"

Her new name still sounded strange to her ears, but she wouldn't have to worry about that for much longer. Emily nodded and said, "And you are, sir . . . ?"

"Samson McIntosh, at your service." He gave her a quick, facetious bow that was clearly meant to poke fun at himself, not her. He straightened, his eyes admiring. "I heard that Delatour had married, but I had no idea that he'd married so well."

Emily smiled. "Thank you. But how did you know it was me?"

"I know well all the fine ladies of Bramble Creek, and you were a beautiful stranger," he replied. "Therefore you must be Mrs. Delatour." This time there was something a bit oily and insincere in his voice that made Emily give him a longer look.

She had grown complacent in this rugged country and had dropped her old defenses. If she were back in Boston or New York and she had met Samson McIntosh at a social event, she would have pegged him as a fortune hunter or, worse, a lothario within the first few seconds. It had taken her a minute of conversation this time.

Thinking of his smoky smell, she leaned over and sniffed him, causing Samson to take an uncertain step away. Good—she wanted him off-balance. "Were you at the shed fire?" she asked.

He shook his head and then nodded. Noticing her perplexed look, he said, "I wasn't there at the beginning, when the fire started, but I helped patch up the shed afterward."

"What's this?" the stationmaster asked. "A fire?"

"At the explosives shed," Samson explained. "Nearly blew up the track and forty men over at the Great Hill curve."

The stationmaster went white. "Good God. Beg your pardon, ma'am."

"My husband, Mr. Winthrop, and Mr. Hendrick put the fire out before the explosives could ignite," Emily said. Yes, she was leaving him, but that didn't mean she couldn't be proud of Lucien.

"Almost got us two beautiful widows," Samson said—a bit too jovially, Emily thought.

"I'm sure many of the other men were married as

well," she said, annoyed. "Had the shed exploded, dozens of families would have suffered unfathomable grief."

"Hendrick put out the word today that someone is trying their hand at sabotage," Samson said, leaning against the stationmaster's desk as if he intended to settle in for a while. Emily gritted her teeth.

The stationmaster stepped backward, as if even the words themselves were lethal. "Sabotage? But why?"

"No one knows why, but Hendrick said that the other two accidents weren't accidents, either. Someone's trying to shut down Winthrop and Delatour's railroad." As if suddenly remembering that Emily was there, Samson said with overdone sincerity, "Now I beg your pardon, ma'am. Hearing about this must be painful for you."

The stationmaster must have sensed that Emily's patience with Samson McIntosh and his gossip had worn thin, for he said abruptly, "What can I do for you, McIntosh?"

"Just came to check on the timetable for the next train heading south toward San Francisco," Samson said. "Mrs. Winthrop said she might want to take a trip down there."

"Again? She came back from there only a month ago."

Samson shrugged, and if he didn't have such an offputting personality, Emily would have appreciated the way his muscles moved in his shoulders and chest. "San Francisco has more appeal to her than Bramble Creek."

Emily frowned. Traveling to San Francisco on the same train as Jacqueline Winthrop would be unpleasant. She would probably congratulate Emily over and over again on her decision to leave Lucien, and possibly even sneak in some references to how Lucien could now marry Susan so that Jacqueline would finally have a friend in Bramble Creek.

In fact, *unpleasant* might be an understated way to describe the trip.

The stationmaster gave Samson the same information he'd given Emily about the best route to San Francisco, and Samson nodded a thank-you to him. Samson turned to leave but then paused in front of Emily. "Can I escort you anywhere, Mrs. Delatour? Maybe back to your house?"

Was that a sarcastic gleam in his eye? Perhaps her separation from Lucien was already common knowledge. She wanted to squirm but instead lifted her chin. "No, thank you, Mr. McIntosh."

"Maybe next time. A lovely woman like yourself should never go anywhere unescorted. Especially now, when there's a dangerous man out there who is determined to make your husband very, very unhappy." He tipped his hat to her and left.

Emily froze as she replayed his words in her mind. Was Samson suggesting that the saboteur might go after *her*?

The stationmaster looked as shocked as Emily felt. Then he frowned and said to Emily, "When you're done here, I'll take you wherever you need to go, Mrs. Delatour."

Emily nodded to him gratefully.

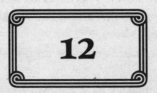

# 12

LUCIEN STOOD BY THE battered desk in his parlor, reading the half-written letter that Emily had penned only that morning. He touched an ink splotch on the upper-right corner with a fingertip before placing the letter back on the desk exactly where he had found it.

And exactly where Emily would find it again when she returned to their home.

Patience and persistence had always been the two keys to his success. He also tried to be honest with himself and clear-eyed about his motivations. Growing up, he had survived by deliberately observing what worked and what didn't, and he'd seen time and again how rash, unthinking behavior led to danger and loss.

And rash, unthinking behavior was what had undermined his marriage from the very start. If he'd just stayed true to his strategy of being patient and persistent and truthful, maybe he'd still have Emily there with him, possibly reading her letter aloud to him and laughing.

A week's worth of *should have*s ran through his mind. He should have insisted on learning who Emily and Annabelle were instead of quickly capitulating to their determination to stay incognito. He should have written to Susan immediately upon realizing that his feelings for Emily went beyond the friendship that fellow travelers tended to strike up, instead of teetering back and forth in denial. He should have talked with Emily before they got married, explaining his lifestyle to her so that she was prepared for the challenges she'd face, instead of rushing her into the wedding ceremony. He should have spent a few nights with her in Bramble Creek so that Emily could adapt to her new surroundings instead of immediately shoving her into their home and isolation . . . and scaring her away.

Lots of *should have*s. Enough to learn from, perhaps.

He stared at the ink blotch on the letter. It looked like a black teardrop. Yes, he was being maudlin, but he was entitled to do that when his bride had just walked out on him.

A bride who—if he was still intent on being honest with himself—was unwittingly helping to bankrupt his railroad.

Emily would still be in Bramble Creek, probably installed at Henry Clark's boardinghouse. The next passenger train wouldn't come through town for at least four days, so he had four days to figure out how to get her back.

Or to decide that he would have to live without her.

For the first time since he and Chuck had cooked up their scheme over a few glasses of terrible whiskey at a smoky saloon in Kansas City, Lucien wished he'd never even heard of the Great Mountain.

The telegram in his shirt pocket crinkled as he turned again to look at the letter Emily had written, and he grimaced. Might as well head over to Chuck's place now and let him know that Macauley Parker and his cronies would not be proud part owners of the Great Mountain railroad.

Ten minutes later, he looped his horse's reins around a fence post of Chuck's corral and approached the house. Jacqueline opened the door before he could knock.

"First my brother and now my husband!" she cried. "This railroad is doomed."

Lucien's feet turned to lead and he stopped in his tracks. "What happened to Chuck?"

"He was almost blown up!"

Oh, right. In all the excitement of Emily trying to pull his clothes off, the arrival of Parker's telegram, and then Emily's departure, Lucien had almost forgotten that he and Chuck had been only a spark away from being messily killed that morning. He started moving again. "Is Chuck here?"

Jacqueline stepped aside, letting him in. Chuck and Jacqueline's place was twice the size of Lucien's house. It was sometimes referred to a bit mockingly by the locals as "Bramble Creek Palace," but no one ever turned down an invitation to visit and admire Jacqueline's bloodred velvet curtains and delicate lace tablecloth. Lucien hardly noticed them now, but Emily probably would have liked to see them, he thought. If he could have offered her a house like this, maybe. . . .

Chuck limped into the parlor, a streak of ash still garnishing his forehead. "Thought I heard your voice," he said.

"I got this today." Lucien handed the telegram to Chuck. "This is trouble. I was relying on Parker to at least not actively undermine the Great Mountain, but he and Highfill hate each other. Parker is probably spreading the word now among all his friends that we're a bad investment."

Chuck dropped down into a chair and groaned. "Hell, at this point, I'm not so sure he's wrong."

From where she stood in the doorway, Jacqueline stated, "It's all that awful Highfill's fault. First he sends his man to blow things up, and now he's squeezing off our money. Chuck, Lucien, we have to face the facts. This railroad is a dead end."

Lucien shook his head. "No. We'll still have some investors—Parker won't scare off all of them."

"But rumors of sabotage will," Jacqueline pointed out. "Who would want to invest in a railroad that's always under attack? Highfill clearly doesn't control his man anymore, or the attacks would have stopped with your marriage, Lucien. The saboteur has gone rogue."

Chuck nodded, and for a moment Lucien was afraid

he was agreeing that they needed to put a halt to building the railroad. But Chuck said, "We need to catch the saboteur. Now. That has to be our highest priority."

"Your highest priority should be staying alive!" Jacqueline said, and then she dashed away toward their bedroom, sobs shaking her shoulders.

"It's hitting her harder than I expected," Chuck said, almost apologetically.

"You'd be acting crazy, too, if you thought Jacqueline had been almost killed."

"True enough." Chuck glanced down at his clasped hands and then looked up again. "Rumor is that the Highfill girl has decided to leave Bramble Creek and go to San Francisco."

Chuck's words felt like a boot in the gut. Lucien of course knew that Emily was leaving, but hearing someone else say it made it more real than it had been before. Hell, having it be public knowledge that his wife had left him was making it feel awfully real as well. "That seems to be the current plan of hers, yes."

Chuck's dark eyes bored into him. "I'm not going to lie to you. This will help fix our problems."

"I'm not going to lie to you, either. *My* plan doesn't involve her leaving. And even if she does leave, we still have to find the fellow who is trying to blow up our railroad."

"It's Highfill who's behind it, and once he realizes that he can't get his hands on the Great Mountain through his granddaughter, he'll give up and leave us alone."

"That's ridiculous. The attacks on the line happened before I met Emily. If anything, I'd expect Highfill to stop blowing up the railroad now so that he'd have something left to own."

Chuck shrugged. "He's always been hard to predict."

"Right, but he's never been an idiot. Think about it, Chuck."

But Chuck clearly didn't want to think about it; he'd fixed his mind on the idea that Emily leaving would solve the Great Mountain's problems. After ten more minutes of trying to get Chuck to focus on other ways they could help the railroad limp along until they found strong investors, Lucien left the house in disgust.

For two days, knowing that Emily had no good way to leave Bramble Creek, Lucien concentrated on tracking down the saboteur and keeping his feelings for Emily locked away.

But after two days of talking with the men till he was hoarse and tracking down every rumor that might lead to the saboteur, Lucien found himself empty-handed. He had directed his attention first at those who had a grudge against the railroad, or him, or Chuck. There were men who had been hurt or had been fired, but he couldn't find anyone who was burning for vengeance—or even simmering with anger. He then looked for people who might be connected to Highfill or who didn't seem to have any good reason for being at Bramble Creek. Again, nothing turned up.

Chuck and Hendrick worked equally hard at turning up leads, and they checked in with each other every morning to compare notes on what they had discovered. Chuck stopped needling Lucien about ending his marriage, perhaps mistakenly thinking that because Lucien hadn't immediately pursued Emily while she was still in town, he had decided to let her go.

Being patient for those two days—and holding himself back from chasing her—was the hardest thing Lucien had ever done.

At night, before going to his empty bed, he would re-read Emily's half-written letter. Something about it kept him awake, staring at the ceiling, until sheer exhaustion knocked him over the cliff into sleep.

After those two days he decided the time was right to approach Emily to persuade her to stay. A few days in the relative comfort of Bramble Creek might have dampened her fear of living on the edge of wilderness, and, knowing Emily, he guessed that she'd made a few new friends by now.

Besides, he just couldn't keep away any longer.

He didn't find Emily at Henry Clark's boardinghouse, so he tried the second most likely place he thought she would be, and he struck gold.

Standing by the back wall of the general store, Emily was fingering bolts of fabric and looking as charmed as if she were in the shop of Boston's top dressmaker.

He stopped in the doorway and just watched her until she finally glanced up and noticed him.

The big smile that he'd fallen in love with lit up her face like a sunrise, and she took a step toward him, eyes blooming with happiness.

The stress that had been riding on his shoulders like evil angels fell away, and Lucien took his first deep breath in days. Good. This was going to work out after all.

Then she snatched the smile off her face and tucked it away, replacing it with a more subdued expression. Eyebrows tucking down in a frown, she approached him, winding her way past barrels, a pair of snowshoes, and bits of a plow. She didn't look delighted or even angry, only determined.

And this was exactly the problem, he realized. Emily had so much grit that he couldn't quite believe that only one day out here in Bramble Creek was enough to make her turn tail and run. He'd never crossed paths with a more intrepid girl, or one who laughed so much at herself and her situation.

He exhaled as a puzzle piece clicked into place. *That* was why he had kept going back to his desk and rereading the letter she'd started writing. Because that letter was not the letter of a girl who was deciding to leave. It was the letter of a girl who'd decided to poke fun at her own shortcomings and give life out here a good try anyway.

So . . . if she wasn't the type to run away, and if she seemed to have made up her mind to try the rustic lifestyle, what had changed her mind and sent her rushing to catch the next train out of town?

The near explosion? It had shaken Jacqueline. She looked like she'd aged five years since it had happened.

But Emily hadn't run screaming at the news of the shed being set on fire. She'd instead kissed him frantically, as if she wanted to reassure herself that he was still alive.

Did she simply not want to be married to him anymore? But in the moments before Mike had arrived with the telegram, she'd been trying to get Lucien out of his clothes. For Emily, making love was her wordless commitment to their marriage.

Was it the telegram?

Emily came close enough to touch, and Lucien took a chance and reached out to take her hand in his. "I thought I'd find you here." There—let her remember that although they hadn't known each other long, in some ways they knew each other well.

She pulled her hand away. "Am I so predictable?"

Or maybe that hadn't been a good tactic.

"But I suppose I am," she said, "in that there's very little else for me to do."

A slighting comment on how tedious Bramble Creek was compared to Boston? He tackled it head-on. "It's not Boston here."

"No, nor did I expect it to be. But I didn't expect how unlike Boston it would be, either. My mistake." She said it simply, as if acknowledging the mistake was the equivalent of saying *I'm sorry for leaving you.*

She hadn't really left him yet, though. Until she got on that train, he would continue to believe that they still had a chance.

*This will help fix our problems*, Chuck had said about Emily leaving him. It didn't.

All Lucien wanted to do was grab her, toss her onto

his horse, and carry her home, where he would peel off her clothes, kiss the tip of her cute nose, and make love to her in their bed.

Wait: Persistence. Patience. Honesty. He had to remember that these were his tools to success.

"I want you to come back and try again," he said. "I can try better, too. I'll bring in a woman to help take care of the house—"

"Cook?" she said, looking hopeful, and his heart speeded up. Was it going to be that easy?

"Yes, to cook, too. And I can do whatever else you need as well, to help you feel more at home." A bold, unlimited promise, and he'd somehow fulfill it.

"And what of the saboteur?" she asked, the corners of her eyes tight with an emotion he couldn't read.

"What do you mean?"

"Can this woman protect me from the saboteur?"

Lucien felt like he'd been gut punched, and not just with a fist but with a railroad spike. He was an idiot—and Chuck was, too. The attempt to blow up the explosives shed was clearly intended to kill dozens of men. How could he and Chuck have overlooked the possibility that the saboteur might not limit himself to targeting those who worked directly on the railroad? The saboteur could set his sights on those who were more precious to him and Chuck than locomotives and gravel and track.

Lucien breathed deeply through his nose. Emily was right to be afraid. And he was now afraid, too.

"Perhaps it *is* best that you go," he said abruptly.

Emily dropped her eyes and nodded, and he thought that her shoulders slumped a fraction.

Was that it? Did she not want to leave but was afraid to stay because of the saboteur?

He nudged her chin upward with a fingertip until she was staring at him again, and to his surprise and relief he saw tears glittering in her eyes. "But you don't have to be gone for forever," he whispered, and leaned in and kissed her.

Her hand came up and seized his lapel, as if to hold him in place, and he covered her hand with his own even as he deepened the kiss, letting his need for her slip its leash for a few wild moments. Then he softened the kiss and, with a reluctant sigh, drew back and disengaged.

Patience. He couldn't forget patience.

He took her hand from his lapel and tucked it in the crook of his arm, turning them both toward the door of the general store. "I'll walk you back to the boardinghouse."

Looking dazed, Emily didn't say anything as they strolled past three storefronts and then through the front door of Henry Clark's house. "I'll see you tomorrow," Lucien told her. He wanted to kiss her once more, to remind her in a physical way that he wasn't giving up, but he didn't think that he could step away from her lips again. He knew his limits.

"Stay safe," he added. "Stay in town." And then he gave her a short nod and fled before he could surrender to any of the five dozen idiotic impulses that were pounding at him. *Patience*, he reminded himself again as he swung into his saddle. Plus he would see her tomorrow, when he could exercise persistence as well.

The next day a new boarder moved into Henry Clark's boardinghouse. And the new boarder was not pleased with the new accommodations or her housemates—at all.

"This is all your fault," Jacqueline accused Emily, her hands on her silk-gowned hips. Jacqueline's eyes had a wildness to them that Emily hadn't seen before, even when Jacqueline had been at her most insulting.

"Isn't everything?" Emily asked. One good thing about leaving Lucien was that she didn't have to be nice to Jacqueline.

She tried to ignore the acidic clutch in her stomach that almost made her double over whenever she thought of leaving Lucien. Three days, and she still hadn't grown accustomed to the pain. She'd hoped the feeling would dull, but Lucien's visit yesterday had revived it, made it sharper.

Maybe she should take the northbound train after all. . . .

"If you hadn't put that nonsense in Lucien's head about your being in danger, then I wouldn't be stuck here . . . with you!" Jacqueline announced to Emily and whoever else happened to be passing the boardinghouse's front porch that crouched right on Bramble Creek's main street.

Oh. Perhaps Jacqueline's presence *was* Emily's

fault—a little bit. Last night, when Lucien had started listing all the things he would do to convince her to stay in Bramble Creek, her determination to leave started to crumble. And crumble fast.

She had said the only thing that she thought would cause him to step back: She was afraid of being killed by the saboteur.

It wasn't a complete fabrication. Men had already been killed by the madman. Sometimes, as she walked along the short main street of Bramble Creek, she thought she felt angry eyes on her. The saboteur?

And while her grandfather might be unscrupulous in business dealings, she wasn't convinced of his guilt here. No one had ever come close to accusing him of murder before. And his ego was immense—he liked to be personally involved in his schemes, as he had been in his last run-in with Lucien and Chuck.

Too many aspects of this situation seemed unlike him.

"Well?" Jacqueline demanded, and Emily realized that she'd temporarily forgotten the other woman's presence.

"Are we sharing a room?" Emily asked. Sharing a room with Jacqueline would be almost as unpleasant as being blown up by the saboteur.

"Absolutely not!"

"Then that's all right." Emily stood and prepared to go. While she could now go toe-to-toe with Jacqueline and holler and screech all she liked without concern for Lucien and Chuck's friendship, the pleasure would be fleeting, and she'd probably feel guilty about it afterward anyway. "Good day to you."

She was descending the porch steps to the main street when a man on a horse tugged on his reins, stopping right in front of her and blocking her escape. "Mrs. Winthrop! Mrs. Delatour! Imagine my luck at seeing both you lovely ladies at the same time." It was Samson McIntosh, a smile on his beautifully shaped lips.

Emily huffed out an annoyed breath. If she had Annabelle here with her, Emily would fling her sister at Samson as a distraction and continue on. Annabelle would giggle and give him big eyes and then toss him aside like a rag doll that had suddenly become uninteresting.

Help came from an unexpected quarter, however. "Oh, Mr. McIntosh," Jacqueline trilled, "you are such a scoundrel." But a welcome sort of scoundrel, apparently, because she did enough eyelash fluttering that Emily was afraid she would sprain her eyelids.

Samson needed no more encouragement, for he swung down from his saddle. He stayed in the street rather than climbing the steps to the porch, though, which showed good sense on his part. Cozying up to his boss's wife in front of all Bramble Creek would not be smart. There was a gleam in Samson's eyes that made Emily wonder if he was contemplating it anyway.

Unfortunately, his horse was still in Emily's way. "Excuse me," Emily said, and gave the beast a gentle shove. It obligingly stepped sideways, and she descended to the street.

"I'd like to stay longer," Samson was saying to Jacqueline, "but my shift starts right after lunch. I'll send you a note, though, about how things are going."

A note? Did Chuck know that his wife was exchanging notes with the most showily handsome man in town?

Well, it wasn't any of her business, and Emily set off for the stationmaster's office, where she was sure to find intelligent conversation. Also, Lucien might not think to look for her there. He'd said yesterday that he would see her again today.

But Lucien didn't track her down there or anywhere else that day, and when Emily returned to the boarding-house shortly before supper, she wasn't sure whether she was relieved or annoyed.

"Pleasant day?" one of the boarders asked as they crossed paths on the stairs.

"Hurrumph," she replied.

All right. So she was annoyed.

Jacqueline had been given the room next to hers, and Emily could hear through the thin walls the noises of Jacqueline moving about, preparing for supper.

Emily also prepared for supper—and potential battle. She slipped into the silk gown she'd worn when she'd sneaked aboard her grandfather's Pullman Palace car only two weeks ago, and tidied her hair in the room's small mirror, which had enough silvering flaking off to distort her reflection into, strangely, someone who looked more beautiful than Emily had ever been.

Emily paused in the middle of smoothing back a fly-away strand of hair and leaned closer to the mirror. Then she sidestepped a few inches and her reflection moved as well. No, that wasn't a distortion in the mirror. That was *her*.

The baby-like chubbiness in her face had been etched away, and her chin looked set and confident. A certain gravity to her eyes gave her the look of someone who had been tested and had persevered.

She snorted and stepped back from the mirror. Tested and persevered? How had she been tested? She'd spent less than a day in Lucien's house, which had hardly been uncivilized, with a roomful of books and a comfortable bed. With practice, she would have mastered the kitchen and the horse saddling and everything else she needed to do. But she had left all that behind when she left Lucien.

Yes, she had left Lucien.

Maybe that had been the test. To see if she could give up what she wanted most of all.

If so, she hadn't passed that test yet. Only when she climbed the steps onto the southbound train in two days would that trial be complete.

A bell rang downstairs, and Emily did a final quick check of her hair, determinedly avoiding looking at her own expression.

When she got to the dining room, she was glad she'd spent a few extra minutes putting on her gown. Jacqueline's sneer fell off her face as she beheld a dress that was of the current season rather than two seasons behind, as Jacqueline's dress was.

The two men rooming in the boardinghouse also gaped as they stood by their chairs. Emily nodded to them as she sank into a seat with practiced grace. She'd deliberately chosen a chair as far away from Jacqueline as she could, and spent the rest of the meal in conversation with the male boarders and Henry Clark, who wasn't quite so grumpy once she got to know him. Jacqueline ate her meal in silence punctuated only by glares in Emily's direction every time she laughed.

And as she shamefully gained enormous satisfaction from annoying Jacqueline, Emily laughed quite a bit.

Jacqueline soon excused herself, and Emily could hear from her footsteps that she had gone into the parlor, leaving Emily the choice of sitting on the front porch or returning to her room. She picked the front porch and settled in to watch the light traffic on the main street as the Bramble Creek citizens returned home to their suppers or finished up a few final errands before going to bed. Mike Vant rode into view, a few ponies in a line behind him, and he raised his hat to her and nodded hello as he passed.

It wasn't until nearly a half hour had drifted by that Emily realized she was focusing her attention on the western end of the street, in the direction of Lucien's homestead. The direction from which Lucien would appear if he really was going to visit her today.

Or had he tried already but hadn't been able to find her? Not that she had been exceptionally well hidden. She was one of only a handful of ladies in town, and everyone here seemed to know exactly where everyone else was. She'd mentioned to the stationmaster that she had met Mike Vant a few times, and he'd said instantly, "Oh, he's over at the Smiths' place now."

Not much was secret here. If Lucien had come to town to find her, he would have had to speak to only a few people to learn her location.

Another half hour passed, the air cooled, and darkness swallowed the town. Finally, Emily stood up, shivering a bit.

He wasn't coming.

"Lady! Lady!" a boy called from below the porch railing. Emily blinked and looked down. She had been concentrating so hard on trying to pierce the darkness that she hadn't seen him approach. "I have a note for the pretty lady!" And he reached up, a white envelope in his hand.

Emily stooped and took it. "Thank you," she said, and he scampered off, disappearing into the night like a ghost gone home.

She flipped the envelope over, but there was no writing on the outside signifying who had sent it. Lucien, almost certainly. But was he explaining why he wasn't here, or was he explaining that he'd realized she was right to leave and wouldn't be coming to see her at all?

She twisted the note in her hands and took a steadying breath.

"You look worried," a familiar voice said, and Emily jerked her head up to see Lucien flip his horse's reins over the porch rail. He mounted the porch stairs, and Emily impulsively stretched out one hand to him. He took it and brought it to his lips. "And now you're smiling," he said, smiling himself. "What's going on?"

She couldn't tell him that she had been thrown into

black despair at the idea that he didn't want her any longer, or that her heart soared at the sight of him. He would then know that her reasons for leaving him were flimsy at best, and an utter sham at the worst.

"I missed you," he said simply.

"Me, too," she whispered. Surely that would be safe enough to say.

He sat in one of the porch chairs and tugged her down to sit beside him. He didn't relinquish his hold on her, instead rubbing his thumb gently in little circles over the back of her hand, causing tiny quivers of pleasure to run up her arm. "Then can we find a solution that involves neither one of us missing the other?" He gestured around them with his free hand. "Is this more comfortable? Do you want us to move into town permanently?"

"But your house—"

"It's just a house. And while it's the first real house I've owned, it's also the thirty-fourth place I've lived since leaving Chicago. I counted it up this afternoon. So I can easily move again."

Lucien had lived in thirty-four different places? He must've moved once or twice a year. "I've lived in only one place," Emily said in awe.

It was nearly full dark, but Emily could see enough to tell that Lucien's eyes were fixed on her. "And you want to return to Boston?" He paused and then said more carefully, "Do you want both of us to go to Boston?" He gave her hand a quick squeeze. "Be honest. I can take it, and it's important."

Emily silently groaned. She *wanted* to be honest with him. But if she was honest with him—

Well, what then?

Then he would have all the facts, and he could make up his own mind about what to do. She hadn't been honest with him before, when she'd learned that he hated her grandfather, and look at how well that had turned out. Lucien had been angry, and half the time they'd been married, they'd fought about her being a Highfill and ruining his railroad.

Or . . . had they been fighting about her lying to him?

For her part, Emily had been less than pleased to discover that he'd been nearly engaged to another woman but hadn't bothered to mention that to her.

Emily's stomach twisted. Lies, deception, and absent truths had poisoned their marriage from the start.

And if she continued to lie to him, to feed him false information so that he'd do what she thought was best, then their marriage would end as a lie as well.

They both deserved better than that. And she'd much rather end a marriage with honesty than with falsehoods.

"I do miss the luxuries of Boston. And I miss my family far, far more than I miss Boston. But I don't want us both to move there."

Beside her, Lucien went still. "You still want to return. By yourself," he said.

He had misunderstood her. Emily said quickly, "No, that's not what I mean. I mean—" She thought through her next words. Honesty here meant brutal reality. "I believe that if you and I stay married—whether we are at your house, or we are here in Bramble Creek, or we are in Boston—your investors will not invest, and your railroad will die."

His hand tightened on hers. "It's definitely a concern, I admit. I don't think the death of the Great Mountain is certain—there are potential investors in Chicago or San Francisco whom I could call on, and who might not be scared off by your grandfather's reputation. Heck, I know of some who might embrace Highfill's reputation, though they aren't the sort we'd normally want to do business with. As we saw with Highfill before, they're as likely to turn around and cut our throats if it means they'd make more money that way."

"What if you didn't allow investments at all? How long—"

"Two months, if we pull back to a skeleton crew. We won't make it to and over the pass, though, if we have a skeleton crew." He shook his head. "Even if we do get some kind of investment now that allowed us to move ahead full steam, the sabotage could do as much damage—or more—as working with a skeleton crew." Lucien turned to her. "Listen, Chuck and I talked about our options today. One of the options is that we shut down the building of the Great Mountain right now and try to sell the whole thing unfinished to an investor."

Stop work and sell the Great Mountain? That didn't sound like a good idea at all. She tried the logical route first to try to dissuade him. "Wouldn't you have the same problem as before, in that my grandfather's investment would scare off buyers?"

"No, because we would be relinquishing control and selling our shares to a majority investor. Family only has priority in the purchase of minority shares."

"But . . . isn't completing the Great Mountain the most important thing in the world to you?"

Lucien was silent for so long, Emily began to think he wouldn't answer. Finally he said, "What's the most important thing in the world to *you?*"

Emily wrinkled her nose. She could be honest, or she could be extremely honest. While the deepening darkness made honest talk easier, she wasn't sure she was ready to be extremely honest with Lucien and bare her heart. "Well, in no particular order, the most important things to me are Annabelle, my mother and stepfather and the rest of my family, and you. What about you?" she asked again quickly, trying to speed past her oblique declaration of love.

"Well, in no particular order," he drawled, "it's Chuck, the Great Mountain, and you."

She was among his most important things? A bubble of hope expanded so rapidly in her chest that Emily found it hard to breathe. But she needed to make sure that Lucien understood what he risked by including her in that list. "If you keep me, you can't keep the Great Mountain."

Lucien sighed. "I might not be able to keep Chuck, either. But if you keep me, you give up Annabelle and your family."

What? No, that didn't make sense. "Just because my family isn't here doesn't mean I've given them up."

"You give up seeing them every day."

"But I knew I would have to. It was my choice when I said yes to your proposal. The problem is, when you asked me to marry you, you didn't know that the Great Mountain could lose all its investors."

"True."

She wanted to add, *And if you knew who I was, you wouldn't have asked me to marry you in the first place,* but it was so obvious and it stabbed her so sharply that she couldn't bring herself to say it.

The stars started peeking out of the blue-black sky, and one falling star zipped across right above the eastern horizon. She made a wish, even while knowing that with her next breath she was going to destroy that wish herself.

"I don't see how we can stay married," she whispered.

Instead of agreeing, standing up, and leaving her, Lucien settled back more deeply in his chair. "I'm going to repeat what I've been hearing us say tonight. Jump in if I get anything wrong. First: I am important to you."

He paused, one eyebrow raised, and she nodded her agreement. She was in love with him: Of course he was important to her.

Looking satisfied, he continued. "And you are important to me. The Great Mountain might die due to lack of investors, or it could die because a saboteur keeps trying to blow it up."

"The lack of investors is due to Highfill being my grandfather," Emily felt compelled to point out.

"Yes."

"*And* you think my grandfather is behind the sabotage as well."

"I'm not as convinced about that as I used to be. Your grandfather knows we're married, so why would he still be blowing up the Great Mountain? In any case, I've gotten sidetracked. The other thing I was going to say is that you still want to leave me, and I still want you to stay."

Enough was enough. She had to stop being mostly honest and start being extremely honest. "Lucien, I don't want to leave you."

"Then why are you going away?"

"For you!"

"But I want you to stay, so how can it be for me?" he said, maddeningly logical.

"The railroad—"

He leaned over and stopped her words with a kiss. "There will always be other railroads to build," he murmured. "But there's only one Emily."

13

THE TRIP UP TO her room was a blur. Thinking back, she believed they had passed one or
two of the other boarders, but she only had eyes for
Lucien.

He shut her bedroom door behind them. Instead
of stepping forward and capturing her in his arms, he
paused there a moment and smiled.

"Are you sure?" Emily asked. This might have been
the third time she'd asked it, but he was still patient.

"Yes. And you?"

"Yes." It was an answer she felt reverberate in her
bones. Yes, she was sure.

Lucien reached out, took her hand, and reeled her in
until she was plastered against him. He bent down and
whispered an inch from her lips, "You'd better be sure,
because after tonight I won't let you go."

Then he kissed her, and she had to grab his arms for
support, as her knees threatened to stop working. How

had she managed to delude herself that she could live without him?

Her silk dress took much longer to remove than her ready-made dresses, but as Lucien stopped to kiss the nape of her neck every time he undid a button, she wasn't going to complain.

As she laid her dress over the back of a chair and shrugged out of her undergarments, a warm, slightly dusty breeze sailed through the window and dashed across her bare skin. It carried the scent of Bramble Creek, which she'd grown to enjoy in the past few days. A scent that she would describe to her sister Annabelle when she finished writing that letter she'd left back in Lucien's house. No, in *their* house.

Without a single stitch of clothing on, she slipped under the bedcovers and waited for Lucien to join her. It didn't take long. As he got into bed, the mattress shifted, and she rolled against him. Sparks jumped under her skin everywhere their bodies touched, and she gasped. She threaded her fingers through his hair and tried to bring his mouth down to hers.

"I will find someone to come in to cook and clean," Lucien said, resisting her pull. "I meant that."

"All right." Emily tugged a little harder on his hair.

"And you don't have to be friends with Jacqueline if you don't want to."

"I don't." She was practically yanking on his hair now so that he would come closer and kiss her.

He winced but didn't move. "We can also go to San Francisco whenever you want. It's not—"

Why was he chattering so much? He sounded nervous, which was not at all like him. "Stop talking," she commanded, "and start kissing."

"It's just—" He sucked in a huge breath, as if he were planning on diving deep underwater, and said, "I love you."

Emily wanted to laugh. So he *had* been nervous.

This time when she pulled his head down to hers, he didn't resist. A fraction of a second before their lips touched, she whispered, "I love you, too, you know."

Lucien's hands skimmed all over her, leaving sensitized skin in their wake as he touched her cheek, her breasts, her waist, her buttocks, and the backs of her knees. Then he pushed her knees apart as if he were unfolding butterfly wings, and he scooted down so he could kiss the hollow next to her hip bone.

A shimmer of excitement raced down her legs, as if her body knew something that she hadn't been clued into yet.

His mouth moved sideways and then south, and at the first flick of his tongue against her, Emily's back arched off the mattress.

Oh, Lord. No one had ever told her that men could make love with their mouths. Was this how Annabelle had been led astray? If so, Emily had a lot more sympathy for her.

She gazed down the length of her nude body, past her pebbled nipples and trembling belly, to watch Lucien's dark head move rhythmically between her legs as his tongue stroked long and hard against her over and over again. Her knees quivered, and a knot of passion tightened underneath his mouth's onslaught. She held her breath and instinctively tried to squeeze the knot more.

Lucien started to kiss his way up her body, and she tried to fight off her disappointment. Then, as his mouth closed over her right nipple, he dipped two of his fingers inside her and slowly pistoned them in and out.

The knot of passion suddenly tautened. Two more pumps with his fingers, and the knot pulled so tightly that it unraveled in pulses of pleasure that echoed in ever-widening circles, pushing on faster and faster through her body as his fingers pressed deep inside her. Emily half sighed, half moaned, and Lucien kissed her mouth again.

Then he rolled off her, and she blinked at the rush of cool air over her skin. "Wait—is that it?" she asked, propping herself up on one elbow to stare at him as he lay on his back beside her. From her perspective—and she had a very comprehensive view of his anatomy—he didn't look like he was ready to simply go to sleep.

"Hardly." He patted the bed on either side of his waist. "Your knees go here, please."

"My— Oh." Yes, that would work. Emily climbed on top of him. Firmly grasping her courage as well as his shaft, she very slowly eased down over him. Lucien bracketed her waist with his hands, causing a secondary ripple of pleasure to beat through her.

Finally he was entirely inside her.

She gave Lucien an expectant look.

He gave her the same look back. "The lady sets the pace," he said.

She liked the sound of that. She lifted herself up and then sank down over him again. Lucien's eyes crossed.

Yes, this was quite nice indeed. She slowly sped up her rhythm. Within less than a minute Lucien apparently forgot his lady-sets-the-pace rule and started guiding her speed with his hands gripping her hips, which was fine, too. At some point—some point soon—she would set the pace and keep that pace without his interference, but she didn't mind his guidance this time.

As she rose and fell, his shaft filling her with a delicious friction, again the knot constricted, though this time more slowly and with a softer intensity. Eyes half-closed, Emily watched Lucien's face tighten, and he picked up his speed, hands hard on her hips. Then he surged up deep inside her and paused, and she felt the knot spill open and release.

She collapsed on top of him, and he chuckled against her hair.

"What's so funny?" she asked, not able to rustle up more than a shadow of indignation.

"We have a nice large bed at home, and we've never shared it."

"Tomorrow," she promised.

"Good. Because I don't want you having second thoughts, Emily Highfill Delatour."

It was the first time he'd said "Highfill" without spitting the word out like it left a bitter taste in his mouth.

She lifted her head and kissed him. Their tongues tangled in a slow dance, and then she drew back and smiled down into his eyes. "No second thoughts here. I love you."

"I love you, too. We'll make it work."

Disquiet spun through her. They had overcome one large hurdle tonight. She wasn't going to ruin the moment by pointing out all the other obstacles, but their path ahead was not smooth by any means.

Wait—she was doing it again: not telling Lucien the truth because she thought he'd be better off not hearing it. Hadn't she learned anything in the past five days?

She sighed and told him, "It's not going to be easy. Chuck is going to be mad. Who knows what my grandfather will do. The other investors—"

"There's nothing we can do about those things now, so let's deal with them tomorrow." He kissed her. "Perhaps you need a distraction . . . ?"

He rolled on top of her and soon was demonstrating again the pleasures of the gentleman setting the pace.

Lucien left before dawn, dropping a quick kiss on her mouth before he padded almost noiselessly out of her room. Emily rose out of sleep long enough to kiss him back and then snuggled deeper into the covers, smiling.

She could get used to starting her day like this.

But later, as she donned a dress and started combing the snarls out of her hair, all the reasons why she and Lucien shouldn't stay married began to crowd her again like thieves eager to steal her happiness.

She sighed, irritated at herself. Why couldn't she just ignore her worries and instead seize Lucien's love for her and hold on tight, determined to never let go? Was she *trying* to make herself miserable?

No, she was trying to make sure that Lucien would stay in love with her three months from now, three years from now, and thirty years from now, whether the Great Mountain succeeded or failed.

If only they had gotten married *after* the investors had bought into the Great Mountain.

Emily paused in midbrushstroke as an idea ricocheted around in her head.

He could marry her again.

But maybe . . . not right away.

Yes. Yes, that would fix everything. If they ended their marriage, Grandfather would no longer have a toehold on the Great Mountain, and Lucien could re-approach Parker and his network of wealthy friends. Then, after the investments were made and the Great Mountain was flush, she and Lucien could marry again.

She could go to San Francisco, stay with her sister Lily, and wait for Lucien to come back to her. Maybe he could visit once or twice in the meantime. Jacqueline apparently went to San Francisco frequently, so it must be an uneventful trip from Bramble Creek.

Emily finished brushing her hair and then pinned it up. She stared at herself again in the mirror. She looked calm, but inside she was shaking.

It was the perfect plan—

—assuming that Lucien would want to marry her again.

Leaving Lucien would be a very, very large risk.

Half turning away, she spied her only fine dress draped over the back of the dressing table chair, where she had left it yesterday after Lucien had peeled it off her. Emily gathered the dress in her arms and something rustled.

Oh, it must be the note that the boy had brought her last night—a note that she had assumed was from Lucien. But Lucien had appeared only a few seconds later, so it almost certainly wasn't from him. From whom, then?

Emily pried open the flap.

*Darling, avoid the westernmost water tank at noon to-morrow. And if you can send your husband there, all the better. I won't be patient much longer.*

A large scribble ended the short note, as if the writer had simply wriggled his pen at the bottom of the page. Then Emily realized it was the letter *S*.

Well, clearly this wasn't meant for her. She wasn't on *darling* terms with anyone in Bramble Creek—or any-where else, for that matter. Lucien had called her *sweet-heart* once but never *darling*.

"I have a note for the pretty lady," the boy had said last night. Perhaps the fancy silk dress had made the boy think Emily was the pretty lady the note was meant for.

But Emily wasn't the only lady staying at this boardinghouse.

Who would write such a note to Jacqueline, though? Ah. Samson.

Emily stared at the note again, and a horrible suspicion of an evil that went far beyond adultery began to grow in her mind.

Mike Vant was happy to lend her a horse, and after he'd saddled it for her, Emily trotted out of town, keeping a concerned eye on the sun. It was sometime between nine and ten, most likely. If Lucien was still at home, she would have plenty of time to warn him about Samson. But if he wasn't, she'd have to ride out to the railroad and try to find him or Chuck.

The railroad surely couldn't be too hard to find. It was south of the house. Somewhere.

Perhaps she should have followed the railroad from town instead of going home first. But it was too late now—she was halfway there, and doubling back would only add more time and lessen her chance—

"Fancy meeting you here all alone," Samson said pleasantly, and Emily automatically yanked on her horse's reins, causing it to shy sideways.

On horseback, Samson moved out of the gloom of a thick stand of trees. "You really shouldn't be out here by yourself without anyone to watch out for you, as I think I mentioned before."

Emily tried to smile. "You startled me." There was no way that he could know she had intercepted his note to Jacqueline, was there? "Aren't you supposed to be working?"

"'I've been working on the railroad, all the livelong day,'" Samson sang, and then laughed. "No, not anymore. I quit yesterday. See, I'm leaving town tomorrow on the train."

With Jacqueline? That would bold. But he had written, *I won't be patient much longer*, and there was a barely restrained energy to him that made Emily think his words might have understated his lack of patience.

"How interesting. I was planning on leaving town tomorrow, too. Perhaps we'll be on the same train." Well, that was a dumb thing to say. There was only one train passing through Bramble Creek tomorrow.

"You won't be leaving town," Samson said, smiling.

Emily felt her hands grow cold. "Oh?"

He held out his hand. "I think you have something of mine. Or rather, something that used to be mine and wasn't meant for you."

Shaking her head, Emily said as firmly as she could, "I don't have anything of yours, Mr. McIntosh."

"Well, maybe you do—and maybe you don't."

Pretending not to hear the menace in his voice, Emily smiled and said, "I don't, I'm afraid. If you tell me what it is, I could keep my eye out for it."

"It's a letter. I was waiting for a response to it, and when I didn't get one, I decided to talk to the recipient directly. And she said she never got the letter." He watched her closely as he spoke.

Emily put on a frown. "A strange story. Is this

person trustworthy?" Chuck, for one, would probably think not.

Samson shrugged. "If she isn't, she's a better liar than you are. Mrs. Delatour, I can smell fear all over you."

Emily momentarily froze and then gave a haughty sniff. "It is fear of being exposed to more bad manners from you, Mr. McIntosh. Good day to you, sir." She kicked her horse back into a walk.

"Oh, no. You're not going anywhere alone." Samson yanked the reins out of Emily's hands and gave her an awful grin. "I warned you before: It's far too dangerous."

Emily hadn't known what to expect. Getting conked on the head, perhaps, or shot in the chest. But being led to a gorgeous house nestled next to a large wood was a surprise. This had to be Chuck and Jacqueline's house, but right now it unfortunately looked completely empty.

Samson prodded her through the unlocked front door and into a sitting room with long curtains and lushly upholstered furniture. It reminded Emily of her family's morning room back in Boston—a room she was unlikely ever to see again, judging from the triumphant look on Samson's face.

"Why am I here?" Emily demanded. If there was any occasion that demanded rudeness, it was being kidnapped.

"You're a loose thread that has to be snipped. And you can serve double duty. If Chuck somehow survives the explosion today, then he'll be arrested for your murder. His dislike of you is common gossip around town and in the crew's camps."

"People think he'd kill me because he dislikes me? That's ridiculous."

"Well, a little birdie might have told a few of the crew about how your unsavory relatives could bring down the whole railroad." Samson winked.

Jacqueline must have told Samson everything, and he was spreading the gossip himself.

Emily decided to stop playing dumb. Samson wasn't convinced, and she wanted to know exactly what was going on before Samson killed her and tried to pin her murder on Chuck. "You and Jacqueline are behind the sabotage, not my grandfather."

"I hadn't even heard of your grandfather until Jacqueline decided he'd be a good scapegoat."

That was a relief, but it opened up another question. "What does Jacqueline get out of destroying the Great Mountain? If it fails, Chuck fails." A thought struck her. "Is she trying to get revenge on Chuck for something?"

Samson shrugged. "Who knows why? All I know is that once this railroad is destroyed, she's going to be with me." But Emily's question seemed to cause him discomfort, or perhaps it made him wonder himself about Jacqueline's motivations. He growled, "No more questions." Then he pulled out his gun and aimed it.

"Jacqueline is going to be upset if you get blood all over her chairs and couch," Emily pointed out a bit desperately.

He hesitated.

Emily threw a pillow at him and darted sideways toward the doorway to her right.

The gun boomed. With a yelp, Emily scrambled through the doorway and into the kitchen. Samson bellowed in anger, for certainly the pillow hadn't hurt him at all, and she could hear his boots thumping across the room in pursuit.

The back door was only five feet away. She could get outside if she moved fast. But what then? Outside, Samson would hunt her down in seconds.

She'd have to stand her ground.

Grabbing off the stove a heavy cast-iron skillet that still had the remnants of breakfast clinging to it, Emily pressed herself against the wall beside the doorway to the living room.

Then the back door opened, and a woman Emily had never seen before began hauling a large bucket inside the kitchen. She stopped short upon seeing Emily. "Who—"

Samson barreled into the kitchen and then tried to slow his momentum when he saw the strange woman standing in the doorway. He growled and raised his revolver, pointing it at the woman, who screamed and dropped the bucket of water.

This was the best chance she'd get. Emily leaped forward and slammed the skillet down on Samson's skull.

He dropped like a rock, but she could tell from the way he half rolled onto his shoulder as he hit the floor that he wasn't completely unconscious.

Kicking his gun out of his hand and then planting her

foot on his upper arm to keep him down, Emily swung the skillet again.

Samson stopped twitching and went still.

The woman shrieked, "You killed him!"

Still keeping her grip on the skillet, Emily eyed her coolly. "Maybe so. But maybe not. Find some rope so we can tie him up in case he isn't dead, and then let's go find Chuck."

Keeping one eye on the men refilling the steam engine from the water tank, Lucien listened to Chuck detail once again why staying married to Emily would ruin the Great Mountain.

"I'm not giving her up," Lucien said when Chuck finally winded down. Chuck's diatribe had been shorter this time. Either Lucien was wearing him down, or Chuck had finally realized that on this point Lucien was immovable.

Even the rail crew had stopped trying to eavesdrop on their arguments, because it was the same thing every day and had become boring.

Chuck grimaced. "You sound very sure today."

Today? Lucien had been telling Chuck the same thing for the last several days. But Lucien knew why, of course, he sounded so confident today. Today was the day he knew that Emily wasn't going to leave him.

And . . . speak of the devil. Apparently she wasn't just not leaving him—Emily was now seeking him out. The familiar figure of his wife was walking down the rutted path alongside the railbed.

As she grew closer, she started trotting. And then running.

What the—

She launched herself at him and inexplicably began to sob against his neck.

"Hey, hey, hey," he said, wrapping his arms around her and half turning away from Chuck to give them a slice of privacy. "What's wrong? What happened?"

"I almost killed Samson McIntosh, but only after he tried to kill me," she said, and another sob caught in her throat. "He's the saboteur."

Samson McIntosh was one of Lucien's least favorite crewmen: lazy and filled with a deep sense of entitlement. He was young and healthy, though, and had done his share of work when watched closely.

Apparently he hadn't been watched closely enough.

"What happened?" Lucien asked again, and this time Emily thrust a crumpled-up note into his hand.

*Darling, avoid the westernmost water tank at noon tomorrow. And if you can send your husband there, all the better. I won't be patient much longer.*

Lucien glanced at the water tank towering above them only twenty feet away. It was the westernmost tank on the line, serving the locomotives that hauled track and ties and gravel to the crew, along with food and casks of beer.

If it blew up or collapsed, it could kill the men nearby. It would certainly cripple construction for several weeks.

And it was only an hour or so until noon.

"Where's Samson now?" Lucien demanded.

Emily slid a look at Chuck. "Tied up at the Winthrops' house."

Chuck didn't bother pretending anymore that he wasn't listening to their conversation. "What do you mean he's at my house?"

"Samson grabbed me on the trail and he took me to your house to kill me. He was trying to get you blamed for my death. I got away and whacked him on the head with a skillet. Your housekeeper, Angela, has gone to the sheriff so that he can be put in jail."

It didn't make a whole lot of sense the way that Emily was describing it, but the "husband" mentioned in the note was helping Lucien put the pieces together. He gave the note to Chuck, who read it with a frown.

"Samson and Jacqueline—" Emily broke off. "I'm sorry, but it was Jacqueline's idea to sabotage the Great Mountain, and she convinced Samson to do it."

Chuck's face grew white and then red. "You're lying," he said before she'd barely finished. "I don't know why, but I know you are." He held up the note. "You're trying to tell me that Samson wrote this for Jacqueline, but there's no proof it was meant for Jacqueline. I bet Samson wrote it to you. We all know your grandfather is behind the attacks on the railroad. So it makes sense that you and Samson are working together. Not"—he snorted—"my *wife*."

Lucien tightened his arms around Emily. "Emily had nothing to do with the sabotage, Chuck, and you know it. Stop being an idiot. But you're right that we only have Samson's word that Jacqueline is involved. Let's go find Jacqueline and talk to her."

But Jacqueline couldn't be found. She wasn't at the boardinghouse, and no one in town had seen her since breakfast. Angela, whom they met with the grim-faced sheriff on the street in front of the boardinghouse, confirmed that Jacqueline hadn't been back to Chuck's house.

A whistle blew twice, and everyone looked in the direction of the train station. "That's the northbound train heading out," the sheriff said.

"Jacqueline had a ticket for the southbound train," Chuck said, but Lucien could see fear growing in his eyes. "She's not on that train."

"One way to find out," the sheriff said. He disappeared inside the boardinghouse and then soon reappeared with a white square of cloth in his hand.

"That's one of Jacqueline's handkerchiefs," Chuck said, frowning.

"Yep. And we're going to pay a visit to Mike Vant."

"But—"

"Chuck, do you want to know where your wife is or not?" the sheriff demanded. "Mike's got the Sight. He can tell us if she's dead or alive, and if she's dead, he can tell us her location."

*If she's dead?* It hadn't even occurred to Lucien that Jacqueline might be dead. If Emily was right, Samson's plans centered on his and Jacqueline's future together, not on getting rid of her.

From the clenching of Chuck's jaw, Lucien wasn't sure if he'd prefer her to be dead or unfaithful.

Mike was mucking out a stall when they all trooped into the livery stable, but he looked up with a welcoming smile. Then he took one look at the sheriff's stern expression and the handkerchief he held, and his smile disappeared. Lucien knew that Mike hated being called upon to find dead bodies, but he thought it his civic duty. He'd once described having a vision of a dead person as plunging his whole body in an ice-cold creek and then breathing in the scent of a rotting grave.

Pulling off one glove, Mike took the handkerchief and closed his eyes. Then he abruptly grinned and gave the handkerchief back to the sheriff. "Alive and well," he said simply. "So, who is it?"

"My wife," Chuck bit off. "Mike, I need your fastest horse. I'm going after that train."

In less than a minute Chuck was galloping north. The sheriff shook his head. "He'll never catch her."

Lucien wasn't sure it would be a good thing if Chuck did catch her. If all that Samson had said was true, and Jacqueline was a partner in his sabotage, then Jacqueline had blood on her hands and didn't deserve much mercy. But her husband shouldn't be the one to administer justice.

"Little Emily?" a voice said from the livery stable entrance.

Lucien groaned. That was a voice he knew well and had hoped against hope that he'd never hear again.

His arm tight around Emily's shoulders, Lucien

turned and squinted against the sunlight. A tall white-haired man strode into the livery stable like he owned it, and the loathing Lucien had tried to tamp down for Emily's sake rose up like a scorpion's tail.

"Grandfather!" Emily cried.

**14**

WHAT WAS HER GRANDFATHER doing here? Was he swooping in to buy a piece of the Great Mountain?

Then out from behind Highfill stepped another man in his forties and a few inches shorter, and Emily's breath caught as she realized that investments weren't the only impetus. "Mr. Grant!" She rushed forward and threw herself into her stepfather's embrace.

"You've sent your mother into three separate fainting fits," Mr. Grant said sternly, but he hugged her tightly and kissed the top of her head like she was a young girl again. Then he set her back and said, "I think introductions are in order."

Lucien stepped forward, his eyes unreadable but his hand outstretched for a handshake. "William Grant? I'm Lucien Delatour, Emily's husband."

Emily frowned. Lucien sounded so possessive, as if he were drawing battle lines and placing Emily on his side. Darn it, she hadn't had a chance yet to tell him her plan of getting divorced and then married again. He was going to spoil everything if he started acting extremely husbandly.

Lucien then introduced Mike Vant, the sheriff, and Angela Jackson. Mr. Grant and Emily's grandfather murmured their hellos, with Mr. Grant raising his eyebrows a hair at the sheriff's grim expression. Then Mr. Grant said, "Why don't you show us around Bramble Creek, Delatour, while we talk? We could use a good leg stretch after traveling for so long."

Lucien took Emily's hand and began leading them down the main street. Emily tried to unobtrusively tug her hand away, but he scowled at her and tightened his grip.

She popped up on tiptoes and whispered, "I have a plan."

"For what?" he asked, not bothering to lower his voice.

"You know. The railroad. Just follow my lead."

Lucien shook his head, but she wasn't sure if he was disagreeing with her request or displaying an overall mistrust of her plan. But he hadn't heard the plan yet and didn't realize yet how it would solve everything.

"I'm surprised to see you," Emily told Mr. Grant. "I mean, I'm delighted, of course!" And she was. Upon seeing his familiar, steady face, she hadn't realized just how adrift she'd felt in the past two weeks, cut off from her family's love and support.

"You didn't think you could get married to a man I

didn't know and—ahem—approve of without my coming to check on you, did you?" But he said it with a twinkle in his eye.

"We're more than two thousand miles from Boston," Emily pointed out.

"Luckily, travel becomes more and more convenient every day," Mr. Grant replied. "I hope you aren't disappointed that I didn't bring your mother. You know how she is about trains."

"Is Emily's welfare your sole reason for this visit?" Lucien asked. The tone and the words were mild, but Emily could read the tension in his shoulders.

Mr. Grant hesitated, and Highfill jumped in. Uncharacteristically, he'd been holding himself back since his arrival, ceding center stage to Mr. Grant, but he clearly couldn't keep himself restrained any longer. "We're interested in the Great Mountain."

"*You're* interested in the Great Mountain," Mr. Grant corrected him mildly, but Highfill talked over him.

"You had New York abuzz with talk of investing in your little railroad, and I can't wait to see the operation. If I recall correctly, and if you and Chuck Winthrop haven't adjusted the partnership, family has first choice in investing."

Lucien nodded tersely.

"And I'm now family," Highfill concluded smugly. He looked around. "Where is Winthrop, anyway?"

"As you didn't send us word that you would be arriving today, Chuck made other plans," Emily said before Lucien could reply.

"No matter. The clause in the partnership is clear: If shares are being sold, family has first dibs on those shares, assuming family pays the price being offered to other investors. I'm willing to pay that price." He grinned. "Looks like the three of us are in business together again, Delatour. Unless, of course, you don't need to sell those shares. . . ."

Lucien's grip on Emily's hand tightened until it was almost painful. She glanced at his other hand and saw that it was balled in a fist.

"Look, here's our general store," she said, trying to distract the men and reduce the swelling tension.

Highfill ignored her and kept his focus on Lucien. "We heard during the last leg of the trip that you've been having lots of accidents. There were even rumors of sabotage. That must have your other potential investors worried." He sounded disapproving, but Emily recognized the gleam in his eye. This was Highfill in full bargaining mode, trying to close the deal.

Emily could feel Lucien's gaze on her, and when she glanced up, he gave her a nod and a smile. It was a strange smile that was both sad and seemed to contain some kind of promise, but she couldn't figure out what the promise was until Lucien turned to face Highfill and said, "That got fixed this morning. We're still planning to get over the summit before the first snowfall, but you're right. We're going to need a cash infusion to get there."

Oh, no—Lucien was going to give in and sell part of the Great Mountain to her grandfather.

"Wait!" Emily cried. "I think that before this goes any

further, you all should know that Lucien and I are getting a divorce."

"What?" all three men replied in various levels of disbelief. Highfill seemed puzzled, Mr. Grant looked shocked, and Lucien . . . well, Lucien was furious.

"We settled this last night," Lucien said, his eyes burning down at her with a fierce mix of outrage and passion. "Remember?"

Emily's ears felt as though they were on fire, but she managed to reply, "I remember. But it didn't solve anything. Not really."

"We need a few minutes alone," Lucien said, trying to pull her away from the other men, but Mr. Grant shook his head.

"I won't have my daughter browbeaten into staying married to you if she wants to leave. Whatever you have to say, you can say it in front of me."

"I'd rather we have privacy, too," Emily said quickly.

Mr. Grant shook his head again.

"Then it should be just the three of us," Emily countered. "Grandfather needs to take five steps back."

"What's this, a children's game?" Highfill grumbled, but he obediently took five steps away.

The other two men took one step in, forming a huddle with Emily. "What's going on?" Lucien asked. Some of his anger had trickled away, as if he'd realized that she wasn't simply leaving him again—she was up to something.

Lucien probably wouldn't want her revealing the financial straits of the Great Mountain Railroad to her stepfather, but she had no choice if she was to convince both men of her plan. "Lucien's investors backed out when they learned that Grandfather would also own part of the railroad," she told her stepfather.

Mr. Grant nodded. "The clause in the partnership agreement that gives family first right to purchase shares. Yes, your grandfather was quite excited about that." He raised his eyebrows at Lucien. "I hadn't realized until Highfill and I traveled west together just how well you two knew each other."

From the way Mr. Grant was speaking, it was obvious that a previous business association with Highfill didn't reflect well on Lucien's judgment.

"It was a while ago and didn't end pleasantly," Lucien said shortly.

Emily kept going. "Yes, well, unless we can find a way to keep Grandfather out of the railroad, Lucien and Chuck are going to have a much harder time getting good investors, and the railroad will suffer. Maybe even collapse."

Lucien grimaced but didn't contradict her.

"So, if Lucien and I divorce—"

"No," Lucien said. "We won't."

"—then Grandfather won't be able to invest. Lucien, we only have to be divorced for a little while, I think. Six months or so."

"No."

"I won't be far. I can go to San Francisco while we wait for things to settle down and the other investors to return."

"No."

She held on to her slipping patience with both hands. "Be reasonable. Our divorce will only be a technicality."

"It won't be just a technicality if you're in San Francisco."

"Then I'll stay here," Emily said, her heart lightening at the idea of not leaving Lucien. "But we'll still be divorced."

Mr. Grant, the traitor, shook his head. "No one will believe it, then. Your grandfather will just wait you out."

Lucien crossed his arms over his chest. "Then it's settled. No divorce."

Desperately, Emily said, "Lucien, you once told me that you would throw your engines down a ravine before you let Highfill get his hands on them. And now you're planning on letting him buy into your railroad without a fight?"

"I'd throw away the engines, Emily, but not our marriage. I don't love my engines, Emily. I love you."

Tears began to fill Emily's eyes. She wasn't sure if they were tears of happiness at Lucien's refusal to let her go, or tears of despair at the thought of Lucien's dreams of the Great Mountain Railroad slowly and painfully being destroyed. She whispered, "Why, Lucien? You wouldn't have married me in the first place if you knew I was a Highfill."

Out of the corner of her eye, Emily saw Mr. Grant stiffen in shock at her words. Then he turned on his heel and strode a half dozen steps away, finally giving them privacy.

Wiping one of her tears away with his thumb, Lucien gazed down at her with serious eyes. Then, surprising her, he grinned. "It might have taken me a little while longer to talk myself around to marrying you, Emily Highfill Delatour, but I would have done it, and I would have tracked you down in San Francisco, or Boston, or wherever you were. After that kiss in the rain on the back balcony, I knew I'd never be able to get you out of my thoughts." His eyes still on hers, he brought one of her hands up to his mouth and grazed a kiss across her knuckles. "I'm not sure if I was destined to bring the Great Mountain over Dead Horse Pass, but I do know that I was meant to get married—and *stay* married—to you."

"Oh," Emily said, completely inadequately. "Then that settles it."

"Finally." Lucien laughed, and pulled her into a kiss that made her knees and heart quiver.

One of Lucien's closest friends—or he had thought she was—had been conspiring to destroy the railroad behind his back. His partner had skedaddled without any indication when, or if, he would back. And Lucien had just essentially agreed to allow his longtime enemy to invest in the Great Mountain.

But he had his arms around Emily, and she had decided—again—to stay with him.

This was the best day of his life.

"Ahem," Emily's stepfather said from behind them,

and Lucien loosened his hold on his wife. But only just a bit.

When he turned his attention to William Silas Grant, he saw that Highfill had also rejoined the group, and the white-haired bastard was rubbing his hands together, clearly eager to start negotiations.

"I know the price that you've been offering folks in New York," Highfill said, "and it seems inflated to me, now that I'm out here and can see the operation for myself. But we're willing to take one hundred shares at twenty percent lower than the New York price."

Charles Highfill had stepped off a train ten minutes ago, hadn't left town, and yet considered himself an expert on the operations of the Great Mountain? Lucien drew in a breath to tell Highfill exactly what he thought of his twenty percent reduction, when William Silas Grant held up a hand to halt further conversation.

Emily's stepfather was shorter than both Highfill and Lucien, but he had a strong, quiet presence that demanded respect. Next to Grant, Highfill seemed like a high-strung windbag. Grant said, "I'm not investing in the Great Mountain, and you don't have the money to, Charles, even with shares at twenty percent off."

Highfill straightened. "I have money. Cash money."

Grant looked around. "Where? I understand that your private railcar was even impounded in San Francisco due to nonpayment."

"Oh, that. A misunderstanding." But his eyes narrowed, and he didn't push his claim of having ready money. "I thought you came out here to look over the Great Mountain, Grant. Do you think it's a bad investment? Perhaps Delatour and his partner are poor managers."

Lucien could already see the wheels spinning in Highfill's head. If Highfill couldn't buy the Great Mountain Railroad, then he'd happily ruin Lucien's chances of getting anyone to invest. They had a score to settle, after all. The fact that Lucien was now part of the family wouldn't make a difference.

Emily grew pale. She had obviously realized the same thing. "You haven't even seen the work being done on the Great Mountain," she objected. "How can you make such a statement?"

"Hush, everyone," Grant said, and like trained circus animals they all shut up. "I came out here to make sure our Emily was happily married, and indeed she is." He raised his eyebrows at Emily and Lucien. "Though it sounds like the path wasn't entirely smooth in the beginning."

Lucien wasn't sure whether to swear or laugh. So he kissed the top of Emily's head instead and decided to let the comment go past.

"However," Grant continued, "in celebration of Emily's wedding, before I left Boston her mother and I agreed to give Emily and her new husband a wedding gift of twenty-five thousand dollars."

Lucien's lungs stopped working. Emily made a squeaking noise like a mouse that had been stepped on. Highfill literally staggered a half step sideways. Twenty-five thousand dollars was twice the money Highfill had initially offered, and more than enough to get the railroad over the pass before winter.

Lucien's lungs unfroze, and he drew in the first clear, clean breath he'd felt in months.

Grant seemed pleased by their reactions. "Wonderful. I'm glad that's settled. Now, what does everyone think about lunch? Charles and I haven't had a decent meal in at least two days."

Emily, feet propped up near the fire and book in hand, lifted her head to listen to the howl of the snowflake-laden winter wind as it raced around their little home, trying to find a way in.

If it was like this here, what must it be like in the mountains? Lucien had warned her that snow on the tracks could delay him. She hoped any snow there was light, but he was already a day late in returning.

She directed her attention back to the page, read it again, and realized she'd already read this same page three times. She closed the book in disgust. Really, one shouldn't be without one's husband for twenty-two days. It did things to the mind.

Then the door blew open and Lucien appeared, stomping mud off his boots and grinning. "It's wild out there."

Emily jumped up, the book dropping to the floor with a thud, and ran to give him a welcome-home kiss. Or rather, about a dozen welcome-home kisses.

Finally he laughed against her mouth and pulled

back. "Let's close the door. Sorry I was late, but Chuck finally decided to talk about Jacqueline, and I didn't want to stop him. We stayed up all night drinking whiskey, and then snow slowed me down on my return. We're lucky that the crew is blasting out the railbeds ahead of schedule, because winter has decided to arrive ahead of schedule, too. I told Hendrick that I'd bring some of your biscuits for him when I returned in three weeks, as thanks for moving construction along so quickly."

Biscuits were Emily's specialty. She was a royal disaster at cooking anything else—and frankly didn't care to become good at it, either, since Angela ruled the kitchen just fine. But Emily had decided that she should learn to cook *something*, and in the last few months she had perfected a recipe for light, fluffy biscuits that made even Chuck smile when he saw them.

Emily helped Lucien out of his heavy canvas coat and tugged him over to sit on the couch by the fire. She snuggled up against him and inhaled the crisp-snow scent that still clung to him.

He tilted her face up to his for another kiss, and his cool lips clung to her warm ones. "I love you," he said, "and I missed you."

She wanted to press him down full-length on the couch, layer herself on top of him, and show him how much she missed him, too. But Angela was in the kitchen preparing supper. Emily would just have to demonstrate her full enthusiasm for his return after Angela left.

"What did Chuck say?" she asked. "Did he finally find Jacqueline?" Chuck had spent a lot of time away from the Great Mountain during the fall, and while he had refused to explain why, Lucien and Emily thought that he was still trying to track down Jacqueline. Currently, Lucien and Chuck were taking turns being on-site at the railhead. Chuck had offered to be in the vanguard all winter, but Lucien had privately told Emily that he wasn't confident in Chuck's focus, so the men had agreed to switch their roles every three weeks, with one of them at the front with Hendrick and the other back in Bramble Creek. It was working well, though Emily far preferred the weeks when Lucien was home.

Lucien rested his cheek on Emily's hair and sighed. "Apparently Jacqueline made her way back to her parents in Washington, D.C., and she and Chuck have been corresponding for months. After he got about six drinks in him, he showed me some of her letters. He keeps them all in an oilskin pouch that hangs around his neck, and the pouch is thick enough to stop a bullet."

"Well, if Jacqueline acquires another bloodthirsty boyfriend, that might come in handy," she said lightly, but the thought of Chuck carrying around letters from his faithless wife made Emily sad.

"In the letters that Chuck showed me, Jacqueline blamed him for the sabotage, saying that he had forced her to do something drastic to make him give up the railroad and move them back east, where it was civilized."

That didn't make any sense, and it brought to mind a loose thread Emily had never been able to tie up. "Then why did she encourage you to marry Susan? Was Jacqueline hoping that if you got enough money by marrying Susan, Chuck would feel free to leave you to run the railroad yourself?"

"No; she thought that Susan would hate it out here, too, and that if both Chuck and I had wives who wanted to move back east, we would finally give up the railroad and decide to move east, too."

Well, that helped explain why Jacqueline had been so furious when Emily showed up. And Jacqueline would have also been afraid that, as Highfill's granddaughter, Emily would eventually find a way to prove her grandfather wasn't behind the sabotage. "What about Samson? How did he fit in? Or did she not mention him at all?"

"Apparently Samson was Jacqueline's tool of destruction—crippling the Great Mountain was her idea, not Samson's. She claimed she wasn't trying to hurt anyone, much less kill anyone. When Samson tried to blow up the explosives shed, and almost blew up Chuck in the process, Jacqueline realized that her plan had spiraled out of control and Samson couldn't be trusted any longer. She wanted Chuck to take her back to Washington, D.C., not a new husband. Samson seemed to have other intentions."

Emily snorted. "The whole plot seems delusional."

Lucien sighed. "I admit, while Jacqueline's methods of trying to get Chuck to return east—the sabotage, the affair with Samson, her attempts to destroy our marriage—are completely abominable, she did initially try other ways to convince Chuck not to get involved in the Great Mountain. They had lots of discussions about it—some of which I was a part of, as a business discussion—and then fights, and Chuck admitted to me that once or twice Jacqueline told Chuck that she'd leave him if he didn't quit the railroad. But he didn't listen or take her seriously."

Was Lucien actually defending Jacqueline? "That's no excuse—"

"No, it's not. And I'm not trying to excuse her actions. But in her letters, she tried to lay a lot of blame on Chuck in between her passionate avowals of her undying love for him. And I think that's why Chuck was missing so much during the fall. He was wrestling with Jacqueline's declarations of love and blame."

"Do you think he was considering going back to her?"

"Yes."

Emily shivered. Lucien's decision to keep Chuck from being the only owner on the front lines of the Great Mountain now seemed especially wise.

"But," Lucien said, "I believe that by telling me about Jacqueline, Chuck was closing the door on their relationship. So . . . I told him that if he still wants to run the front end of the Great Mountain for the rest of the winter, he can."

Emily sat up straight and turned to face Lucien, who was grinning at her. "You mean, you'll be here for the next few months?"

"Exactly."

She kept staring at him as plans whirled through her

head for spending the cozy winter months together, and he finally chuckled. "Have I made you speechless? That's a first."

"I'll show you speechless," she growled, and launched herself at him. Forget Angela in the kitchen. She was going to give her husband a taste of how wonderful their winter evenings together were going to be.

Several minutes later Lucien raised his head, eyes dazed and hair mussed. "Now, that's what I call a magnificent welcome home." Then a smile gleamed in his dark eyes. "Remember how we first met? You took one look at me and screamed."

She smiled back. "I had good instincts. You turned my whole world upside down in less than a week. But now I like this way of saying hello much better than screaming." She leaned in and gave him a slow, lingering kiss.

"Hel-lo," he murmured against her mouth, and that was the last thing either one said for a very, very long time.

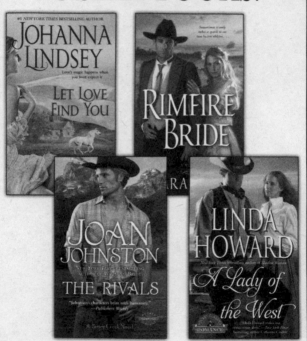